---- ★ ----

She screamed. At first, he thought a scorpion bit her. He had forgotten to warn her about scorpions. Then he saw what she saw.

The bones were yellow-brown and bits of clothing still clung to some, but insects and small animals had removed anything resembling either flesh or features.

"Shh…" he said.

"It is a person?" she whimpered.

He lifted the canvas a bit more. Insects scurried over the bones and away into the desert. He made out the distinct outlines of a pelvis and more fabric.

"Yes, I think so. I'm guessing a woman. We have to call the police.

"Police?"

"Yeah. I'm just an anesthesiologist and a long way from freshman gross anatomy, but that jagged hole in the cranium is not supposed to be there."

Her face took on the ashy expression one sees just before people faint. He grabbed her just as she collapsed and kept her from falling into a jumping cactus.

---- ★ ----

Acknowledgments

I want to thank Barbara and Robert of the Poisoned Pen Press, who continue to support me in this peculiar calling, this novel writing, which is a preoccupation as addictive as the strongest opiate and as compelling as holy orders. I know something of the latter, absolutely nothing of the former, but as a fiction writer, I can imagine how that must be.

And I want to thank my wife, Susan, who always stands behind me as my reader, line editor, critic, and primary support.

I have the good fortune to be encouraged by a host of friends, neighbors, critics, and other authors who say enough kind things to me to keep me plugging along. If I were to attempt a comprehensive listing, I would invariably forget some. To them I now apologize. Nevertheless I need at least to mention my critique group—past and present, David Bishop, John Rundle, Fran Cohen, Bette Dowdell, and Nancy Clarke, and all my friends and colleagues at The Southern California Writers Conferences, especially Michael Steven Gregory, Jean Jenkins, Bette Abell Juris, Raymond Straitt, Wes Albers, and Cricket Abbott.

IMPULSE

Frederick Ramsay

WORLDWIDE®

TORONTO • NEW YORK • LONDON
AMSTERDAM • PARIS • SYDNEY • HAMBURG
STOCKHOLM • ATHENS • TOKYO • MILAN
MADRID • WARSAW • BUDAPEST • AUCKLAND

Recycling programs
for this product may
not exist in your area.

IMPULSE

A Worldwide Mystery/July 2011

First published by Poisoned Pen Press

ISBN-13: 978-0-373-26759-0

Printed in U.S.A.

To Campus Kids, those fortunate enough to have spent at least some of their childhood in the shadows of ivied school buildings. And especially to all the boys and girls, now men and women, who like me roamed the McDonogh School campus in Owings Mills, Maryland. Its nearly nine hundred acres became our backyard. We roamed in packs of three, four, or more and we knew it as others, even our parents, did not. We were gifted with acres of fields, woods, and streams where we built forts, hideouts, dams and tree houses. Overall, we had the rare good fortune to grow up in a very special world.

Scott Academy is loosely modeled after McDonogh School, but I hasten to add that neither the events nor characters portrayed in this book are anything more than the product of this author's imagination. The mystery described in this story is fictional as are the people involved in it.

ONE

FRANK SMITH STEPPED TO one side at the top of the escalator, turned and studied the passengers behind him struggling with their luggage on the moving stairs. He inspected each in turn, looking for telltale signs, for any indication that one or two might be following him. But they all seemed painfully normal. None appeared even remotely interested in him. He resumed his march toward the security checkpoint. Sky Harbor, Phoenix's busy airport, teemed with men and women, many more than he would have expected on a Wednesday morning. He glanced backward once more and marginally increased his pace. He muttered to himself for his foolishness. If Ledezma or anyone else, for that matter, wanted to know where he was going, he would only have to step up and ask. Four years of suspicion and guilt had made him paranoid.

The whole idea was ridiculous, of course. No one chased anybody through airports anymore. No more O. J. Simpson careening through crowds to get to a plane on time. It was O.J., wasn't it? Time and circumstances changed so many things, made memories dim, and O.J. has been reduced to the quintessential *persona non grata* in the civilized world.

He reached the security checkpoint and joined the hundred or so men and women standing in the sixteen ranks of a serpentine line, waiting for their turn to show an ID, a boarding pass, and be handed off to one of four screening stations. He had a brief Mel Brooks moment as he inched forward a few feet at a time—a movie scene, two men tearing through the airport, one in hot pursuit of the other. The first drew up at this slow-moving line and stepped in. Then the other man joined it four or five places further back and together they moved slowly forward, two feet at a time…shuffle, shuffle…shuffle, shuffle. Finally, the first cleared the X-ray and screening, and resumed his mad dash through the airport. The second followed a moment later, hopping on one foot as he struggled to get his shoe on. Frank smiled and looked over his shoulder one last time.

THE PLANE WAS NEARLY FULL, but he managed to get a window seat.

He'd used his computer to print his boarding pass the night before and had made a point of being one of the first to board. He wanted to scrutinize the other passengers as they made their way between the seats, dragging their carry-on luggage down a cramped aisle scant inches too narrow to allow that to happen. A damp man in a rumpled suit squeezed into the seat next to him. He stowed his laptop and what appeared to be lunch under the seat in front of him. Frank squirmed around in his now more confined space. He wished he could have flown first class or at least business, but this trip did not qualify for a tax break and Southwest didn't offer first-class seating anyway. He envied his row mate's foresight. He should have packed a meal. Now he would have to resign himself to a narrow seat, a bag of peanuts, and a snack pack. They'd dueled for the best elbow position on the common armrest. During the course of this unacknowledged combat, his seatmate recognized Frank. The good news, he'd been awarded the best spot. The bad news, he had to engage in a conversation he'd sooner have avoided. The man turned toward him with a too familiar look.

"Let's say you're a murderer…." Frank flinched. "How do you do it? I mean, I bet you must get that question all the time." For a split second, Frank wondered if it were possible this man had, in fact, followed him on the plane, if his question was more than idle curiosity. He decided to play it straight and see.

"I do, get the question, that is. Well, in my opinion, murder, real murder, is ordinary and boring. Most of them are committed by desperate, angry, or demented people who've slipped out of control and are acting on impulse. Typically, they leave a trail a mile wide and they are almost always caught. The few who do get away with it are either lucky or someone or something interfered with the process. No, murder is pretty dull stuff."

Frank knew better—knew that the vast numbers of murders were never solved, that in Los Angeles alone, the last time he looked, something like eight thousand murders were unsolved and the number grew daily. The process, as he'd called it, bogged down more often than not, because there were many more killers than there were homicide detectives to catch them. L.A. had more cops in its internal investigation unit than on the street as detectives.

"It's means, motive, and opportunity," he replied, trying to look deep and wise, and at the same time not appear pompous. "If I were plotting a killing, for example, I would find a way to mask all three and then do it. The last thing I want is for those characteristics to stick out and attract the notice of a detective. Otherwise, it's 'find them and book them'…dull stuff."

"That's it?" His companion pushed back a pale lock of his comb-over and looked disappointed. "I mean, I would think anything as important as killing another human being is pretty serious stuff and involves all sorts of—"

"No, that's a common misunderstanding. In real life, murder is almost always mundane. It's rarely planned, premeditated, or thought out."

"But in books…I mean, I read a lot of mysteries…yours, for example, and the murders are so elaborate and, well, elegant."

"I don't write about real life. I write fiction. You wouldn't buy, much less read a book, that accurately described most of the killings that cross a police blotter every day. Writers like me make up complicated and sometimes very shocking ones, serial killers, hatchet murderers, and the gorier the better. We describe autopsies with horrific precision. Don't ask me why, but people seem to be fascinated with the graphic details of that process. Watch *CSI* some evening. Anyway, we're in the entertainment business, not the truth business."

"Oh. Well, then, what if you had to solve a mystery? I mean, with all the times you've written about them, I bet you could solve a real one. Do police departments ever ask you to?"

"Never."

He did not mean to sound abrupt. This man could not possibly know what had happened and asked a perfectly reasonable question. Why wouldn't people who studied and wrote about crime be good at unraveling them? Why indeed? Because writers solved their crimes backward. They always knew who'd done it before they did it. He'd toyed with solving one once or twice, a long time ago, and thought he might like to again someday, but not today, not here, and certainly not under the present circumstances. He picked up the brochure from his lap and turned toward the window, hoping to signal an end to the conversation. The man looked crestfallen. He had a three-by-five card and a pen at the ready. Frank smiled and signed the card, *Best wishes, Meredith Smith.* The man nodded his thanks and left him to read his brochure.

He turned and stared out the window. The ground fell steadily away. In the early morning light, shadows etched the desert floor, giving texture to shrubbery too far away to see clearly. Among the shadows he could make out longer ones, some branched, attached to thousands of saguaros, which looked like Gumbys marching northward toward Sedona and red rock country. They would never make it. Fifty miles out I-17 they would come to an abrupt halt, their northward migration from Mexico stopped by temperature and altitude.

Soon the morning heat would send columns of air shimmering across the expanse below, distorting the shapes, tricking the eye into seeing things that weren't there. And somewhere down in that dead, brown Arizona desert lay the bleached bones of his wife, missing now for four years and presumed dead. Another of those murders he'd so blandly dismissed moments before, one that went unsolved. No motive, no body, no suspects—except, of course, the most logical one, the one always favored by the police—him.

The plane leveled off, its engines settled into a low whine, and it turned its nose east toward Baltimore.

TWO

Brad Stark inspected the twelve watercolors on the walnut-paneled wall. He'd seen them a hundred times, when they were raw and fresh in Albert Magarry's art classroom. That would have been before Magarry had been discovered by the art world and left the school for better, or at least more exalted, company. Next, for several years they hung in the school's art gallery, and now they adorned the walls of the headmaster's outer office. Mixed in with them and set at regular intervals along the walls were plaques extolling the headmaster for services rendered to a plethora of worthy causes, organizations, and institutions. He thought they looked like Stations of the Cross and wondered if the boss might not perform some private ritual in front of them from time to time. He inhaled the scent of freshly cut roses bunched in a Waterford crystal vase. The headmaster's office always had fresh-cut flowers. He didn't know whether that came about because the headmaster or his secretary arranged for them to be delivered. The latter picked up the phone, murmured something Brad couldn't make out, and looked up at him.

"He'll see you now, Mr. Stark."

He nodded to the secretary and pushed open the heavy mahogany door that separated the headmaster from the world. More than a metaphor, he thought. Darnell, *Doctor* Felix Darnell, had assumed the headmastership of Scott Academy after a career that included teaching posts at several private schools and dean of a prestigious prep school in Massachusetts. His chief attraction at the time seemed to be his doctorate. A month after his installation as the school's twelfth headmaster, it came to light that the degree was not a Ph.D. or even an Ed.D., but a D.Litt.—an

honorary degree bestowed on him by an obscure university in
northern India, which had a reputation for selling them to rich
or ego-needy Americans. Nevertheless, Darnell used the title
that came with it and insisted staff and students do the same.
In his favor, he had a talent for administration and fundraising,
the chief attributes needed for a headmaster in this day and age.
But he was not a naturally warm and friendly man, a fact which
distanced him from his students and annoyed his faculty. Brad
served directly under him as the Academy's chief development
officer and alumni secretary.

"Dr. Darnell, we need to talk about Frank Smith," Brad said,
without waiting for an invitation to speak. Darnell liked to control conversations and expected his visitors to respond to his
cues regarding both the content and direction of any interviews
he had. Brad knew this, but today chose to ignore the protocol.
Alumni would be arriving soon and he had work to do. Class
gifts to be totaled and, hopefully, increased in size with the
right amount of gentle pressure—one-third charm, one-third
guilt, and one-third luck. He did not have time to fence around
with Darnell. The headmaster waved his hand in the general direction of a crewel-upholstered wing chair, inviting him to sit.
Brad knew from experience that the cushions in that chair were
exceedingly soft and he would sink into it, allowing Darnell to
look down on him. Power games. He remained standing.

"Which Smith are we talking about? We have many Smiths.
The phone book's full of them."

"Frank Smith, Franklin M. Smith, here for his fiftieth."

"Okay, Frank Smith. What about him?"

"Well, this is the first time he's communicated with the school
in any way since he graduated. He's never attended a reunion,
never responded to any of our fundraisers, and never completed
an update for the directory. Nothing, until now."

"I can't see that's so odd. Many graduates disappear. They
drift away, don't recognize the value of the experience they
had—"

"Frank Smith is the son of one of our more distinguished

former faculty members, Doctor Charles Addison Smith." Brad laid an emphasis on *doctor*. Smith's degree was earned, a Ph.D., a relative rarity for a prep school in his day and one the Academy touted all the years he taught there. "He taught English and retired when he hit sixty-five."

"Oh, yeah, the ascetic looking guy hanging in the teacher's lounge."

"His picture, yes. We should move it, by the way. It was painted from a photograph. He refused to sit for a real portrait."

"Really? Why not?"

"We kicked his other son out of the Academy. The kid committed suicide later that year and Dr. Smith was never the same after that."

Brad finally sat and scanned the office. Darnell had it built as part of his agreement to accept the headmastership. With the paneling, oriental carpet, and custom desk and bookcases, Brad guessed a six-year full-boat scholarship could have been offered for what it cost.

"Why'd we bounce the son?"

"Not sure. Record says, 'for behavior unbecoming a cadet.' When we functioned as a military school we were a much more rigid institution. That's all they ever put in the record."

"Do you know why?"

"Just rumors, and even if we knew, there's nothing we can do about it now."

"No, I suppose not. Still, it would be good to know since he's coming. He might bring it up. Find out for me, will you? Someone ought to know, one of the old-timers, maybe."

Darnell fiddled with an ornate letter opener, turning it between his fingers, sending a splash of light darting around the room's dark paneling. Brad thought he could make out *Presented to Doctor...*on the haft.

"Did you have him?" he asked.

"Who? Dr. Smith?"

"Yes, who else are we talking about?"

"No, he was long gone before my time. According to the yearbooks they used to call him 'Jolly Cholly.' I think in the end it was more like 'Angry Addison.' He took what happened pretty hard."

"So the problem with Frank Smith is…? I assume you came in here to fill me in on a problem," Darnell said, sensing, Brad guessed, a chance to assume control of the conversation.

"Frank Smith is an author of a couple of dozen mystery stories. You may know him as Meredith Smith—"

"Meredith Smith is a man? I read her…um…his stuff all the time. Great storyteller, and there was the TV series based on his Episcopal minister detective—what was it called?"

"*Collars.* Smith taught English like his father. Ended up in Phoenix at some prep school out there. Then his books hit and the TV show went big-time for three or four years—I think it's still in syndication on PAX. He's made a lot of money but we haven't been able to squeeze a dime out of him. That's the problem. My guess is he's been angry at us all these years, but he'll be on campus this weekend and I thought you'd—"

"I'll have a word. No, let's put him at the High Table at lunch next to Elizabeth Roulx. She's our English maven now and she's a reader. I'll have her butter him up. Then I'll pitch him and you can close. Anything else?"

"No, sir, that'll do it. Well, there's his portrait. We should hang it in the dining hall so he can see it, Smith, that is…and—"

"And? Please don't tell me you have another problem?"

"Dexter Light. He may show up again. Unlike our Frank Smith, he loves reunions."

"Loves a free lunch and a chance to embarrass us, you mean. God, I'd have thought his liver would have exploded by now. Give me a heads-up if he comes on campus. And then call security."

"Yes, sir."

Brad left the office complex and stepped into the bright sunlight. He wandered over to the quadrangle. From there he could see the progress made for the next day's festivities. The big tent was up. Men from the rental company unloaded folding chairs from a van parked nearby. Women in aprons laid tablecloths on the trestle tables under the tent. The temperature hovered in the low seventies. The heavy humidity that would characterize the area later on had not yet arrived, and it promised to be a splendid weekend. Sunlight streamed through old maples, dappling the tent and the grounds. By Friday night there would be four bars, two long tables laden with catered food and desserts, and best of all, no rain. At least none predicted. A reassuring bit of news, although they said of the area, "If you don't like the weather in Pikesville, wait an hour." Still, he felt safe enough.

He returned the greetings of a half dozen students moving from Old Main to Armiger Hall, smiled at a gaggle of kindergarten students like goslings following their teacher to the art gallery. A cloud drifted across the sun, the day went gray. He pivoted ninety degrees and his eyes focused on Old Oak Woods a mile away, down the hill past the chapel. His smile faded. For the hundredth time since he'd arrived at Scott, he asked himself why. Why had he come back? Of all the places in the world he wanted to settle, Scott Academy would have to be near the bottom of his list. Yet here he was.

The invitation to join the staff at Scott had been wholly unexpected. He'd been active in the Pittsburgh alumni chapter and raised some serious money for the school. He supposed that must have played into their decision—that and the school's peculiar habit of bringing back "names." His father had been a popular teacher there at one time. At the time, he wallowed in what he thought of as an unappreciated life, and so the offer gave his sinking ego a boost. The call had tugged at him, but not enough to overcome its dark side. He had no desire to face memories that haunted him even at the remove of more than two decades; memories that crept in during the small hours of the night to rob him of his sleep. Then again, his job provided something of a push. He hated it. He'd never wanted to be a stockbroker. He sometimes wondered if he even understood the concept. But his wife, Judith, had pressured her father to give him the job. Judith had a way of getting what she wanted, always, and crossing her inevitably ended in recriminations that might linger for months, even years. His options were limited in any event. An attempt at law school proved an expensive disaster. The only other job offer he'd received involved a two-hour commute only to manage the sporting goods section at a Walmart. So, with no other real job prospects in sight, and in the face of Judith's insistence, he'd accepted her father's offer to join his firm.

They settled in Squirrel Hill and he sold securities. The past drifted further away. He never felt really secure, and not exactly happy. But he soldiered on as a mediocre stockbroker whose only sales came from referrals handed down to him by Judith's father. His boss/father-in-law disliked Brad almost as much as Brad disliked him. Only Judith kept them in some sort of reasonable relationship. Days slipped by as each month flowed seamlessly into the next. Sometimes he felt like a sleepwalker wandering aimlessly and unconnected to the world around him.

Then one gritty spring afternoon, his father-in-law asked him to lunch, an unusual request on any day. They'd found a small eatery at Station Square, well away from the office. They ordered lunch and his father-in-law proceeded to fire him before his iced tea arrived.

"Bradford, I can't carry you anymore. You haven't built your business, you're not earning out, and the rest of the sales force are unhappy—ticked off at me, in fact. Sorry, but you have to go. I'll let it be your choice, resign or be fired. If you resign, your stock options and 401(k) stay in place. If I fire you, they're off the table. Oh, and you'll have to be the one to tell Judith. She's my daughter and resident Princess, but I don't have any intention of being within a mile of her or what she will do when she gets the news." He showed a lot of teeth and bit into his bacon cheeseburger. Brad recalled with some small satisfaction the glee he'd experienced when a dollop of ketchup dribbled down the old man's chin and onto his white shirt.

So, he resigned and took the job at Scott. He did not tell his wife why, no way he'd do that. The single point he and his father-in-law had in common involved Judith's volatility when

she didn't have her way. Besides, he told himself, once again, he
had no other viable choice. For a while he even believed it. As
for the memories—well, it had all happened a long time ago, a
quarter of a century, for crying out loud, how bad could it be?
Nobody remembered anymore, nobody cared.

Twenty-five years ago. Had it been that long? Teddy, Ned,
Bobby, and Tom, all gone. When the memories slithered in to
steal his sleep, he dreamed about Old Oak Woods, saw their
ghosts dancing in the trees, forever young, beckoning him to
join them. Not now. Not yet. He shook his head like a cow shaking off flies. He needed to focus. That was then, this was now.
The sun emerged from the cloud. He didn't notice.

THREE

IF THE STATE'S GOVERNOR has his way, Baltimore-Washington International Airport, BWI in the trade, will be renamed Thurgood Marshall Airport in honor of the late Supreme Court justice who grew up on Baltimore's mean streets when it was still just a segregated southern town. How the late justice would feel about the honor was problematic. His opinions of Baltimore were a matter of record and mostly negative.

The airport turned out to be the first of a series of culture shocks for Frank. He remembered when it was Friendship International. He remembered when they'd built it. He remembered its predecessor, Harbor Field, for goodness' sake. The last time he'd flown east, he had landed in Washington at Reagan National—the airport that congressional vanity and self-importance kept open as a full-service facility in spite of warnings it was a time bomb ticking away, a disaster waiting to happen. And when it did, public outrage would be followed by public wringing of hands and great crocodile tears from the body whose self-centered need for a quick exit from the district kept it going. It would work fine, he thought, if they limited Reagan's traffic to corporate aviation and smaller, commercial commuter aircraft. They could manage the river approach. But that wouldn't happen anytime soon, and in the meantime what price would the nation be asked to pay to maintain the privileges, the reserved parking spaces, and perquisites assigned to senators and representatives too busy, too important, or too self-absorbed to take a cab and spend the hour it required to get to Dulles or BWI?

But BWI—what a transformation. Construction equipment

cluttered the access roads. Buses and cabs fought with each other for a few feet of curb.

"This place is a mess," he said and looked around him. A limousine nearly knocked him down even though he still stood on the sidewalk.

"It's like a cathedral," his daughter replied. "They're never finished. At least that's what they tell me."

"Ah, airports. America's twenty-first century spiritual centers."

"I don't think I'd go that far."

"No, neither would I, but it's a thought."

"You could use it in a book."

"Maybe I could at that. Remind me later."

Barbara Thomas was a well-put-together forty-something. As tall as her father at six feet and celebrating the same thick, glossy hair that prompted envious thoughts by both men and women. But where hers curled and glistened with chestnut highlights, his lay flat, straight, and gray. She steered him to the garage and her car.

"Take me through the city," he said. "I know it's dark and I won't be able to see very much, but I'd like to see downtown."

"You got it, but we can't stop. I told the kids they could wait up for you and it'll be nearly ten before we get home."

They drove in silence while she negotiated the various detours and lane changes occasioned by construction. Once on Route 295 she relaxed and settled back in her seat. Frank waited for the question he knew was coming.

"So, is there anything new?"

"You mean have the police made any progress on your mother's disappearance?"

"Well, yes. But surely they don't still think she just disappeared?"

"No, they don't. They believe she was murdered and they think they know who did it, and so they're waiting for him to make a mistake."

"They're not pursuing leads—?"

"They've settled in to wait."

They drove on in silence. When Route 295 became Russell Street, she moved to the right lane. She swept around Oriole Park at Camden Yards and turned east on Pratt Street. The Inner Harbor appeared in front of them. Who would have believed the dingy waterfront he knew as a child could be transformed into this elegant retail center?

"I used to buy my suits over there. This whole area was Baltimore's garment district. Joseph A. Banks, that is, the man himself, mind you, used to make suits right over here, before his company went big-time."

"I know."

"They had this manufacturing facility on that corner, and you just went in and tried suits off racks made of pipe. Old Jewish guys cut fabric and stitched them up in the next room."

"I know. You told me."

"If you didn't find what you liked, you got to go through the swatch book. 'Make me a thirty-nine long in this,' you'd say and they would. Need two pairs of pants? No problem, a vest—"

"Dad you've told me that story a hundred times. I know, I know."

"It's not a story. That's the way it was. Hof-Tex was around the corner but I didn't like their clothes as much, no style. Your grandmother did, though, mostly because they sold their suits cheaper."

They turned north on Calvert Street and past row houses with marble steps, some boarded up, all a little shabby, until they crossed North Avenue. Then the real estate steadily improved. They continued past the Union Memorial Hospital, veered north onto Charles Street, and finally turned into Homeland. Whereas downtown Baltimore had undergone a metamorphosis, its residential neighborhoods remained unchanged, in an urban time warp. He relaxed.

"So, with no off-the-pipe-rack Joseph A. Banks to supply you, where do you shop now?"

"Goodwill."

"No."

"Oh, yeah. I go across Bell Road to the Goodwill near Sun City. Those old folks know how to dress and when they die… You see this blazer?"

"Very nice. You didn't—"

"Seven dollars and fifty cents."

"It has a patch on the pocket. What's it for?"

"No idea—came with the coat. A country club in Illinois, I think."

"Dad!"

"Relax, I only wear it around the house. I have another one for the shindig at the school. It cost—"

"I don't want to know. Here are the kids. Don't tell them about Goodwill. If you do, they'll want to do all their clothes shopping there, too. They think you hung the moon."

"WHAT TIME DO YOU NEED to be at the Academy tomorrow?"

Frank shrugged and wiped the yolk of his egg from the plate with a toast crust. His grandchildren were noisily gathering their books and lunches. School would go on for another three weeks. He wished the reunion had come later in the year, after the schools closed. Then he could have enjoyed the kids' company more. He basked in the cacophony of children's voices and breakfast's aroma. The combination of frying bacon and perking coffee is the finest fragrance known to man, he thought. Society's ambergris.

"More coffee?"

"Yes, please. A continental breakfast is scheduled for eight. Then there are activities of various sorts during the morning, a luncheon with the headmaster at noon, a bus tour, and some athletic events after that. Are you sure you won't need the car? I could rent, you know."

"I know. No need. The kids should go there."

"Go where? To Scott?"

"Why not?"

"Do you have that kind of money? I don't know what the tuition is but I bet it's huge."

"It's seventeen thousand dollars a year…each."

"You have that kind of money?"

"No, but you do."

Frank stared at his daughter. In all of her adult years, she'd never asked for anything from him. Even when she and her husband, Robert, were young and struggling, she never asked for help. Frank assumed his wife sent her money from time to time, but he never did. His son was another story.

"Yes, I suppose I do. And you think that would be a good investment?"

"They're your only grandchildren, Dad. I work. Bob works. We manage, sort of. We don't need or want your money. But we can barely keep them in the schools they attend now and certainly not Scott. But they're bright and Jesse will be moving to middle school next year—"

"Not Scott. Send them to Saint Paul's, Boy's Latin, any place but Scott."

"Dad, it happened fifty years ago. Let it go. Times change. You can't hold those people accountable for what happened to Uncle Jack."

Frank sipped his coffee. It tasted bitter. She rose and moved into the living room to referee the departure of her children. He listened to their bright young voices and her cautious one. She did not return right away. He heard her moving about in the front room.

"What would you like to do today, before your big dinner at the Maryland Club?" she called.

"Don't know. I have no plans. Read through these, maybe." He waved the brochures from the reunion committee.

"Right. There's a new Michael Connelly book on the coffee table. You read the competition, I guess." She appeared in the doorway and stood contemplating him, a small frown on her face.

"You didn't do it, did you?"

He looked at her, tried to read what lay behind her eyes. "Do you think I did?"

"No…no, of course not."

The hesitation in her reply lasted no more than a heartbeat, but he heard it. Once, researching a story, he'd watched a pathologist prepare a frozen section in liquid nitrogen. The tissue went from slippery pink to rock hard, frozen solid in less than a second. That's what that pause did to his heart now. Barbara's eyes betrayed nothing; there was just that tiny pause.

"The police think I did."

They were silent a moment. Finally she turned and marched to the front door. "I'll see you this afternoon. I have to go to work. You know where everything is."

He guessed he did.

The door slammed behind her.

YOUR 50TH REUNION. MEET YOUR classmates for dinner Thursday night, and then join them for a full day at the Academy. Talk with Dr. Darnell about the school's future. Join your "pen pal class" for lunch….

Fifty years! Who would he recognize? What would he say? Frank's mother had died in an assisted living facility, one of countless Alzheimer's victims, a fact which made Frank considerably more sensitive than most to things like memory lapses. And now he had to face his own advancing decrepitude by attending his fiftieth high school reunion. Of the sixty-five members of his graduating class, fifteen were already dead, and of the remaining, he guessed another dozen or so had the proverbial "one foot in the grave." The knife edge of despair began its near daily intrusion into his consciousness—the low-level panic he felt whenever reminders of his advancing age invaded his thoughts. He closed his eyes and tried to push them away.

He had not set foot on the campus in fifty years. He leafed through pictures of buildings and fields, most of which he recognized only with difficulty. New buildings screened out remembered vistas, distorted the familiar lines and landmarks of what was once familiar topography. So many changes, so much newness. As he scanned through the photographs, it seemed as though his past, his youth, had been methodically erased and replaced by the shiny new physical plant that now defined Scott Academy.

He'd grown up on the campus. It had been his home, its woods and streams his backyard. He'd roamed over every square acre of it. He knew where the springs of ice-cold water gushed out of mossy stream banks, surrounded by beds of tangy, crisp watercress. He could tell you where you could trap rabbits, hide from parents, or just loll in the sun on a lazy Saturday afternoon unseen, unharried, invisible. The nearly nine hundred acres of woods and fields were as familiar to him as streets and alleys were to the city born and bred.

Of course, his memories of the school differed significantly from those who only experienced Scott as students. His father taught at Scott for thirty-eight years, twenty-five of them as a beloved English teacher, "Jolly Cholly," his final years as plain Dr. Smith, taciturn, sometimes rude, and usually angry.

Growing up as a "campus kid" had its advantages and disadvantages. On the one hand, you had access to all that land, the playing fields, barns, and woods. Few of his friends could boast such a playground. On the other hand, there were the frustrations of being different, of being Dr. Charles Smith's kid. There were many days when he thought the balance sheet, advantages versus disadvantages, tipped heavily toward the latter. There existed among some of his fellow students, particularly the slower, duller ones, an impulse to bully a teacher's offspring. He had endured his share of fights—won some, lost most, and learned to run like the wind.

In Frank's senior year, the Academy expelled his younger brother, Jack. It caused a small sensation. Some anonymous students accused Jack of homosexual behavior. Whether he was, in fact, gay, not a word used in that way then, had never been addressed. Fifty years ago, suspicion and rumor sufficed, indeed, were cause enough. No one ever attempted to discover the truth. No one offered to defend him. After all, everyone knew Jack was a little fey. And that was that.

Frank went off to college that fall. His brother committed suicide over the Christmas holidays and Frank vowed he'd never return to the Academy. Never. It took him nearly thirty years to forgive his parents and deal with his own guilt. He'd kept his vow until this year. But now, as he finished off his sixty-eighth year, and mellowed somewhat by his own tragedy, he decided he needed to forgive the school and have one last look, to touch his past one last time before the judicial system or old age had their way and succeeded in closing him down forever.

FOUR

SCOTT ACADEMY PROVIDED housing for as many of its faculty and staff as possible. Young couples, without sufficient down payments for houses, and older men and women consolidating their assets for retirement found this possibility an attractive perquisite, and that, in turn, helped the school recruit many above-average teachers. Brad and Judith Stark occupied an end unit in a row of six town houses. The complex had been built into a hillside so that the front door and first story were at ground level facing the main campus but the basement door also opened at ground level in the back. On the whole Brad seemed satisfied with the arrangement but said he missed the annual deduction from his Schedule A for interest and taxes and the equity build home ownership provided.

This morning he sat in the tiny kitchen amidst disorder and clutter. He valued order while his wife, Judith, had a cavalier attitude about housekeeping. In fact, she hated it and put off doing it as long as possible. She sat across from him in a kelly green robe. Its tie had come loose and the robe was perilously close to falling open. As much as he enjoyed looking at his wife's naked body, it made him uncomfortable with the children tumbling around the house gathering their school things.

"The twenty-fifth-year reuners may be a problem," he said, more to himself than to her.

"Well, you can hardly blame them. It must have been a big deal at the time."

"Yeah, but it's been twenty-five years. Enough is enough."

"Brad, you are too sensitive about that day. I mean, it was in all the papers and television news then. What'd you expect?

For some of those guys, it might have been the only important thing that ever happened to them."

"It was for me. They were my friends, Judith. More than that. I could have been—it could have been me...."

Judith nodded. She'd heard it all before. She had not wanted to move to Scott Academy. She liked her job and her home in Squirrel Hill and did not understand Brad's insistence on returning to the school where, by his own admission, he had been desperately unhappy as a child. His descriptions of life as a teacher's kid, a TK, were anything but glowing. Yet, when the offer to move east and become the school's development officer came along, he'd jumped at it. No consultation, no "should we," just pack up and go. She had to admit he seemed happier than he was as a stockbroker. And the pay was good. Good enough so that with the housing provided by the school and other perks, free tuition chief among them, she reckoned it a positive exchange. Still, when reunion weekends came around, she wondered. And then there was the unhappy fact that Brad had not yet distinguished himself as a fundraiser. Selling securities to people ready to buy anything is different from prying dollars from alumni. She wondered how much longer they'd be at Scott. She made up her mind to call her father, just in case.

Brad pushed back from the table, frowning.

"Four boys go into the woods and disappear forever. No sign of them. No bodies, no motive, no suspects. No one ever figured it out. It *is* a big deal," he said.

"It'll be fine," she replied. "Wait and see. A few ghost stories and some wild speculation, maybe. The further away in time it moves, the dimmer the memories. By their fiftieth, they won't remember a thing."

"That's where you're wrong. The one thing I've learned in this business is this, as the alumni become increasingly geriatric, their memories about their school days become sharper. It's a law of nature; the memories retrieved are directly proportional to the gray cells lost. Some of those old geezers can repeat the dining hall menu from September to June of their senior year."

"You're exaggerating."

"Only a little."

"Look, you had better get used to it. Every class for the next several years will have that incident on their list of school day memories, right up to your own."

"That's a happy thought."

"Why don't you have a second coffee? I'll walk the kids up the hill to school today."

"Thanks, I'll do that. I have a ton of things to do. I need time to figure out how to approach Meredith Smith."

Judith Stark moved like a ballerina, which at one time in her youth she'd dreamed of becoming. Five foot eleven in her stocking feet, hair as black as obsidian, thin and elegant, she dominated any room she entered. She rose and glided toward their tiny foyer. The children were waiting, backpacks slung low on their spines.

"Tighten your straps."

"Mom!"

"I mean it. Put the weight of those packs up high. You'll all turn into Quasimodo if you don't."

"What's a Quasimodo?" Lillith, the youngest, asked.

"The goofy-looking guy who rang the bells, stupid."

"I'm not stupid."

"Be still. Pull up those straps.... Don't even say it. I don't care what the other kids do."

She imagined in the next decade or two, there would be legions of deformed men and women hunched over at bus stops, in offices, and on street corners—victims of a peer pressure that insisted that backpacks should be worn like fanny packs—an orthopedic disaster waiting to happen. She glanced back at her husband. He stared, eyes out of focus, off into space, lost in his private world. Where was he now? she wondered.

"C'MON NED, LET'S GO."

"Shhh... Wait a minute. There's someone over there in those trees."

"Who?"

"I think it's Light and Hot Pants."

"No way! What would they be doing out here?"

"Shhh."

"Don't be such a jerk, Bobby. What do you think they're doing?"

"They're doing 'it,' you dope."

"Oh, you know so much, Tom, like the time you said we could sneak in the Pikes Theater through the back door."

"Well, we could have if you hadn't been such a jerk."

"Jerk? You could have gotten us arrested and anyway, who let the door slam?"

"Shut up, you guys, they'll hear us."

"I gotta go."

"In a minute. Let's sneak up and watch them do it."

"Are you crazy? We're not even supposed to be here. You know what your dad said."

"I'm going to look."

"Jeez, Ned...okay, if you go, I will, too. Who else?"

"Shhh."

"They're not doing it."

"Shhh."

"They're just talking."

"Well, she's old enough to be his mother."

"That makes him a mother—"

"Shhh."

"Maybe they'll do it later."

"Well, I'm not waiting to find out—Light'll kill us if he catches us."

"Big deal. What's he gonna do? We could tell about him and Mrs. Parker. Then what?"

"Shhh."

"I really gotta go. I'll be late and I can't get more demerits or my dad will kill me. Never mind Light."

"Okay, okay, in a minute. You still have time. Listen, follow me. I found something really neat last weekend."

"What now, Ned?"

"Wait and see."

They followed him along the west bank of the small stream that wound through the thick canopy of oaks and maples. They pushed their way through the underbrush carefully at first, until they forgot all about the couple behind them. Then they kicked at the leaves and tossed stones at frogs.

"My dad said these are sugar maples. We could come out here in the spring, you know, like early when there's still snow, and collect the sap and make syrup and sell it."

"Tom, you dork. How are we going to make syrup? You need equipment to do that."

"We could make it in Shop."

"Oh, sure. 'Hey, Mr. Simpson, we want to make stuff to go into the maple syrup business, can you help us?'"

"Shut up."

"Make me."

"Come on, you guys."

"Look, here it is."

The stream, one of those meandering creeks that carve their way through the woods and countryside in the area, made a gentle right turn. For the last several decades it had slowly cut into the earth to the left. Roots of trees ready to fall dangled in the cold water where it undercut the bank. Opposite, on the right bank, the stream had deposited a sandy delta. Above that, an embankment rose nearly six feet to form a minor escarpment, evidence of the stream's original course. A wilted bush punctuated its center.

"I found it and put that bush in front so nobody else would."

"What's the big deal about a dead bush?"

"Not the bush, moron, behind the bush."

The boys clambered up the bank and pulled away the bush.

"Wow! That is so cool."

"Nobody knows it's here except us."

"Well, somebody else must know. I mean this is not natural."

"Maybe a bear did it."

"Bobby, you are so dense. There haven't been any bears in these woods since, jeez, colonial times, I bet."

"Like you know."

"My dad said he saw a bear in Cumberland."

"Well, that's not near here, is it?"

"Boy, if the Empire ever attacks, we could hide out here and be like guerillas."

"Like Ewoks?"

"No, like Luke—"

"Teddy can be R2-D2."

"Yeah, and you can be Darth Vader, peabrain."

"We could get a machine gun."

"Maybe we could fix up the one in the museum—"

"That was an old World War I machine gun. I don't think they make ammo for that anymore."

"Tommy could make us some in Shop."

"Shut up."

"Boy, this is so neat. We could light a fire."

"I gotta go now. What time is it?"

"You have fifteen minutes. If you hurry, you'll make it."

BRAD STARED AT THE COLD coffee in his cup and let his mind return to the moment. He still wasn't sure how he would approach Smith. He wasn't sure about anything. He shook his head to stave off the tears that threatened to spill out over his cheeks. Tom, Ned, Teddy, and Bobby. He caught his breath, wiped his face, and looked at his watch. What happened to time? he wondered. Where did it all go? If he hurried he'd make it.

FIVE

THE CHESAPEAKE CLUB SURVIVED Baltimore's historic cycles from antebellum overindulgence through Depression-era austerity. Many of its members could trace their ancestry through that same history. The years had not been kind to the exterior of the building, a flaking brownstone, but the interior retained much of its past elegance. The club endured over the years as a reminder of an earlier, gentler age, a men's club complete with squash courts, Turkish baths, and a smoking lounge reeking with decades of accumulated cigar smoke. It boasted dining facilities featuring crab cakes, terrapin soup, and all the imagined traditions of those same bygone eras. Frank parked his car in a lot, paid the attendant, and walked two blocks to the stately, if somewhat city-begrimed, building. He paused on its gray granite steps and wondered for a moment if he hadn't made a mistake. What could he possibly gain from eating dinner with twenty-five or twenty-six superannuated preppies whose names he could barely remember? Names he'd spent the last fifty years trying to forget.

The door swung open and Don Hudson, exuding the aroma of alcohol and tobacco, bald but still recognizable, stuck out his hand, his grin amplified by expensive dental work.

"Frank Smith, Smitty, you're here."

No one had called him Smitty since he left Scott. Smitty!

"How are you, Don?" He did know one name. Maybe this wouldn't be so bad after all.

"Great, great. The guys are inside working the bar, telling lies about the good old days, the usual stuff. You're the last."

They crossed the marble-paneled lobby and turned left into

a smallish dining room. He heard the babble of voices and the clink of glasses. When he entered, twenty-five pairs of eyes snapped his way and beamed in on him. A moment later they were followed by another fifteen pairs—wives who'd decided to tag along. Frank managed a weak smile and a wave.

"Bar's over there," Don said and waved toward the corner where an ancient black man poured drinks and kept up a steady stream of chatter with his customers. Hudson moved off to schmooze with someone else. Frank made his way to the bar and asked for a Coke. He'd given up booze three years ago when its siren call to sink into mind-numbing oblivion nearly destroyed him. He looked around at the room. Dusty animal heads and hunting gear hung on the walls, nearly lost in the gloom of high ceilings. He counted a moose, two bears, and a couple of animals he took to be gazelles or elands. His knowledge of African fauna was limited. The horns were straight and spiraled and he felt certain they were neither elk nor deer. Fascinating. He sighed. The walls were painted a deep red, or perhaps they were some other color but time and grime had combined to create a dark terra-cotta. Either way, he thought, the room must be oppressive in the daylight. At that moment, however, candles lighted tables and lowered the visual perspective. It appeared warm and welcoming. He sipped his drink.

"Hi, remember me?" A woman's voice.

He turned and looked into a pair of soft brown eyes. *Her eyes were brown and playful in a shiny boyish face*…who wrote that? She must have been sixty-five or six, but could have passed for fifty-something.

"I'm embarrassed, but no. Sorry."

"Rosemary Mitchell."

He scoured his brain, opened every one of the cluttered file drawers that constituted his memory, and still drew a blank. He thought about early-onset Alzheimer's and whether it began here.

"Rosemary *Bartlett* Mitchell," she said. She smiled. Perfect small teeth.

In the years before he started the third grade, he and Rosemary Bartlett practically lived in each other's apartments. The

Bartletts lived on the first floor of a building long ago demolished to make room for more classrooms. The Smiths occupied the second floor of the same building. He and Rosemary played on its big L-shaped front porch, shared sleds, candy, and secrets. They drifted apart when the Bartletts moved off campus. He would have been nine or ten, Rosemary a year younger.

"My God, Rosemary! Where did you come from? Mitchell? You're married to George Mitchell? Wait, I thought he…I'm sorry. I've been out of touch."

"It's all right. He died six years ago, just long enough for me to be okay with it. Widows get invited to these shindigs. This year, when I heard you were coming, I decided to accept."

Someone tapped a water glass with a knife.

"At ease," Don Hudson barked. "You all have assigned seats. There are name cards at the tables, cleverly placed there by our alumni secretary, Brad Stark. Dinner will be served in a moment. The Reverend Alistair Forsythe will say grace." A rotund clergyman in a Black Watch tartan rabat muttered a brief invocation asking the Almighty to keep an eye on the gathering and ended with an Amen. Hudson then cleared his throat and intoned, "Cadets… Attention… Seats."

Heels clicked together as two dozen dried out, paunchy men attempted to snap to attention.

"You can take the boy out of military school but you will never get the military school out of the boy," someone shouted. Frank smiled and began to relax.

People moved in and around the tables, laughing and searching for their places.

"Listen, Rosemary, this is great. Can we catch up, after dinner maybe?"

"No need to wait. I switched your name card so you're next to me now instead of Mr. 'Dialing for Dollars' Stark."

"You always were a naughty girl."

"You remembered."

THERE WERE ONLY TWO THINGS Frank ever really missed when he left Maryland—crab cakes and the Baltimore Colts. When the latter were shanghaied to Indianapolis, only the crab cakes remained. The Chesapeake Club made what were undeniably the finest crab cakes in the state, well, in Baltimore, anyway. The rest of the meal was merely adequate.

Frank surveyed the room, trying to connect names to ancient faces. He found a name badge at his place—his senior yearbook picture next to his name. Very cute, he thought, but he would have preferred a roster of current pictures with names to study first. Someone waved to him. Who? Too far away to make out a name, and the face did not ring a bell. He wondered what all these men would look like with a full head of hair. He imagined the waver with hair. Whilamon, Sam Whilamon.

"Hey, Sam," he called, and waved back.

"When did you decide to become Meredith instead of Frank?" Rosemary asked.

"When my first book came out. My publisher said since most books were bought and read by women, I ought to consider writing under an assumed name. He thought Ellen Carstairs would work."

"Ellen Carstairs? Where'd he come up with that one?"

"No telling. Anyway, I balked and we settled on using my middle name. It is sufficiently gender nonspecific to go either way. They didn't put my picture on the dust jackets for years."

They ate and caught up on five decades of news. Rosemary had children living in Denver and Houston, and grandchildren. The children rarely came to Baltimore, so she was left with flying out to them. She had more house than she needed but couldn't bring herself to sell.

"It's hard to let go of things."

"Unless there's a reason, a push to change, we'd all stay right where we are, hang on to friends, familiar routines…doesn't always work, though."

"No, it doesn't. Not always."

They finished eating in relative silence. Frank tried and failed to identify a man across the table from him. He stole a glance at Rosemary. He remembered her as not beautiful, but pretty in a tomboy way, button nose and round face and freckles, he definitely remembered freckles. She still had the nose and the face, but the freckles were gone.

"Too bad," he said.

"What's too bad?"

"I remembered you as having freckles and now they're gone. Stupid thing to say, sorry."

"Sorry the freckles are gone or sorry you mentioned them?"

"Both, I think."

"Well, if it makes you feel any better, I've still got them. They're under a layer of makeup. And you don't need to be sorry on my account. I'm happy you remembered them. Do you remember anything else?"

"Yes, I do. You could throw a ball like a boy and you could lay down a bunt better than any of us and could spit through a gap in your teeth."

She blushed. "My orthodontist put an end to that trick. You're a widower? Is that right? I looked you up on the Internet. There's a lot about you on the Internet."

"And the Internet said I was a widower?"

"Yesss, well, sort of. They were a little vague. Are you?"

"A widower?" Frank looked down at the linen tablecloth. His appetite dropped into his shoes. How to answer that question?

"My wife disappeared four years ago. She's presumed dead. That's how the reports read. But—"

"I'm sorry." She knit her brows and added, "This is personal. I shouldn't…I'm sorry. I didn't know. The Internet…"

He looked up and measured the sincerity in her eyes. "She's dead." He paused, checked the eyes again, and added, "She was murdered."

FOUR MEN STOOD TALKING in a small cluster, occasionally darting a glance in his direction. He waited—for what, he did not know—but his antennae were up and he felt something coming. He listened with half an ear to Dr. Darnell. Accepted his invitation to sit at the High Table, whatever that was, the next day. He kept Rosemary in his peripheral vision. Now, there was a turn. She did look good. Not tall but still slim with hair gone completely white. He thought of Sandy and felt something like early guilt creeping up his spine. Three of the men detached themselves from the fourth and headed his way.

Darnell excused himself and Frank turned to face the men. He recognized two and guessed he'd figure out the third after they talked awhile.

"How are you, Smitty?" Bill Powers was the all-American boy fifty years ago—all conference football, wrestling team, baseball team. You name it, Billy did it. He also had a sister, Frank remembered, who excelled in a different sort of sport, and in her way, managed to be more popular than Billy. He wondered what happened to her. He decided not to ask. Charlie Eveleth and, aha…Tank Forward stood next to him. Fifty years ago he would be looking at power. Now they were just three old men with imposing but irrelevant résumés.

"We've missed you, Smitty. You never came back."

"No."

They shuffled their feet and two stared at the floor.

"Look, I don't know how to say this, but we're sorry for what we did," Powers mumbled.

"Excuse me?"

"Oh, hell, here's the thing. We are the ones who reported your brother to the assistant headmaster."

"You?"

"Us. Yeah, and O'Conner over there. He's afraid to face you. We didn't know it would end the way it did."

"You turned Jack in for being—"

"A fairy, yes."

"Why? He wasn't anything, just a kid who acted a little different, thought about things differently. Why?"

"I don't know. It was stupid and mean and one of those spur-of-the-moment things kids do, you know? Just some dumb idea that got out of hand and—"

"He killed himself because of you."

"Hey, we couldn't know. Hell, we didn't think anything would happen to him. We thought Old Man Bartlett would just ask questions and, you know, call your dad.... It would be funny and...that would be that."

"But when he was expelled, why didn't you say something then?"

"Long gone. We graduated and left. The expulsion came after."

"That's no excuse. You could have saved him."

All three men looked past Frank at a spot on the wall behind him. They studied the spot as if their lives depended on it.

"That's the problem, Smitty. Lying got you tossed out, too. We could have lost our diplomas, college admissions. Our parents...it was damned if you did, damned if you didn't. So we, you know, let it slide."

Frank wanted to lash out, to hit something. He wanted to grab Billy Powers by the throat and wring the life out of him. Tears filled his eyes.

"You bastards," he croaked, "you spineless, cowardly bastards."

"Jeez, Smitty, we were just kids, we didn't know. For God's sake, we were scared, we didn't know...and then, later...it was too late."

He spun around and headed toward the door.

"Give me a lift?"

"What?" He turned only to see Rosemary, a faint smile on her lips that did not cancel the worry in her eyes.

"I saw you with those guys. I guessed what they were saying and I thought—"

"You guessed? You guessed what?"

"My father was the assistant headmaster, remember? He nearly died when Jack had to leave. The headmaster—you remember 'Black Jack' Perry—he had a thing about homosexuality. He made the decision to expel Jack and there wasn't anything my dad or yours could do about it, except quit. That didn't seem like a good option then."

"Those idiots killed my brother."

"They were young and not too bright and they had lots of help from people who should have known better, Frank. Let it go."

"I thought I had, a long time ago. Now I have to start over. It won't be easy."

"If you need to talk—"

"Why are you doing this, Rosemary?"

They had made their way outside to the street and the chill May night. She shivered and folded her arms across her chest. "I forgot how chilly it gets at night in May. I didn't bring a coat."

"You said something about a lift."

"I came with the Starrs. They want to stay. I want to go... with you, if that's okay."

"Sure, yeah. I'm parked two blocks away. Here...wear my coat."

They walked to the car in silence. He opened her door. "It's been a long time."

She turned to face him, her face serious, but he thought he caught a glint in her eye.

"For a lot of things," she said.

SIX

"YOU LOOK AWFUL. WHAT were you up to last night, anyway?" Barbara Thomas stared at her father. He thought she looked like a tall version of her mother. He winced.

"I'm still on Arizona time. It's five in the morning there."

"Is that why you were so late coming in last night, Dad? One o'clock is only eleven your time?"

"You clocked me in? I don't believe it."

"Well, it got late and the brochure said the dinner ended at ten, so I thought—"

"Actually it ended at nine forty-five, at least for me it did. I left early."

"So what were you doing from quarter to ten 'til one?"

"You sound like a cop I know. Am I under investigation here? If so, you'll have to get in line."

She had been leaning forward over the breakfast table. At this, she sat upright and frowned.

"I didn't mean anything. I was worried. Forget I said anything." She stood and started to leave the room. "I've got to get the kids moving," she said.

"Wait. I'm sorry. It's just…I get a lot of that now. Every couple of weeks Sergeant Ledezma finds me. I can't eat a meal in peace. No matter how hard I try to hide, he pops up. 'One more question, Frank,' he'll say. We're on a first name basis now, you see, and always, it's a game. Will I say something that will contradict something I said before? After a while, I just might, because he's asked so many questions in so many ways that by now I don't remember what I said."

"They still think—"

"That I did it? Yes. But that's only part of why I'm grumpy. Sit down. I need to talk to you about your uncle Jack."

She sat, her hands folded on the table. "Uncle Jack, he committed suicide, right?"

"It was a bit more than that."

"Well, I know he was expelled from Scott, and then he did it, and you and Granddad blamed the school and you never went back and Granddad didn't either after he retired. There's more?"

"Your uncle Jack was expelled because someone reported that he was gay. In those days, being gay got you kicked out, period. Last night, four of my classmates allowed as how they were the ones who turned him in."

"That's awful. What did you do?"

"I thought about knocking a few heads together, but I didn't."

"Was he gay, Dad?"

"That's not the point, and no, he wasn't—at least not practicing. What he might have become when he took the time to explore that part of his life, I can't say. Who knows about those things? But then he was just a little…well, he wasn't gay. Do you understand?"

"I don't know. Maybe."

"Your uncle Jack was effeminate. What else he was, if anything, hadn't surfaced. But that characteristic brought him a lot of grief. I spent some serious time duking it out with some of the morons in the school—a lot of morons, actually. I hated your uncle Jack sometimes for that. 'Why can't you stop being so swish?' I'd say, and he'd apologize, like it was his fault everyone else acted so stupid."

"So what happened last night?"

"Well, these guys told me they were the ones and wanted to say they were sorry."

"You were gracious and forgiving, of course."

"Don't get smart with me, girl. I'm still your old man. No, I yelled at them and if I had been ten years younger, would have decked the four of them, then and there."

"That's why you left early."

"Yep."

"So what were you doing from quarter to ten 'til one?"

He studied the woman who began her life as an eight-pound wiggling pink blob in his arms and now had grown into the image of her mother. How much could he tell her? How much like her mother was she really? He weighed the risks against the benefits and decided to equivocate. At least for now. Her mother would have understood, but not his daughter, not with her mother missing and only presumed dead.

"I met some friends. We went drinking."

"You don't drink."

"Soft drinks. They did the heavy lifting, and so I had to drive them home."

She stared at him a long time. He saw the doubt in her eyes and realized she didn't buy it.

"Okay," she said. "When you're ready, I'll be here." She left the room.

Oh what a tangled web we weave, when first we practice to deceive. He never liked Sir Walter Scott. Maybe it had something to do with his name.

AT FIRST HE'D GONE ALONG with the police. They had a job to do. If they were less than sensitive about his loss, well, that's police business. But as the weeks wore on, he grew less tolerant of their coldness, their disbelief. He finally asked them what leads they had, how far the investigation had gotten. That's when the silence and the looks began. That's when Sergeant Ledezma became part of the furniture. Manny Ledezma studied him. The game seemed to be: if I stare at you long enough, you will confess to whatever crime I think you committed and I can go home to the wife and kiddies. Frank wasn't playing. He stared back.

"You think I had something to do with my wife's disappearance, don't you?"

"Did you?"

"Would I tell you if I had?"

More silence.

"You aren't looking at anyone else, are you?" Frank knew the answer but wanted to hear it from Ledezma.

Ledezma had those dark brown eyes that romance writers describe as pools women drown in. Soft and inviting. They were set in a fairly ordinary Hispanic face. Deeply tanned and mustached, Ledezma seemed a model police officer, orderly, methodical, and patient. A little short for a cop, he thought. Not the sort you'd cast in a TV show—he knew something about that—but obviously strong and fit.

"The case is still open."

"You didn't answer my question."

"No."

"No, you didn't answer my question, or no, you're not looking at anyone else?"

Ledezma rose and let himself out the door. "I'll be back if I have more questions."

Frank slammed his fist on the table. How much longer did he have to put up with this? Sandy disappeared years ago. No trace. The insurance company would not pay unless and until the police found a body or made a determination that she was dead. One million dollars in death benefit sitting in an office in Boston. Twice that with the double indemnity. They didn't want to pay. He got up and slid open the door to the patio. He stood a moment, his back still in the air-conditioning while he acclimatized to the hot air outside. His son, down from Seattle, once compared it to walking into a blast furnace. That was before, when he and his son still spoke.

He stepped onto the patio, closing the door behind him. He watched two overweight golfers three putt the green that served as his backyard…well, he thought of it as his backyard. The smell of cigar smoke drifted over to him and drove him back indoors. What was with this cigar/golf thing anyway? He knew at least half a dozen men who never smoked in their life who now cranked up a stogie the minute they cleared the clubhouse. "It's a guy thing, I guess," Sandy had said. "Guys do stuff like that for no reason that I can see. They smoke those terrible cigars, own guns they never shoot, and have to hold the remote. It's obviously a Freudian thing with you all."

"I don't smoke cigars," he'd said. He did hold the remote and he did own a gun. The gun no longer lay locked in the desk drawer. Missing, like her. Presumed…

Ledezma kept after him about the insurance. Well, of course he would. Any cop would. Motive and opportunity, that's all the DA wanted. Frank had both and no alibi. They weren't giving him any credit for the stupidity factor. If he were going to kill someone, wouldn't he have managed all those loose ends better?

Murder, real murder, is boring, it's ordinary, and lacks excitement. Most killings are done by desperate, angry, or demented people out of control. They leave a trail a mile wide in their wake and are usually caught. The few who do get away with it do so because someone or something interferes with the process of finding them.

He'd recited those lines a hundred times in bookstores and libraries—his stock speech. Who'd have thought they'd come back to haunt him?

"You'll be late for your continental breakfast," Barbara called from the living room.

"Going to take a pass on that. I'll go out for the lunch. The headmaster invited me to sit with him at the High Table, whatever that is. I guess I'll do that and find out what's on his mind. Plots and counterplots, *la vie academique. On ne change pas.* Or something like that."

"Well, try to behave. If the kids are going to enroll at Scott, I want him to have a good impression."

"Who said anything about the kids going to Scott?" He sighed. She would wear him down. He knew that. Wear him down with equal parts of "They're your only grandchildren" and guilt. What a combination.

SEVEN

BRAD STARK WIPED THE STEAM from the mirror, peered intently at his reflection, and then adjusted his tie. He ran his finger up its center. The dimple should be tight, but obvious. Satisfied, he stepped back, turned his head right and then left, inspecting each profile out of the corner of his eyes. He ran a hand over his jaw to check for stubble, any miss by his razor. He shifted his weight forward and rose up on his toes. It made him an inch and a half taller, as tall as his wife. Judith Stark spent her life in flats because of him, although she had several pairs of high heels in the closet. She only wore them when she went out without him or when she wished to make a point after one of their fights. Then she'd wear them in his company. It usually worked, and whatever they were fighting about got resolved with an apology from him. He frowned at the thought and considered clearing the shoes from her closet, tossing them all in the trash and laying down the law, once and for all. But he knew he wouldn't. She knew too much about him; knew how to push his buttons.

Brad's strength lay in his ability to compartmentalize. It had served him well, had kept him sane, in fact, at a time when he could easily have crashed. He could shut one door in his mind and open another. His focus would then be wholly redirected and singular. He could even close them permanently, if he needed to.

Now he refocused. Judith and her shoes and any threat she might pose to him evaporated. In their place, he summoned up Frank Smith—Meredith Smith. If he could extract a sizable donation from him—Lord knows Smith could afford it—then the fiftieth-year class gift could be a record and that would please

Felix Darnell, which in turn meant Brad could relax a little, his job would be secure for the time being. He had not put up the numbers Darnell and the Board of Trustees expected. He could be replaced. Baltimore had a reputation for having one of the densest populations of fundraisers and development professionals in the country. Hiring someone to replace him would pose no problem at all. He took a last quick glance in the mirror, braced his shoulders, and left the bathroom.

Last night he'd set out the place cards so that he and Smith would sit next to each other. Somehow Charles Drake ended up beside him. Drake talked his ear off about the summer camps he'd attended at the school fifty years ago, tennis camps, lacrosse camps, band camps, the gamut of summer-filling self-improvement ventures. Drake's parents must have found him as boring a child as Stark did as an adult, and shipped him out to Scott whenever they could. He asked if Brad thought they should revive the camps.

"Some serious money there, Stark," he'd said.

Drake lived in an antique world where haircuts should cost a dollar and a generous tip was a quarter. Brad had no choice but to listen to his drivel and smile through it. He had a lot of nerve, changing those cards and then turning around and boring him with camp nonsense.

He wondered if an honorary diploma for the suicide, for Jack Smith, would help. A diploma, backdated, of course, and a formal apology…no, an apology and a disclaimer stating that the charges were… He shook his head. Darnell would never buy it.

"Come up with a real plan, Stark," he'd probably say, "something that will work this time, something sensible."

Brad chafed under Darnell. He thought that when the Board of Trustees finally found out how incompetently he managed the school, there'd be a sea change at the top levels. He had ideas and Darnell couldn't see them.

Back to Smith. There were rumors about Smith—bad things. He couldn't remember what or how bad. Maybe he could find them on the Internet, the mother lode of information and factoids. Maybe he could find the key to Smith's bank account there. Not blackmail. After all, it would be from the public domain. Anybody could access it. Intelligence was not about what you knew, he believed, but how you used what you knew.

MEREDITH SMITH: BIRTH DATE, family information, book credits, and TV shows. Personal stuff would be harder to find, but not impossible. She surfed three more sites and then found what she was looking for.

Smith's wife of forty years was reported missing in the fall. No evidence of foul play was ever found nor was her body recovered, and it is still unaccounted for. Smith had no explanation for her disappearance and no alibi for the time the police believe that she dropped out of sight. Speculation surrounding his possible involvement in the mysterious disappearance and presumed death continues. Police will only say he remains an investigative lead in the case.

At issue is a substantial life insurance policy taken out on Saundra Smith. Meredith Smith is the only beneficiary and its value is reliably reported to be in seven figures.

They think he did it, she thought. Did he? Could he? People change, but Frank? Rosemary tried to conjure up a murderous Frank Smith. She could not. She remembered only the boy who wept over the naked birds that fell from their nests and whose parents no longer fed them. The boy who, forlorn but dry-eyed, took his nearly blind and crippled dog to the vet to be put to sleep because he couldn't bear to see it suffer.

THE LIFE INSURANCE HAD BEEN Sandy's idea from the start. They didn't need it. Residuals and royalties still arrived quarterly. Movie options from his books and the possibility of turning *Collars* into a full-length feature film promised to bring in even more. On top of that, he had enough new material on his hard drive to keep the flow going for the next decade. He knew his limits and he recognized the possibility his brain could turn to peanut butter in the years to come, that he could follow his mother into dementia, so he wrote steadily. He had six manuscripts in various stages of completion. In his latest books, he'd made it a point to leave out anything that could date them. If he died he figured his wife could pull the next in the series from the file, have a book doctor smooth it out and ship it, and the next, and the next after that, to his publisher.

But Sandy said she wanted the insurance and she wanted it now.

"Both of my parents died of cancer, Frank. My two aunts and three cousins did, too. I'm a medical disaster waiting to happen. This will make what happens bearable."

He read the determination in her hazel eyes. He wasn't going to win this one.

"I'd have to take a physical, see. I want to get this done while I can, while I'm still healthy, before the cancer finds me. When it comes—"

"Don't say when, Sandy. You're inflating the importance of your genetic pool. Your chances of getting cancer are no greater than mine."

"You say. But I know better, and what about you and your obsession with Alzheimer's?"

"That's completely different."

"Not in my book, it isn't."

Frank settled into the sagging end of their sectional sofa. He knew that when she got hold of an idea, there'd be no stopping her. "Okay, okay," he said, surrendering.

"It's like I'm being stalked, you know. Like I've got one of those stalkers the movie stars have, only mine is cancer."

He started to protest but she waved him off.

"It found them and it will find me. I need to get this done now."

He thought her overly dramatic, but gave in to appease her, not out of any sense of either impending death or financial need. If it made her feel better, she could have it. The face amount had been an afterthought. "What do you think? A hundred thousand, two?"

"A million. Let's do a million dollars like one of those pampered athletes you're always complaining about."

The premium on a million dollars turned out to be affordable and she laughed.

"I'm your million dollar baby. Do you remember that song, Frank? *I found a million dollar baby, in a five and ten cent store,*" she sang.

"Nat King Cole," he'd said, and they danced around the living room while she hummed the rest of the tune.

EIGHT

DEXTER LIGHT REACHED into the drawer in the bedside stand. Ragged light streamed through tears in the yellowed blinds on the window. Shadows and light, the story of his life, he thought. Mostly shadows. A bus accelerated outside, leaving a plume of diesel exhaust which would, in a moment or two, seep into his rooms. The picture lay next to the gun. He removed the picture and squinted at its faded images.

She stood next to the front fender of an antique automobile. He never figured out what make. Probably an old Buick. She held the baby in her arms and smiled at the camera, a wide toothy smile that showed a little more gum than one might consider attractive. No *Vogue* model, but her smile always captured him, in spite of its pink surround.

"Who's your daddy?" he said to the picture. His head throbbed. He dropped the photo back in the drawer, looked at the gun, and repeated, "Who's your daddy?" He glanced at his watch. Too late for the breakfast and the luncheon. He rubbed his temples and contemplated the disorder that he called home, at least until they tossed him out of this one-room kitchenette and bath, miserable excuse for an apartment. That could happen soon if he didn't find rent money. If he went to work today, he'd get his pay. There ought to be enough in commissions this week to cover rent and allow him to retrieve his cleaning. There'd be enough, that is, if he could get past the Ironman Tap or Cal's Sports Bar, or any of the half dozen taverns and taprooms that, like bad boys, stuck out their legs and tried to trip him on his way home every day. He guessed if he promised himself a good drunk at the Scott Academy cocktail party tonight, he could avoid them, certain eviction, and his daily contemplation of a premature death.

He sorted through the clothes lying on the floor, selected a relatively clean shirt, unknotted the tie next to it, and tossed them both on the bed. His slacks hung over the back of a chair in front of what would be a usable desk except for the ten inches of unopened mail, official-looking notices from various government organizations, and old newspapers.

Four aspirins and a shower later, he began to feel better. He dressed, found his sport coat behind the sagging armchair in the corner, and put it on. The thought of breakfast made his stomach turn over, so he left for work. He would be on the phones early. That would make Janetta happy. She worried about him. She was the only person who did. Janetta supervised the boiler room where he and a dozen tired men and women sold things. Right now it was security systems. Business tailed off a bit after the Do Not Call List went into effect, but Secure-4-U sold burglar alarms by selling fear, and the people who responded to that, the poor and the aged, were the same group that had not figured out how to get their names on the list, so business was reasonably good, and Dexter managed to stay ahead of his landlord.

"*Tonight, tonight…*" he sang and then couldn't remember the rest of the lyrics. He once owned the tape of *West Side Story*. She'd given it to him. She said it was her favorite show. He cherished it because she did. But he'd lost it somewhere.

"ROSEMARY BARTLETT," she said to her reflection, "what in God's name are you playing at?" She inspected the dark circles under her eyes. Without makeup and the flattery of dim lighting, she looked old.

"You're an old lady, Rosemary, and you should get used to it."

Who says so? Aren't you only as old as you feel?

"That's a myth foisted off on an unsuspecting geriatric public so they will not draw down their Social Security at sixty-two when they are entitled, thereby helping the politicians in Washington to keep stealing from the trust fund."

My, aren't we cynical this morning.

"Shut up and leave me alone."

This is not Victorian England. You're not required to mourn forever, you know.

"I'm not mourning. Not anymore."

Right, so why are you feeling guilty about last night?

"I am not feeling guilty. Yes, I am. Rats!"

She spun around from the dressing table and bunched the silk of her dressing gown in her fists. She felt the tears slide down her cheeks and stamped her foot.

"This is so dumb. The kids are grown and gone. They've been saying for years I should go out. Men have called. One or two of them were even fairly attractive. Why am I feeling this way?"

She turned back to the dressing table and made a face at its clutter. Bottles, boxes, blush brushes, and lipsticks fought for counter space. Too much stuff, she thought.

"Who am I kidding? I'm over sixty-six years old. No amount of this stuff is going to change that, and who'd want an old bag like me anyway?" Who indeed? She left the table and its convicting mirror. She'd get dressed and work in the garden. Then she'd read and…and go to bed early.

And alone?

"Yes, and alone." She went down the wide staircase to the first-floor landing. Sunlight streamed in through the double hung security doors that were made to look like leaded glass but which would stop a bullet from a .357 Magnum, she'd been told. George used to worry about her. She paused to glance at yesterday's mail, neatly stacked at one end of an ornate mahogany credenza. The reunion brochure winked at her.

"What do you want?"

She'd started talking to herself shortly after her husband died. Her home had always been filled with noisy conversation, even after her children left to make homes of their own. But when

George died, the silence descended like fog on the Chesapeake Bay. It nearly drove her mad. So, she filled it with her own voice. Voices, actually. Sometimes when she talked she felt like the little cartoon characters who had a devil on one shoulder and an angel on the other. They'd argue back and forth and she'd be caught in the middle. Once, in the middle of one of her conversations, she realized the meter reader was standing ten feet away listening to her. She blushed and retreated into the house. She wondered if he had any other batty old women on his route. She hoped so.

She ran her eye over the schedule. Earlier she had checked off the events she thought she might attend: the dinner, the party Saturday at the Nichols', and a cocktail party at the Academy tonight. She'd made her selections a week ago when it seemed more like an adventure. Not an adventure, really, but a chance to satisfy her curiosity. She and Frank had been childhood sweethearts. She wanted to catch up, that's all. Now she debated whether to close it down before she slid into a situation that could hurt. Well, maybe not hurt, what could happen, really? But embarrass…?

Yeah, right.

"I told you to go away. And it could, it might."

And so your decision is?

"I'll decide later, not now."

She went back upstairs and began sorting through her dresses. She laid out the red one she bought in Hawaii. George never liked it. She'd wear it tonight.

"I WON'T BE BACK UNTIL late tonight." Frank watched his daughter out of the corner of his eye.

"What time?"

"Barbara, I am an adult, not your teenaged son. You do not have to worry about me. I don't know when. I might meet up with some people and we might go somewhere."

"Okay, I won't worry about you. Did you know almost no one wears Arpège anymore?"

"Wears what?"

"It's a perfume. Mom used to wear it."

"Oh, that. 'Promise her anything, but give her Arpège,' they used to say. I didn't do a lot of scent."

"I picked up your shirt to wash it. It reeks of Arpège."

"Reeks? Are you sure it reeks?"

"I can smell it."

"I don't think that qualifies as reeking. There were ladies at the dinner. One sat next to me. You probably smell cigars and booze, too."

She made a face. "Don't be too late, Dad. I'll wait up."

"Don't you dare."

"I have a right to worry. Why are you always so secretive about things? All the time when I was growing up, you never... I only heard about your brother, Jack, just now."

"You didn't need to know before now."

"But I'm family. I have a right to know."

"Did hearing about your uncle Jack, a man you never knew, could not have known, make you feel better? Would your life have improved if you'd known about him all these years? What is the point of burdening people with the dark side of life if you don't have to?"

"Right now I guess I want to know what else you haven't told me. What other secrets are you keeping?"

"None you need to know about," he said and thought about Sergeant Ledezma.

NINE

FRANK MANAGED TO HOLD his temper in check the first time he missed the turn. After all, things can change dramatically in five decades. The second time, he wondered again about his memory. Anger began to give way to frustration. On the third try, he gave up any semblance of patience and rehearsed the four-letter vocabulary he'd learned in the Academy's locker rooms. His landmark, an abandoned streetcar, had stood on that corner for as long as he could remember. For a while, it functioned as a vegetable stand where fresh produce could be bought at prices lower than at the market. Later, new owners used it as an outlet for their Silver Queen corn crop, fresh picked from adjacent farms. But the farms were gone, replaced by condominiums and town houses, and God alone knew what happened to the streetcar. In fact, the intersection now lay a hundred yards to the north, complete with traffic lights, turn lanes, and strangers. On his fourth pass through the intersection, he spotted a van with the school's seal on its door turning right. He cut across two lanes of traffic accompanied by blaring of horns and verbal abuse and followed it to the Academy.

SCOTT ACADEMY CELEBRATED its one hundred and thirtieth anniversary in 2004. By American standards, that made it an old school. And like most things American, it had drifted significantly from its traditions and origins. It began life as The Maryland Academy for Boys, intended as a haven for poor boys from Baltimore. In the 1870s, that meant street urchins, orphans, and the discarded children the age produced. At the remove of well over a century and in an era of relative abundance, it is difficult to imagine the fate children suffered in the late nineteenth century. Dickens' *Oliver Twist*, with its London scamps, presented a prettified picture compared to the reality of street life in urban America in the era between the Civil and Spanish American Wars.

The boys selected for the Academy and sent to the country received, for the most part, a reprieve from an early death, the result of poverty—malnutrition, rickets, or any of the myriad diseases that plagued a pre-antibiotic world. They were taught penmanship, learned to read, and given a smattering of the classics. More importantly, they acquired practical skills that prepared them for a return to the city's streets, ready to assume a productive life free from crime—the latter being the probable fate of too many of their contemporaries.

The school's first headmaster, Colonel Anselm Quentin Armiger, served with General Robert E. Lee at Gettysburg. He lost an arm in that tragedy and sat out the remainder of the Civil War in Richmond, working in the army's quartermaster corps. He'd accepted the position as headmaster primarily because his wife had developed consumption and her doctors believed fresh country air would afford her at least a respite from the ravages of the disease if not an outright cure. The fact that he was also the second cousin of the board chairman and a man of unrelenting piety didn't hurt his case, either.

Faced with the first contingent of ragamuffins that climbed the hill to the school, and still without a decent classroom building or facilities to house them, he dressed his boys in uniforms—that being the simplest way to replace their rags. Each boy received a pair of butternut linen trousers, two shirts, and a high-collared tunic, all of which looked suspiciously like Confederate army uniforms. Over the years, the uniforms evolved and ended looking like those worn at West Point.

For the first six weeks of their stay, those first students lived in tents and met for their studies in a barn. Several, seeing no significant difference between their country and urban environments, and homesick, ran away. Armiger's first faculty mem-

bers were predictably male, and, like him, the shattered waste
product of war. A few younger men possessed more education
than ambition and needed work. He ordered the boys by age into
companies and appointed older boys as their officers. He formed
the companies into a battalion. Later, as the school grew and
younger, paying students were added to the mix, the battalions
grew into a corps.

The senior students elected a corps commander, who wore,
at first, a half dozen gold stripes on his shoulders, later a lieutenant colonel's silver oak leaf. The officers descended in rank
from there and in the same order as the army. It would be an
awkward arrangement and one attacked periodically by alumni,
parents, and faculty, all of whom yearned for the more easily
recognizable president, vice president, student council model.
But it held until the mid-seventies, when the school's board decided to drop the military program. Any semblance it once had
to West Point disappeared forever.

Colonel Armiger spent most of his first year writing letters
to the board asking for money, buildings, and the services
of a medical man. They, like so many groups entrusted with
substantial sums of other people's money, took to believing it
was theirs and, like Silas Marner, guarded it like gold, granting
Armiger's requests reluctantly and only after endless debate
and haggling. When two boys died of pneumonia and the
county coroner threatened to report the school for child abuse,
a relatively new breach of the law at the time, the money began
to flow.

The school languished as a mediocre military school until
Franklin Scott, a Midwestern railroad mogul and multimillion-
aire, at a time when even a millionaire was reckoned a rare com-
modity, visited the school in search of a lost nephew. Finding him
in good health and safe, Scott endowed the Academy handsomely
with the stipulation it be named after his errant nephew. The
board, exhausted by the irksome duties of managing a school
for ungrateful boys, agreed. Scott quickly applied his consider-
able managerial skills to the school, impaneled a new Board of

Directors, and set it on a path that ultimately led to its recognition in 2000 as one of the country's premier prep schools. Generations of young men salvaged from the mean streets matured and, for the most part, repaid with gratitude and endowments the school that had lifted them out of the gutter and from a life that held no possible future.

Armiger died before his wife and was replaced by another former army officer, this one from the Union side but who carried more substantial educational credentials and experience. Later, in the 1920s, the school began accepting paying students and the evolution from a unique institution to a college preparatory school began. Fifty years ago, when Frank attended, it had been male. Half of the student body lived in dormitories and went home only on weekends, if at all. Somewhere in the seventies, in the confused effects of Vietnam, it shed both its uniforms and all-male status.

FRANK FOLLOWED THE VAN to a parking lot behind Main. He didn't remember the lot ever being there, but then half the buildings that stretched out before him were new also. He looked in the direction of the chapel, seeking the familiar bulk of the three-story building where he grew up—where he and Rosemary Bartlett grew up. Gone. In its place, a blockish building with too much glass and too little style had been erected. He checked his map and discovered his old apartment complex had been replaced with a building that housed a kindergarten and grades one through five. He thought that appropriate.

"Can I help you?"

He turned to see a young woman, a very young woman, in a blue blazer and khaki skirt. She balanced a stack of books in her arms and looked inquiringly at him. She looked to be twenty but could have been older or younger. Everyone looked young to him now. He thought his new general practitioner couldn't be more than twelve.

"Thanks, Miss...ah—"

"I'm Elizabeth Roulx. I teach English literature, and you must be Meredith Smith. Am I right?"

"Yes, but…well, I'm impressed. How did you know?"

"No mystery there…sorry, no pun intended…. Dr. Darnell asked me to keep an eye out for you. He said he hoped you'd come early and if you did I should ask you to speak to my classes about writing."

"No, well, that might have been fun, but I couldn't get away any earlier."

"Maybe some other time," she said. He didn't detect any annoyance in her voice so he guessed the plan to speak had been an impulse on someone else's part, not hers. At least it never made it onto his agenda.

"There's a luncheon somewhere," he said, consulting his map a second time. It felt strange needing a map to find his way around a part of the world he once knew so intimately.

"Come with me," she said. "We're at the same table."

"The High Table, Dr. Darnell said."

She chuckled. "Felix is an Anglophile. He wants to make believe he's at Eton or Oxford. He had a low platform built and set one table in the front of the dining hall reserved for himself and department chairs. All veddy Brit. Next he'll have us in hoods and gowns."

They made their way around a mound of very old lilacs. Frank remembered the lilacs. His mother planted them a long time ago. Somewhere in the middle should be a birdbath set in the ground with mortar he and Jack had mixed for her.

"Do you mind?" he asked and pushed his way into the thicket. The shallow dish lay in pieces but it was still there. A touchstone.

They resumed their walk, rounded the power plant, and headed toward a remarkably ugly building.

"That's Perry Hall," she said. "If half of what I've heard about Black Jack Perry is true, I think the good colonel must be spinning in his grave over that architectural monstrosity."

Frank looked at the boxy lines and alternating glass and rob-in's egg blue panels and decided it had all the charm of a toll booth.

"Perry was a hard man," he said.

She glanced at him, one brow up. "You're next to me, I think."

They stepped into the dining hall. It had an under scent—that's the only way he could describe it—fried food and spilled milk, but barely strong enough to overcome the Lysol. Too late, Frank realized he should have taken a miss on lunch, too.

TEN

Elizabeth Roulx ushered him into the dining hall. People milled about, looking for place cards that didn't exist and faces they no longer recognized, their smiles vague but hopeful.

"Your father used to head up the English Department, didn't he?" she asked, leading him to the front of the room to a table set on the platform raised an inch or two above the black-and-white tiled floor. The High Table.

"Yes, a long time ago. I doubt anyone would remember him now."

"Oh, but you're wrong about that, Meredith…may I call you Meredith?"

"I think you already have." Frank hoped he didn't sound short. He didn't intend to be, but something about the room and its confusion set him on edge. He couldn't think why. It might have been the odor.

"I am the school's archivist, too. The responsibility of cataloging and filing all sorts of documents falls to me. I recently came across your father's old teaching notes. Your father is over there, by the way." He looked in the direction she indicated. Sure enough, his father, or what passed as a portrait of him, smiled back.

"Dad got a light," he said, surprised. It looked new. An extension cord connected it to an outlet in the next panel over. Apparently electrical service only went to every other panel. You got position first, he thought, the light went with location. He formed a question: What criteria determined location? Then the obvious struck him. His father had received the lamp only recently.

"Yes, well, he's highly thought of, did you know that?" Ms.

Roulx looked nervous, like something, some task assigned to her wasn't going very well and she needed to regain her position.

"I didn't know. When did he get his light?" he asked. Meanness did not play a significant part in Frank's personality as a rule. His wife used to complain about that. She thought he rolled over too easily. But today he still smarted from his confrontation with Powers, and even his time with Rosemary had not completely erased that. And then, this morning's session with his daughter had stirred it up all over again. Now, he smelled a rat and gave in to the opportunity to stick it to the school.

"Pardon me?" Ms. Roulx had the decency to blush. Maybe he should be a bit easier on her.

"The light over his portrait…it's a terrible rendering, by the way…when did you all decide to light him up?"

A tall, thin man wearing a carefully worn and patched Harris tweed coat sidled up to them. "Smith, isn't it?" He stuck out his hand. "Paisley Rehnquist, here. I am, if it can be so stated, your late father's successor."

Frank shook the slightly damp, limp hand of Paisley Rehnquist and surreptitiously wiped it on his trousers.

"I think it's a very decent likeness," Rehnquist said, peering over his half-lens reading glasses. Rehnquist had body odor.

"You never met him—how would you know?" Frank stepped back a foot or two.

"Well, I…people who knew him said so."

"I see…and that is sufficient?"

"Um, yes, certainly."

"Then you should know, as his successor, so to speak, that the artist painted that disgrace from a photograph. My father refused to sit. The only reason it's there at all is that one of his former students paid for it and the school had to accept it as part of a sizable donation made by said student. This is the first time I've seen it and I assure you, it is perfectly dreadful. When did he get his light?"

Elizabeth Roulx looked embarrassed, but Paisley Rehnquist charged ahead.

"Really, well…times change. We don't use the old methods anymore, you know. Your father taught the classic way. We are into the new."

Frank thought he said *the new* like he'd discovered an addition to the periodic table of the elements.

"New? As in what, exactly?"

"Ah, no more doting on dead white men, literary fossils. I'm sure you had that introduction to literature, and many did, but it's over, passé. We are contemporaneous now."

"Which dead white men were you referring to?"

"Oh, you know, Hemingway, Steinbeck, Faulkner—"

"James Baldwin?"

"Um…well, yes, if you wish."

"Paisley—may I call you Paisley? Here's the problem—when I read Hemingway, Steinbeck, Faulkner, Kerouac, and the aforementioned Baldwin, they weren't dead, and Baldwin wasn't white. They were…what was that word you used? Contemporaneous. If you wish to divorce yourself from your cultural heritage, that is your right, but I think it intellectually disingenuous to shortchange your students, as well."

Elizabeth Roulx glanced to her left at Brad Stark, apparently seeking some help. Frank could not be sure if Stark had been listening to their conversation or not. He guessed he had.

Stark stepped forward and smoothly disengaged Rehnquist from the group and then led them to their places at the High Table. They sat. Frank picked at his salad. Perry Dining Hall presented as bleak a face on the inside as it did out. Portraits of faculty members, mostly long forgotten, hung on panels between sheets of plate glass. Some had lights attached to their frames; some did not. He wondered again what constituted the criteria for being awarded a light. Elizabeth Roulx watched him, followed his eyes.

"Brad," she said, showing more teeth than necessary, "Meredith has been telling me about his father's portrait."

"Really?" Stark leaned forward to peer around her so he could say something. Frank noted that as he did so, his tie drooped into his salad. Considering the amount of oil and vinaigrette applied in the kitchen, there would be a stain—a big one.

"Your father meant a lot to the school," Stark said and showed a lot of teeth, as well. Everyone seemed to be a graduate of smile school today.

"Did he? How nice. He did not leave here a happy man."

"No, I suppose not. But that doesn't change the way the students felt or the important impact he had on the school. He wrote our first textbook. We used it for years."

"Yes, *An Introduction to American Literature,*" Frank recited. "He made a little money on that book. It helped pay for my mother's constant care—Alzheimer's," he added, seeing the question on Elizabeth Roulx's face.

"I'm sorry," she said. Her smile faded but the confusion remained. Her head rotated back and forth between the two men as she tried to follow the exchange. Frank leaned back in his chair to break contact with Stark and made an attempt to eat. Stark gave up trying to catch his eye.

"Yesterday," she said, softly turning toward him.

"What?"

"The light...yesterday."

"Thank you, I thought so. And I can expect some personal attention from Felix Darnell before I get out of here?"

She smiled. "Yes. They think you have money and hope you will contribute or something."

"I make a comfortable living, but I am not rich, not the way they think."

"But your books, your TV show?"

"I do not write blockbuster bestsellers. I am a moderately successful writer of small mystery stories. What do you know about writing and publishing?"

"I teach creative writing."

"That's not what I asked. What do you know about the business of writing? Very few writers live on their royalties. Most teach, practice law or medicine—keep their day jobs, in fact. I am one of the few lucky ones who makes enough to live on from writing. I am not rich by anyone's standard. Is that what you all think? I will make a big gift to the school?"

Elizabeth Roulx looked at him, evidently disappointed. He wondered if she realized she had a shred of spinach on one front tooth. He heard Stark's chair scrape back, saw him move toward Darnell's end of the table. Darnell, apparently misreading his intention, stood and tapped his knife blade on his plate. Before Stark could deliver what Frank assumed must be the bad news, Darnell launched into his speech. Stark scribbled furiously in a little notebook he pulled from his hip pocket while Frank contemplated the spreading stain on his tie. Stark proffered the note he'd written. Darnell took it and slipped it in his vest pocket without reading it, never missing a beat. Stark rolled his eyes and returned to his seat.

"Elizabeth, it's been very nice meeting you, but I'll be going now," Frank said.

"Now? But the headmaster planned to speak to you after—"

"Our prodigal, so to speak," Darnell intoned and gestured in Frank's direction, "has returned. The son of our beloved Dr. Charles Addison Smith and a writer of national reputation in his own right, Meredith Smith has joined us today."

Darnell led a polite round of applause. Frank nodded and sat down again and contemplated his lunch.

"I might as well eat this. It seems I'm stuck here for the duration," he said.

ROSEMARY ATE HER SANDWICH while she read her paper. She, unlike most people who devour their morning paper with breakfast, saved hers for lunch. She believed that people's minds worked too slowly early in the morning to absorb anything important. She'd come to that conclusion after she discovered that crossword puzzles that had her stumped before ten in the morning were a breeze after two in the afternoon. She relegated nonmental tasks to mornings—gardening, laundry, and so on. Her late husband thought the whole notion silly. He had been one of those early risers who didn't require an alarm clock to bounce out of bed at five-thirty. He'd be showered, dressed, and out the door about the time she began to have the first inklings that a world existed on the other side of her closed eyelids.

The front page of *The Sun* carried the same depressing news it had the day before. Shootings, terrorists, political corruption. Nothing changed. She tried to remember if it had always been that way. She didn't think so. Years ago, crime and violence seemed far away. They never locked their doors and left the car keys in the ignition. She frowned.

You sound like an old lady.

"We've had this conversation once already. Leave me alone."

Her thoughts drifted, to Scott, to another, gentler age, and finally to Frank Smith.

He's a man with a lot of hurt.

"I suppose so. Is that why I'm feeling this way?"

It doesn't matter why you feel that way. Carpe diem.

"Oh, please, I'm not some thirty-something, perky breasted, one-hundred-twenty-pound career woman. I'm old and subject to the laws of gravity. I can't just move in and out of relationships depending on the state of my hormones. I don't even have hormones."

Right. You're an old bag ready for the scrap heap. Come on, the buzz on the street is fifty is the new thirty, so what does that make you, forty?

"That is horse hockey. Boomers, unwilling to admit they're getting old, are in mass denial. They think they drank from the fountain of youth at Woodstock. But when the cartilage disappears from their knees and arthritis kicks in, they'll give up that nonsense and pay attention to what their body is trying to tell them. So, I'm not young and people my age just don't… whatever."

Where is it written that people in their "golden years" aren't allowed to fall in love, have sex, or enjoy themselves?

"That's not what I was thinking about."

Yes, it was, you hussy. Stop feeling guilty and go for it.
"Go for it? Go for what?"
Should she? Could she? Well, why not?

ELEVEN

LATER, FRANK WOULD COMPARE the evening's events to four cars speeding toward each other at an intersection, none aware of the other's approach. When they met, the collision would be spectacular. He admitted the simile contained more hyperbole than truth, and the events he found so spectacular would seem ordinary to anyone not intimately involved with what followed. As it turned out, there would be five players involved in the collision, but he didn't like the image of a five-cornered intersection, and besides, Darnell played only a minor role. Nevertheless, for the families of four missing boys and a few members of the Scott Academy faculty, the cocktail party set in motion a series of actions and reactions that would forever change their lives.

Guests started arriving shortly before six. Alumni, alumnae, wives, and husbands dressed in blazers and slacks or cocktail dresses flowed out of parking lots and along the Academy's brick walkways like bright flower petals bobbing downstream. A large green-and-white-striped tent, set up with tables, two bars, and the aroma from an extensive buffet drew them inexorably with its promise of refreshment and fellowship.

Frank calculated the time the round trip back to Baltimore would take—too long and not worth the trouble. Instead, he'd brought a fresh shirt and electric razor, and, borrowing one of the school's soap-scented washrooms, freshened up and changed. The marquee was nearly empty when he entered; no waiting at the bar and a free run at the buffet, two activities that would become increasingly difficult as the evening progressed and more guests crowded under its green and white stripes. Newcomers, for the most part, clustered together by class year. Occasionally they would shift and merge only to separate again like a human lava lamp. Frank nibbled finger food and sipped tonic water. He had learned that to avoid a zealous host's insistence on his having a "real drink," he needed a look-alike drink in his hand. So he sipped his ersatz gin and tonic and studied the crowd.

Rosemary made a splash of color as she entered. Heads turned. No mean feat for a sixty-six-year-old woman. Frank waved. She saw him and beamed. It took her a full five minutes to make her way through the crowd. She had friends and acquaintances to greet and one or two approaches from recently widowed men to fend off.

"I need a drink," she said when she'd finally run the gauntlet.

"What'll you have?"

"What you're drinking will do."

"I doubt it. This is a virgin gin and tonic."

"Really? No, get me the real thing. It's way too late in the game for some of us to have thoughts about virginity, liquid or otherwise. Get me a Jack and Ginger."

"That's not a drink, that's a dance team."

"Trust me, it's a drink, but you're right. It does sound like one."

"Okay, come with me," he said and took her elbow. "The bar is crowded and this could take some time. I could lose you in the interim."

"I'm not going anywhere."

"Indulge me."

They plunged into the crowd around the bar, greeting the people they knew, nodding to others. Five minutes later they emerged, only slightly disheveled but with drinks in both hands.

"This ought to hold us for a while," he said.

"Yes, but how do I eat with a drink in each hand?"

"We'll grab some space at a table—that one," he said, pointing at the table marked with a large *50th*.

DEXTER LIGHT STOOD BEHIND the woman in the bright Hawaiian dress and the old man with her and smiled when he saw them push out of the scrum at the bar, each with a drink in both hands. He guessed they'd be loopy by seven-thirty and in need of medical attention by eight. He enjoyed watching the characters that annually descended on the school, the old ones in particular. They spent hours getting tight and retelling stories about teachers now long dead and escapades that grew more and more exotic with each passing year as details were invented and the stories expanded. He vowed that he would not become one of the old geezers. When his mind went, he decided, so would the rest of him.

He wandered over to the tables marked *25th*. A few of his classmates had arrived. The rest would come later. They had important jobs and families. Twenty-fifth-year reunion or not, reunions received a low priority on their to-do lists. He recognized most of the men at the table. The women with them, he supposed, were wives or girlfriends. Women did not enroll at Scott until two years after his class graduated.

"Dex," Marc Antonio called out, "our peerless leader."

"Hello, Marc. Who's the babe?"

Antonio's face flushed.

"You must have hit the bar early, Light."

"Like voting in Chicago…early and often, Marc," he said and turned to the woman with him. "Hi, I'm Dexter Light and I'm a little drunk, but not too drunk to see you are young enough to be this guy's daughter. Tell me you're not."

"I'm his wife. And you *are* drunk. Is that why you're so rude or are you always this way?"

"Can't say, darling, I'm never sober long enough to find out."

She gave him a pitying look and turned away. The others at the table averted their eyes. Conversations around him resumed. None included him.

"Marc," he interrupted, "do you know the old coot with the woman in the red sarong over at the fifty table?"

"Why would I know them?"

"I thought you knew everyone. You're our alumni representative, aren't you?"

"I think that's Meredith Smith, the writer," a big blonde in a blue-and-yellow sack dress warbled.

"That's Meredith Smith? I thought Meredith Smith was a woman." This from a short guy that Dexter couldn't place.

"What's he write?"

"Mysteries, and he had that TV show for a while."

"I guess that's why Darnell is talking to him. Trying to pick his pocket."

"If he's a mystery story writer, someone ought to ask him to figure out what happened to the campus kids."

"What happened to who?" Marc's wife had rejoined the group.

"Dexter, you ask him."

"No," Dexter snapped.

"Aw, come on, Dex. You're our leader. You're the class golden boy, Most Likely to Succeed, Corps Commander, Mr. Big, et cetera, et cetera. You can do it," Antonio said.

The sarcasm was not lost on the group or Dexter. Where they had arrived fresh and neatly pressed, he looked like he'd been dragged backward through a keyhole. Where they were conspicuously successful, he stood before them a rumpled, yellow-eyed failure.

"No," he repeated, this time softly, and added, "let it go."

Harvey Byrd looked up from his scotch on the rocks. "Don't you want to know?"

"No, I don't." But he did. He hadn't been able to run away from, drown, or forget that afternoon. Maybe, it would be better to get it over with. "Okay," he said, finally. "I'll do it. Antonio, you have to come with me to be my witness, and you, too, sweetheart. What's your name anyway?"

"Denise, and if you call me darling or sweetheart again, I'll kick you where what's left of your gene pool resides."

"Right. Good thought."

The three of them started toward the fifty table. Dexter made them wait while he secured another drink from the bar.

"WHO'S THE DISHY OLD BABE in the gorgeous scarlet dress?" Judith Stark pointed across the expanse of the marquee. "At the fiftieth-year table." Her husband turned and stared.

"That's Rosemary Mitchell with Meredith Smith."

"Oh, so that's the mark you and Darnell are working on."

"Judith, please, someone will hear you. He's not a mark, he's a potential donor. An important one, I hope." He didn't sound too sure. The conversation he'd overheard at the luncheon raised some doubts about that. But Darnell assured him that rich people always talked that way, were always poor-mouthing. He, that is, Brad, just needed to check out Smith's financials and make the pitch.

"Well, if he is, and you don't want to lose him, you'd better hustle over there before Dexter Light drives him off the plantation."

Brad's heart sank. Light and other members of the twenty-fives were heading straight for Smith. Dexter, as usual, unsteady on his feet.

"Be right back."

"No hurry." His wife turned and sidled up to the bar. "I'll be right here."

He scowled, started to say something, and then turned and left. She had on her heels.

ANTONIO INTRODUCED HIMSELF, his wife, and Light to Frank. He, in turn, introduced Rosemary. In the awkward pause that followed, Brad Stark arrived.

"Ah, Stark," Light said, "you're just in time—"

"I hope so."

"We were just going to proposition Mr. Smith, our imminent author and expert on crime."

"Look, Mr. Light—" Brad began.

"Since you were planning to do the same thing, only for a different cause, you will appreciate what we have in mind."

"I don't think Mr. Smith is up for any of your—"

"It's all right," Antonio said and looked at the group for support. "We just want his expert help to solve the mystery."

"What mystery is that?" Frank asked. He searched the faces of the people in front of him for a clue. All he saw were young-ish forty-somethings who seemed a little too pleased with themselves.

"The missing boys. You must have heard about that."

"Sorry. No."

"Well," Antonio said, "when we were seniors, four...is that right, four?"

Light nodded. "Four."

"Four campus kids went into Old Oak Woods and disappeared. Not a trace. You know what we mean by campus kids, Mr. Smith?"

"Oh, my, yes, Mrs. Mitchell and I know all about campus kids."

"Well, we thought that since you deal in mysteries all the time, and with the wisdom that comes with age, you should give solving it a shot."

"I see." Frank waited. There had to be more to it than that.

"You have a reputation. The question is, is it wisdom or se-nility that comes with age?—sorry, no offense intended. But can you do it?" Light started to leave.

"Wait, don't go," Antonio said.

"You don't look so good, Light," Denise added.

"Cheap booze."

"I think you've bothered Mr. Smith enough already," Brad said. Frank thought Stark didn't look perky, either.

"Everybody sit down and tell me what happened." Frank gestured for the others to join his table.

Antonio started. Light interrupted. And finally Rosemary told the story.

"One spring afternoon, late May, about this time of year, twenty-five years ago, a Saturday afternoon, four kids, four campus kids, that is, were seen going into Old Oak Woods. I don't remember the time exactly, it's probably not important—"

"Two o'clock," Light said. Stark nodded.

"Well, then, two o'clock they were seen going into the woods and they disappeared. Gone. Not a trace, not a clue, just vanished into thin air. The police and hundreds of volunteers searched the woods. They brought in dogs and even a psychic—nothing."

Frank listened and frowned. Why were these shiny-brights after him to solve a twenty-five-year-old mystery?

"Well, I'll tell you. The people police least want messing around in an investigation, even an old one, are mystery story writers. The truth of the matter? We are poorly equipped to solve a case, any case. The only crime we know anything about is the made-up kind. We write mysteries, but we know the solution before we start. The clues are ours, the crime is ours. Now, someone else's…not that this is a crime exactly…but that's another story entirely."

"Well, that settles it," Stark said and looked relieved.

"You're sure?" Light asked, and smirked. Frank studied him—saw the rumpled clothes, the bloodshot eyes, and the failure. "Probably not up to it. Keep you all up past nine. Age slows you down. Like, I read somewhere that old people have a higher rate of alcoholism because they don't realize they can't handle the three martinis they were used to having before dinner when they were active and forget—"

"I expect you know a good deal about alcoholism," Frank snapped. What was with this jerk? Stark looked angrily at Light and started to speak.

"Light doesn't mean—"

"I think you should do it, Frank," Rosemary said.

He turned and studied her face. Her eyes flickered—with excitement or anger? He couldn't be sure. He turned back to Stark.

"Would the school support me in this?"

"Umm…I'd have to check into that."

Rosemary smiled at Stark. "I imagine the school would have the same interest in his work as it does his potential as a donor."

"Touché," Light said, but he wasn't smiling. Stark swallowed and nodded.

"You'll help?" he asked Rosemary, hoping he'd correctly read her excitement.

"Just call me Miss Marple."

"Effie Perine is who I had in mind." *Her eyes were brown and playful in a shiny boyish face*...Hammett, of course. And she could pass for Spade's secretary, plus forty years.

"Not good enough. She just answered the phone. How about Nora Charles?"

"We're dating ourselves."

"Some things are obvious, Frank."

TWELVE

Sergeant Manuel Ledezma started his career in the Los Angeles Police Department. He grew weary of urban warfare and the department's top-heavy bureaucracy. Each day seemed like a week and the possibility of promotion further away. When the scandals seemed to have no high-water mark, he joined the growing number of officers and detectives who bailed out—left the department. He moved his family to Arizona and signed on with the McMicken Police Department. He never regretted the choice—until now. He sat across the desk from a lieutenant newly promoted to head up his division. A stack of folders sat in the exact center of the desk. Ledezma recognized them as his open cases.

"Ledezma," the new guy, Phelps, said, "you have twenty cases pending, is that right?"

"Yes, sir."

"That's a lot."

"Yes, sir." Not by L.A. standards, it's not, he thought.

"They call you Manny?"

"Yes, sir."

"Okay, Manny, here's what I need you to do. I want half of these babies closed by the end of the month. If there're perps out there, you find 'em or forget 'em."

"Sir? You want me to just shut them down?"

"Yep…I know, I know. Some bad guys are going to get away with murder, but you know what? They are anyway. I've read over most of these. They're dead in the water. No leads, no suspects, nothing we can wait out—nothing. It's time to turn them over to Cold Case."

"But some will break in time. I'm only keeping the ones I'm sure will pop."

"Like which?"

"Like Frank Smith."

"The writer guy? Why do you think that one will, as you say, pop?"

Ledezma paused, wondering if he would have to justify the whole stack. "He did it. I know he did it, and he knows I know. Sooner or later he's going to make a mistake and then we'll have him."

"What makes you so sure he's the guy who clipped his wife?"

"Classic case. He had a motive—life insurance in seven figures on the wife, recently in force, and he's the sole beneficiary. Opportunity—he and his wife lived quietly, no close friends, no kids at home. No alibi—he can't account for his time for the day his wife disappeared. And there is one other thing. He had a gun registered in his name and it's missing."

"What'd he say happened to the gun?"

"He said he got rid of it, tossed it in the lake, he said."

"Why would he do that?"

"He didn't say."

"Did you cross-check the wife's disappearance with any other activity in the area that might turn up a lead—besides Smith?"

"We canvassed the neighborhood, asked the helicopters to keep an eye peeled when they flew the desert, yes, we did."

"You're committed to Smith being the guy?"

"Yes, sir. He's the guy."

"I'll make you a deal, Manny. You nail this guy by the end of the month and you keep your files. If you don't, the case goes cold, along with the rest of these turkeys, savvy?"

"But—"

"That's it. I need manpower on hot cases and I can't allow the division to get any thinner by tying you up on these old ones. The population in this sector has doubled in the last five years and we have the same staffing. I can't afford to have you off the street. That's it."

Ledezma left the office, and when he cleared the corner where he couldn't be seen, he removed his tie and unbuttoned his collar. Ledezma knew the expression "hot under the collar" intimately. He wondered if it was too late to take up L.A.'s new chief's offer to go back. Many of his friends had. He said no the first time. There'd been no second invitation. He returned to his desk and slammed the files on it. Dominic Pastorella jumped.

"What's up with that?"

Ledezma explained what happened.

"I'm getting to like this new guy less and less," Pastorella said.

"I have fourteen days to get Smith or he and all the rest in the stack walk."

"What're you going to do?"

"Start over. From the very beginning. Somewhere in the file I've missed something—something that didn't seem important at the time." Ledezma opened the file and leafed through its pages. "How come nobody ever talked to the insurance company? You could start there. And I want to know what happened to his gun. Threw it in the lake, my ass."

"Hey, it's quitting time. How about grabbing a beer and a burger?"

"Not tonight, Dom. I only got two weeks and no time to waste if I'm going to fry this guy."

"WHERE DO WE START?" Rosemary asked. For the second night in a row, she'd ditched her ride to go home with Frank. They were heading south toward the beltway and to Ruxton. She guessed there might be some talk this time.

Who cares?

"Who cares, indeed? Let them talk."

"What?" Frank said. "Who cares about where we start—talk about what?"

"No, sorry, I…never mind—senior moment," she said, embarrassed.

"You know," he said, "I hate that expression. People our age use it all the time when we can't remember a name or a movie title or something. We grin sheepishly and say, 'senior moment.' Young people smile back and think we're going dotty. And all the while we're scared to death that someday the police will find us wandering down some street in our pajamas in the middle of the afternoon and we won't know how we got there or who we are.

"The funny thing is, memory is the one thing everybody thinks is infallible, in spite of reams of research to the contrary, and when it falters, we panic. We begin to doubt ourselves and our ability to cope. People not faced with lapses start making lists for us, become our minders. They get ready to pat us on the head and say, 'There, there, I'll handle it.' We're not useless or demented, Rosemary, we're just old. We can still tell a good story, make love, and carry on a conversation with consider-ably more substance than those thirty-something yuppies who think the greatest loss to American culture was the termination of *Friends*."

Are you listening to this man?

"Yes."

"Yes?"

"My children think I should act my age," she said. "They're all for my going out and so on but if I ever hint that maybe I'd like to…you know…they look as shocked as I must have when they broached the topic to me when they were teenagers. Role reversal."

Good job, Rosemary. Now you're getting it.

"Thanks."

"You're welcome," he said and gave her a sideways look, one eyebrow cocked. "There are two reasons I said I'd look into the mystery of the missing kids. You know the first? Because those young people don't think I can do it."

"I sort of guessed that. I thought they were interested, maybe just as a hypothetical, but—"

"No, you're right, but not at first. There was something else going on. That's the odd part. I would have sworn that the sandy-haired guy, what's his name? Light? I think he didn't want any part of it at first. But after he saw you and the look in your eyes and heard you volunteer, he changed. He thinks we are an old, ludicrous couple. I'm a has-been celebrity. You are a sixtyish babe wearing the kind of dress he'd expect to see on a younger woman. To him we are…what?…geriatric Ken and Barbie. The other guy and his trophy wife were just indulging me. Tomorrow they will have forgotten all about it. It ticks me off."

"Young people don't understand what it's like to be discounted, do they? If we were feebleminded, and some of us are, or silly, as they believe most of us are, I could understand it, but they dismiss us simply because we are old and therefore irrelevant." She sounded like she'd only that moment realized the truth of what she said.

"Not all of them do, just too many of them want to lump us all together as dinosaurs, as superannuated couch potatoes. They expect us to sit around on our assets while they wait to inherit."

Frank turned into Rosemary's driveway. He killed the ignition, and instead of exiting the car and walking around to open her door, he leaned across and unlatched it from inside. She laid her hand on his shoulder.

"Come in for a minute?" Less a question than an invitation. "I'll make you coffee and you can answer my question."

"What question is that?"

"The one I asked before you started your rant. Where do we start?"

"Was I ranting?"

"Just a little."

"I'd like very much to stop, but I can't drink coffee at night."

"That's okay, I don't have any coffee."

THIRTEEN

"WHY DO YOU PUT UP WITH HIM? He's rude, obnoxious, and a drunk."

"You should have known him twenty-five years ago, Denise. He was everything the rest of us were not. Top of the class, captain of the football team...I tell you, the guy had an arm like a cannon. He was recruited by Big Ten schools, ACC schools, and Notre Dame. Turned them all down to go to the Naval Academy."

"That doesn't change what he is now, Marc. What's he doing now? Look at him."

"I don't know, exactly. He lives downtown off Eastern Avenue somewhere. He managed to get himself kicked out of Annapolis. Joined the army after that, I think. Now...I don't know. It looks like he's trying to drink himself to death."

"And succeeding. It's late. Let's go home."

Light staggered over to them. His tie hung loosely around his neck. The top buttons on his shirt had come unbuttoned. He'd lost his blazer somewhere. He waved a beer can in their direction. "Not leaving, are you?" he yelled. Beer sloshed down his arm.

"Time to go," Marc said, taking his wife's elbow and placing himself between her and Light.

"But I want to dance with your beautiful wife."

"Not tonight, Dexter. We have to go."

"One little dance is all."

"Aren't I a little too young for you?" Denise asked.

"You have a point," he replied.

"That's right, Dex. You always preferred older women. Whatever happened to Hot Pants Parker?"

Light pulled up short. Denise could have sworn he sobered up in that instant. If looks could kill, she thought, Marc's a dead man. He spun on his heel and walked from the tent and disappeared into the darkness.

"What was that all about?" she asked.

"I'll tell you later," her husband said. "Like I said, he could do anything in those days." They left him, a dim shadow, staring into the darkness toward the woods, seemingly lost in thought, in another time and place.

A CLOUD CUT OFF THE BRIGHT mid-afternoon sun streaming through the trees. In an instant the day turned gray. He rolled onto his side. The ground still held the residual cold from the previous night. She'd brought a thin blanket so no dirt would smudge her clothes. It would rain that night, he thought. Rain to wash away any evidence they'd ever been there. For some reason, that thought made him sad. He sat up.

"I've got to get back," she said. He loved her soft, honeyed accent. "Now, you wait five minutes, you hear? And then you can follow, but be careful." He once asked her if everyone from South Carolina talked that way. She'd laughed and said, "You should hear an Alabama accent."

Dexter watched as she buttoned her blouse. The cloud moved on and the sun returned. The forsythia burst back into bright yellow, the green leaves moved up one full tone. She smiled, and for a moment it seemed the sun's return was intimately linked to that smile, glowing ever brighter as she held it. He thought she might not leave after all. But she stood, smoothed her skirt, and squared her shoulders. She'd stuffed her bra in her purse rather than put it back on. When she stood that way, angled slightly to his right, her breasts pushed at the fabric of her blouse. She knew the effect it had on him. She spun. He reached for her.

"No more, Dex, honey, but next time we'll be back in bed," she murmured. "Marvin's classes start up again Saturday and the apartment will be ours." Marvin, her husband, went to night school and took some Saturday classes at Johns Hopkins University. Dexter and Luella Mae had been meeting in her apartment for a month. But not the first time. That happened in the library.

He had permission to stay up an hour after lights-out to complete his essay. As the assistant librarian, it fell to her to wait with him and lock up. They started to talk. He remembered every word of that conversation and how it ended in the little storeroom behind the checkout desk where books were processed or repaired. She'd asked him to help her lift a box up to a shelf. He stepped in looking for the box. Finding none, he turned to ask her a question. She'd closed the door. The only illumination came from a night-light. She seduced him then and there, surrounded by the smell of rubber cement and stamp-pad ink. After that, when her husband had classes, he'd slip into her apartment and they'd use her bed. Once they did it on the couch and one memorable time, on the kitchen table.

But this day her husband had stayed home with a cold, so they met in Old Oak Woods in a copse formed from wild forsythia and honeysuckle. It circled them like a huge green-and-yellow doughnut with a grassy clearing in its center. Bees and insects filled the air with their humming. Ants and other crawly things marched across their blanket and eventually their bare legs.

The copse had been his suggestion. She grinned at the thought of an *alfresco* tryst—her words. He knew from experience, the copse would screen them from the road, but he still worried. Others knew about the clearing. Too many others. Cigarette stubs, "roaches," tobacco papers, and an assortment of cans lay about. The older students called it the Smoking Lounge. No, meeting in the open like this carried too many risks. He thought he'd heard someone in the brush a while back. Probably the campus kids he'd seen on the road near the main gate, but it could have been anybody or anything. Kids. If they had come into the woods, they could easily have stumbled onto the two of them. The little creeps were like ants at a picnic. And if one saw and were to tell a parent…

She pulled on a shapeless green sweater, bent over, and kissed him on the lips. "Remember," she repeated, "five minutes."

"Did you see some kids on your way here?" he asked.

"Oh, yeah, that group of brats that are always sneaking around. You know I caught them peeking in my bedroom window one night."

"Did you tell on them?"

"No. I didn't want any trouble. Five minutes."

"Okay, five," he said. And you didn't want the parents to know you'd left the blinds up again, either, he thought. Those kids weren't the only ones who checked out that window.

She stepped through the wall of shrubbery that sealed them off from the path and disappeared. He buttoned his clothes and tucked in his shirt. He listened but did not hear the crackle of branches or her moving away. He slipped out the other side of the thicket and walked deeper in the woods. His watch said quarter to. He still had time. If those kids had been there, he needed to know. Somewhere ahead of him he heard their voices. He had to find out. He couldn't afford even a hint of trouble. He had graduation and his appointment to Annapolis to think about. Too much to risk. He had to know. He crept forward toward the voices.

"MR. LIGHT, ARE YOU all right?"

"What? Oh. I'm fine, Stark. Just dandy. How about you leave and let me sit here for a moment."

Dexter sat slumped on a cold iron bench and stared back into the marquee. The crowd had thinned. People who earlier filled the night with laughter had all gone back to their lives and would not mix and mingle again for a year, five years, ten…. The catering crew busied themselves with clearing off and packing up. A guffaw and a woman's voice raised in mock indignation drifted back through the night air. Light held his head between his palms as if he thought it might otherwise fall off.

"You were one of them, weren't you, Stark?"

"One of whom?"

"One of the bratty campus kids. You were one of them."

"A long time ago, Mr. Light, and yeah, I was a campus brat."

"You were there that day."

Stark sipped his cola, ingenuousness plastered across his face. "What day would that be?"

"*The* day, Stark. Don't be cute. You know what day."

"Just in the beginning. But I had to go to DISH, so I left them before—"

"I had to monitor Detention Study Hall that day. You were there?"

"Me and ten other guys."

"So, if it hadn't been for that—"

"I might have disappeared, too."

"Really?"

"Yeah. I think about that sometimes."

"I bet you do. But you didn't have anything to say about that day to our celebrity sleuth to help him…do whatever sleuths do…crack the case."

"No, nothing. And what about you, Mr. Light, did you have anything for him? A mention of a meeting, perhaps?"

"No, nothing," Light said, ignoring the last part of Stark's question. "Just that that day was the last good day of my life."

FOURTEEN

ROSEMARY PLACED HER CUP carefully on its saucer, which she in turn put on the coffee table in front of her. Still leaning forward, brows knit, she swiveled her head around and scrutinized him like a jeweler appraising an expensive antique necklace. How much value lay in its history, how much in the gold and diamonds alone? Frank returned the gaze, face expressionless except for the smallest trace of a smile.

"Do I pass?" he asked.

"I don't know. I'm not sure what I'm looking for."

He placed his half-filled cup and saucer down next to hers. Hot chocolate from a paper packet, decaffeinated at that, could not replace the real thing. The aroma seemed chocolaty but that was it. He'd accepted it only because she'd offered and it seemed as though he ought to.

"You said you looked me up on the Internet."

"Yes." She sat back and directed her gaze at the wallpaper on the opposite wall.

"And you are wondering about my wife?" Those amazing brown eyes shifted to his.

"It's none of my business, is it?" She resumed her study of wallpaper.

"No," he said, almost sadly, "it's not, but you can ask anyway."

"The report said you were a suspect in her disappearance. Is that true?"

"Disappearance...and probable homicide, too, don't forget that part." He lifted the cup and then put it down. "I'm their best bet. Something over eighty-five percent of disappearances and deaths of this sort are perpetrated by family members. I'm family. I had the means, motive, and opportunity. They can't find anybody else who does. That leaves me. They don't have anywhere else to go."

"Oh."

"The problem with surfing the Internet," he said, as much to himself as to her, "is that there's no control on what gets put there. Newspapers, TV, and radio have filters. Editors or owners screen what gets said and what doesn't. Even in the face of the obvious bias of some media outlets, there are limits. But the Internet has none. Anybody can post anything. The truth is mixed in with lies like diamonds with sewage. There is no sure way to sort them out."

"No, I suppose you're right. So how do we find out the truth?"

Frank shook his head and shrugged. They sat for a moment, lost in their own thoughts.

"I thought about you last night after you left," she murmured. "I didn't get much sleep wondering how I'd ask you about her. It scared me a little, too. What if it turned out that…" She plucked at a fold in the fabric of her dress.

"She had cancer," he said. "She had these stabbing pains and no appetite. Her doctors sent her to the Mayo Clinic, the one in Scottsdale. They did tests and…ovarian cancer. She expected it, you see. She just knew cancer would find her and it did. Do you know how ovarian cancer works?"

"It's every gynecologist's favorite topic for women over fifty. So I've heard the lecture more than once. It's a silent killer."

"By the time they made their diagnosis it was already at level four. There was no way they could attack it. All they could do for her was write prescriptions for painkillers and set up a hospice program. They gave her three months to live."

"The report didn't say anything about that."

"I didn't mention it to anyone."

"Your children?"

"No. She wanted to hold off as long as possible. There was nothing anyone could do about it. She said they should be called at the end, but only then. She wanted them to remember her as she used to be, not the doped up, gray scarecrow she would become. You didn't know her. She could fill a room with sunlight. She moved like a swan. She had all this energy. I never knew anyone who could tackle so many different things at once. Even on the day she disappeared, she went for her daily walk—only, this time she didn't return. I thought…I called hospitals thinking she might have collapsed." He paused, closed his eyes, and took several controlled breaths.

"She enjoyed life so much…and then…suddenly, she found herself worn-out by noon. It was like watching ice melt."

Rosemary's eyes filled with tears. "I don't think I want you to say anything more, Frank. I don't need to know the rest."

"I'd better go," he said, but didn't move. She upended her purse on the table in search of a Kleenex. He handed her his pocket handkerchief.

"Stay," she whispered.

"DO YOU THINK YOUR MAN Meredith is hopping in the sack with the fabulous Mrs. Mitchell tonight?" Judith Stark leaned in the doorway. She had a hairbrush in her hand poised in midair.

"Judith," Stark protested, "what a thing to say. They're pushing seventy. I expect they're sitting around drinking hot chocolate and reminiscing about old TV shows or life on the campus in the fifties."

"You think? Well, I don't have any intention of giving up sex until I die. So consider yourself put on notice, sweetheart."

He blushed. His wife could be embarrassing in public and private. Not that this particular threat bothered him. On the contrary, it might signal an end to their spat. He looked up but she turned her back and left the room.

"I'm in the guest room tonight," she said over her shoulder. He heard the door click shut. He sighed and pulled on the green paisley robe she hated.

The master bedroom boasted a tiny balcony. He stepped out onto it. He shivered in the chill May air, reached into his pocket, and extracted a pack of cigarettes. He did not smoke often. Judith did not let him smoke in the house, but when he felt the world closing in on him he'd sometimes go outside and light up. And at that moment the world weighed heavily on him. He lit the cigarette and watched as the smoke curled upward. At the eaves, it dashed away, caught in an invisible air current. The land fell away from the back of the house. A long, shallow hillside that ended at the state road. He could just make out the streak of white concrete shining in the moonlight. Beyond it, Old Oak Woods. He closed his eyes to shut it out, but the boys came out to dance for him anyway.

"Leave me alone!"

"Okay, if you insist," Judith said from the bed, "but I started feeling horny and thought better of my decision to sleep alone. And I hoped you'd be in the mood for some atoning." She could not see the expression on his face in the dark. Had she, she would not have been quite so flippant.

THE POLICE PUT DEXTER LIGHT in the drunk tank for the night. They'd found him wandering around the Owings Mills Mall. He seemed harmless enough but clearly in no condition to navigate his way back to Baltimore.

"Who's your daddy?" he asked. "Who's your daddy?" Then he burst into laughter. "That's what I want to know, Officer. Can't be Marvin, that's for sure, so, who?" He collapsed on the steel bunk and passed out.

"I swear this is the same guy we get every year from Scott. Let's see…" The cop, a veteran of nearly twenty years, rifled through Dexter's wallet. "Driver's license, Dexter Light. That's our guy." He carefully inventoried the contents of Dexter's pockets and put them in a manila envelope.

"Now, here's an old picture," he said, holding a crinkled black-and-white photograph of a pretty dark-haired woman up to the light. "Not a bad-looking broad, either."

"I DECIDED THAT I HAD TO make a choice," Rosemary said, wiping her eyes. "If we were…if I…" She trailed off.

Just say it, you idiot, he won't think badly of you, and what if he does? You haven't seen him for fifty years and might not again for another fifty. Didn't you say this morning you were old? So, stop acting like a teenager.

"Am I acting like a teenager?"

"I don't think so, but then it's been a long time since my kids were that age and I had any real contact with one, and I didn't understand them then, either."

"Here's the thing. If I condition whatever relationship that may develop between us on first making sure you weren't involved in your wife's…disappearance, then it would seem like I could never trust you. I'd have to cross-check every detail and that would mess up everything. Oh, God, I'm making a fool of myself, aren't I?"

"You aren't if what you're saying is—you want to feel safe, but by asking the question, you will have already put a precondition on whatever follows. Is that it?"

"Yes. That's nicely put. How do you do that, anyway?"

"I'm a writer."

"I'll try to remember that."

"Nevertheless, if you asked the question that sits like the proverbial elephant in the corner, I would say, 'No, I didn't have anything to do with it.' But I might be lying, you see. Is it likely I'd confess to something like that?"

"I don't think you'd lie. I don't think you even know how."

"I write fiction, remember. I'm very good at inventing stories."

"Then I was right," she said. "I'll never know for certain. I'll have to follow my instincts."

Good for you.

"And they're telling you…?"

She straightened up, rose, and walked across the room to a small desk painted dark green with a thin gilt line edging its fold-up writing surface. She reached into a drawer and removed a bulky envelope. She resumed her place on the sofa and handed it to him.

He opened the flap and peered in. Newspaper clippings, old photographs—all about him.

"What's this?"

"It's for you. My secret, now it's yours."

"I don't understand."

"I have been keeping track of you for years, Frank."

"Really? Your husband…?"

"He didn't know. He wouldn't have understood. To even care about someone from far away would have seemed like infidelity. Men think if a woman is interested in a man it must be about sex."

He sorted through the clippings. One very yellow one, no more than a column inch, announced that Frank and three other boys had won the one-hunred-yard freestyle relay in the ninety-five-pound class at Meadowbrook Swimming Pool. He looked up.

"Now what?" he asked.

"Now we see," she said and kissed him lightly on the mouth.

FIFTEEN

"YOU WERE LATE AGAIN last night." Barbara busied herself with wiping the kitchen sink, although, as far as Frank could see, it didn't need it.

"Not too late, I don't think."

"It was after two. More drinking with your old buddies?"

"Not this time. I had a long conversation with someone from my past." He smiled and turned his head away, remembering that once upon a time to have intercourse with someone meant you had had a conversation.

"You're smiling," she said. "Does that mean you are spinning more bullshit?"

"Barbara, how you talk. Your mother and I never taught you to talk like that!"

"Mom, no, but we all heard you use language a lot stronger than that."

"Well, just a few words I picked up in the army. By the way, where's Bob?" Frank tried to change the subject.

"Up at a normal hour and running errands somewhere."

Always a tip-off. If she'd said hardware store or barbershop or any of a half hundred destinations, he would have let it pass, but *somewhere?* Somewhere could mean anything, but at that moment, it meant his daughter and her husband were not communicating.

"Somewhere?"

She resumed cleaning her sink, her back to him. "He went out. I don't know, Dad. He took his car and left early this morning. He said he had things to do."

"Most stores don't open until ten." She stopped wiping. Her

shoulders sagged. "I'm your old man," he said gently. "What's going on?"

"Nothing." She turned to face him and then he noticed the red eyes, the fatigue. "I didn't wait up for you, I swear. We were arguing until one-thirty. Then I couldn't sleep. That's why I know."

"You two been fighting a lot lately?"

"It's that time in our marriage, I guess. Pushing twenty years and all of a sudden the dreams, the fancy plans, all seem so far away, so unlikely. The kids are growing up so fast. There are big decisions ahead for us and—"

"Money is tight and getting tighter."

"How'd you know that?"

"Been there, honey. Is there anything else you two fight about, besides money, that is?"

She tore off a square of paper towel from its roller under a cabinet and wiped her face. "I don't know. It usually starts with something trivial, you know? Then it sort of spirals up and away, but in the end, everything seems to come down to money."

"That's it?"

She crumpled the towel into a small ball. Outside, a mockingbird began its borrowed litany. Somewhere down the block a lawn mower coughed to life. And somewhere Bob Thomas was breaking his daughter's heart.

"I don't know. How can I know? He never says anything. He comes home late, eats dinner, and retreats into his little den. We don't make love and when I ask him what the matter is, he says, 'Nothing' and clams up even more. I think there must be someone else. Isn't that what all that usually means?"

"No, not necessarily. But something's not right. Do you want me to talk to him?"

"What good would that do? You're leaving tomorrow morning and you have some hoop-de-do to go to tonight."

"Oh, yeah, I meant to tell you. Would it be okay if I stayed on for a few days, a week, maybe?"

"Stay on? Here?"

"Well, I could go to a motel if that won't work," he said. She unfolded the ball of paper towel and began to shred it into the sink.

"No, no. That's not what I meant. It's just…" She scooped up the bits of paper and deposited them into the trash bin. The lid dropped with a clank. "Why?"

"Long story. I promised some people at the party last night I would look into the mystery of the missing boys."

"That sounds like a title of one of your books. Is it?"

"Who knows, it could be. That possibility crossed my mind, but no, it's a real mystery this time. Do you remember hearing about four boys disappearing from the Scott campus twenty-five years ago?"

"Not at the time. We lived in Chicago then, didn't we? I think one of the Scott parents may have told me something like that a while back, but I'm not sure. Is that what you're investigating?"

"Yes."

She squeezed her eyes shut like someone trying to shake off a mild headache. "Of course you can stay. But I'm not sure about the car. I have to be out of the office this week."

"No problem. I have a friend helping me who can drive."

"Well, it will be nice, then. You can see something of the boys."

"We're going to the lacrosse game at Loyola this afternoon, apparently," Frank said. "They said their dad promised but couldn't at the last—"

"No, he couldn't, could he? He's too busy doing whatever the hell he does nowadays that nobody knows about."

"Well, it's a good thing, actually. We'll walk over to the game—have a big time."

"Okay. That'll be good. I only wish that I—"

"I'll talk to him, Barbara. It may not be anything. Money problems always make people do funny things, act crazy."

She sat at the table and began her shredding again, this time a paper napkin. "What is it about men? They keep secrets. They think they can't let on they need something, so they pull away from the people who love them and then go dippy over the first woman who gives them a kind word and a smile."

"Well, you're assuming a lot there. First, you don't know if there is a smile with a woman attached to it or not. And—here's the part you won't like—most men will not go for the smile from a stranger if there's a better one at home. How have you been lately?"

She bristled and tore another napkin in half.

"Oh, I see, it's my fault. I work an eight-hour day, sometimes ten hours. I come home, make dinner, and do all of the housework that every other woman has an entire day to get done. I help the kids with their homework and I'm tired at the end of that. What do you expect? I should put on a tape and do a strip-tease for him, too?"

"I merely said—"

"I'm tired. I get up at five-thirty. I go to bed at eleven. You do the math, Dad. I can't keep this up." She picked up the last napkin on the table and blew her nose. "And he's in the study. Working, he says. Or he eats and leaves the house. He says he has work to do. Work! What the hell does he think I'm doing all day and all night?"

"I'll talk to him, Barbara. There may be some very simple explanation for the whole thing. In the meantime, let me loan you some money."

"I don't want your money, Dad, I want my husband back."

He got up and found a clean cup in the cupboard. He filled it with coffee. He put it in front of her and poured himself another, as well.

Bob Thomas started life on the wrong side of the tracks, as they used to say. He did not have the advantages of private schools, summer camps, and parents who were connected to the power structure in one way or another. He grew up within sight of the old Baltimore and Ohio roundhouse, now the Chessie System Railway Museum. He worked his way through the University of Maryland flipping burgers, washing cars, and delivering pizzas 'til 3:00 a.m. He got his CPA at night school.

He worked hard, kept his thinning hair and expanding midriff in as much control as he could, and wore a look of permanent confusion when he was around his wife, whom he held in awe. In no way did he fit the uptown mold.

"We fight over the Scott Academy thing, too," she said, ignoring the coffee.

"How's that?"

"I want to send them to Scott. I told you that. If they went there, I wouldn't have to arrange for someone to watch them in the afternoon, and…Bob says, 'No way can we afford it. Not on what I make.' I said, 'You make? What do you think what I bring in is—chopped liver?' And he says it helps. It *helps?*"

She finally gave way to the tears she'd been holding at bay. Frank leaned over to the counter and grabbed a fistful of napkins and handed them to her.

"Dad," she said, her words muffled by napkin balls, "solve my mystery, too. What is he doing? Is he seeing someone? I need to know. I'm going crazy. Stay as long as you need to. Find out for me, please?"

"Sure. I'll talk to him. Follow him around town, if I have to. I'll find out. In the meantime, you need rest. I've got the boys this afternoon, then the party tonight. You take the day off and rest a little, read a book, take a bubble bath."

"Easier said than done. Can you get a ride to your party? I don't know when or if Bob is getting back and I have a job to do at the church. Well, if I have to, I could cancel but—"

"No need, I have a friend picking me up."

She sighed, gathered her flannel nightshirt closer, and gazed at the clock.

"You know, I think I will just rest for a while," she said. She got up, somewhat awkwardly. She hadn't inherited her mother's grace, only her regular features and smile. A smile little in evidence lately. She turned and pursed her lips as a new thought seemed to cross her mind. She frowned.

"Who's the friend you're going to the party with?"

"Just an old friend, a piece of my childhood." He regretted the use of the word *piece*.

"Who?" she said, not quite insisting.

"Well, if you must know, I'm going with Rosemary Mitchell." He buried himself in the morning paper. He felt her eyes burning holes in the middle of the op-ed page.

"The friend who's driving you around town while you do your *investigating*—that wouldn't be Mrs. Mitchell, would it?"

He shrugged.

"And that someone from your past, the one you had a *conversation* with, that wouldn't be Rosemary Mitchell, too?"

He lowered the paper. "Barbara, what's the problem?"

She glared at him for what seemed a full minute. "Where's Mom?" she hissed, and her tears began again.

SIXTEEN

"I DON'T KNOW WHY WE HAVE to do this so early." She was tall and very blonde, the kind of blond that usually comes from a bottle, but in her case, it was the real thing. He'd discovered that the night before when she came back to his room.

"You said you wanted to go hiking. We're going hiking."

The dead dry desert stretched to the horizon. The sun just cleared the mountains to the east. He squinted and said, "It's supposed to hit triple figures again this afternoon. Morning is the only safe time for a beginner to tackle the desert. If we want to do ten miles, we have to start early. By noon, it's going to be well over a hundred degrees out here."

"Ten miles! You said, like, a hike. I don't want to go…. If I wanted to travel ten miles, I'd call a cab."

"Well, let's see how it goes. If it's too much for you, we'll turn back, okay?"

She rolled her eyes and smoothed her baggy shorts. They were his. She'd met only a few men whose waist matched hers. Most of the ones she dated were paunchy businessmen and agents. But this guy seemed nice, and Joey, her minder, had ticked her off, so she'd gone with him last night and then allowed him to talk her into this hiking thing. It must have been the line of coke she did in the bathroom before she let him seduce her. She had what she called her loose moments, usually after a snort.

"I have to pee," she said.

"There's a privy over there," he said and pointed to the Spot-A-Pot on the edge of the pull-off.

"No, thanks, those things stink."

"Well, there's nobody around. You could go behind a saguaro. Just don't get too close."

"I'll use the facility." It did have an odor, but not too bad. The dry air seemed to do something to Spot-A-Pots in the desert. She discarded her thong down the hole. She did not need that thing riding up on her, and she knew it would. A wedgie in the desert. "These thongs aren't made for walking…" she sang.

"What?"

She watched him slather sunscreen on his arms and legs. "You next." He handed her the bottle.

"What number?" she asked, inspecting the bottle and seeing no indicator.

"Forty. You need it out here."

"How can you get a tan with forty? I never use anything stronger than fifteen. Usually, none at all. I'll pass."

"You're not here to get a tan. You're in the desert and the sun can fry you like an egg. Besides, if you don't, you'll have tan lines or worse, you'll look like a dancing lobster. That won't go too well on the runway, will it?"

He had a point. She did not need a farmer's tan. And it would be pretty obvious two minutes into her act when she dropped the shortie raincoat and got down to the leopard-skin bikini. She squeezed out the liquid and began to apply it.

"Get behind your knees," he said. "People always forget that and then they are miserable."

"You want to help me here?" She flashed him a smile.

"Sure. Where do you want me to put it?"

"Here." She slid her shorts down.

He laughed and obliged. "I don't think this part is in danger of sunburn."

"Maybe not now, but who knows what might happen out there."

He gave her a water bottle fitted with a belt clip and took a rucksack with three more and slung it over his back.

"Water?" She made a face. "I need coffee this time of day."

"Coffee's no good. It's a diuretic and will speed the dehydration process. Water is what you get. One more thing," he said, and produced a shapeless wide-brimmed hat and clapped it on her head.

"What's this for?" She caught sight of her reflection in the SUV's window. "I look like a bag lady." The idea stopped her. She knew she needed to change her act. Everybody did what she did. Prance out in some fantasy costume, drop it piece by piece, and work the pole. She needed a gimmick if she wanted to book into the big clubs, Vegas, maybe. A bag lady. She'd come out all hunched over in crappy clothes and the guys would boo maybe, or think it was comedy act, but then as she peeled off each layer of rags, they'd get it. Yeah, a bag lady—something like that—sweet.

"Let's go," he said.

She looked at the scrub brush, cacti, and air already shimmering off the desert floor and wondered what possessed her to agree to this craziness.

"You're the doctor. I'm right behind you," she replied, but without much conviction. They marched away from the parked car and made their way along a barely discernable path westward into the desert. It was already too hot for her.

AN HOUR LATER, HE SLOWED DOWN. She had fallen twenty yards behind him. He stopped and waited for her to catch up. Her water bottle was nearly empty. She sat on a boulder and pulled off her cross trainers. She frowned in annoyance. The shoes used to be white but now were the same dun color as the desert floor. They were not the best things to hike in, but he made a point of staying on the level path. If she had been better equipped, he would have taken them farther east and hiked up a small mountain.

"Are you okay?" he asked. Then he saw the red marks on her feet, markings that would soon develop into a set of very nasty blisters. He dug around in the rucksack and found the moleskin he kept there in case something like this happened. He knelt in front of her and picked up one foot.

"Here, let me take care of that." He cut strips of the soft fabric and applied it to her feet. "Where did you get these shoes, anyway?"

"I'll have you know they are very expensive designer cross trainers," she said and inspected one foot.

"Expensive, but very bad for your feet. Look at these marks. Next time you buy shoes, get ones that fit and are good for your feet, not ones with a fancy label. We have to get you back or you won't be working tonight."

"Will that stuff keep it from getting worse?"

"Yes, but I don't want to take any chances. Besides, you look like you've had enough for one day."

"Suits me," she said and leaned back. "Let me rest a minute, then we can go back."

He nodded and wandered a few yards farther along the path. He squinted and shaded his eyes against the sun and scanned the horizon. He focused on a large rock fifteen or twenty yards away. He couldn't be sure but he thought he saw an inscription.

"Put your shoes on and come with me," he shouted.

"I'm tired. Let me rest some more."

"No, this is important. You can rest later. Come on." He heard her grumble in the background and he set out toward the reddish boulder. She scrabbled up behind him.

"Look at that," he said and pointed.

"Some kid scratched a picture on a rock. Big deal."

"No, no, it's a petroglyph."

"Huh?"

"A picture carved into the rock by a Native American hundreds of years ago. Maybe longer."

He walked closer to have a better look and stumbled over the canvas tarp. It had been bleached the same color as the gravel and sand around it. He gave it a kick and flipped the corner back. She screamed. At first, he thought a scorpion bit her. He had forgotten to warn her about scorpions. Then he saw what she saw.

The bones were yellow-brown and bits of clothing still clung to some, but insects and small animals had removed anything resembling either flesh or features.

"Shhh…" he said.

"Is it a person?" she whimpered.

He lifted the canvas a bit more. Insects scurried over the bones and away into the desert. He made out the distinct outlines of a pelvis and more fabric.

"Yes, I think so. I'm guessing a woman. We have to call the police."

"Police?"

"Yeah. I'm just an anesthesiologist and a long way from freshman gross anatomy, but that jagged hole in the cranium is not supposed to be there."

Her face took on the ashy expression one sees just before people faint. He grabbed her just as she collapsed and kept her from falling into a jumping cactus.

SEVENTEEN

DEXTER LIGHT WOKE WITH A class ten hangover. He'd started classifying his hangovers in the army. A class one might be annoying but not debilitating. He could function normally and it would usually disappear in an hour. The scale and degree of debility were directly proportional to the size of the indicator, and at the nine or ten level could include vomiting, sweats, and any number of equally unattractive bodily functions. He groaned and tried to sit up. He failed.

"On your feet, sunshine," the burly cop said. "The judge says he's not interested in party drunks this morning, so you're free to go."

"Say, Barney, you wouldn't have a little something to kill the grizzly bear that's eating my brain, would you?"

"Sure, but not what you're thinking of. And don't call me Barney unless you want to spend a month or two in the slammer. You'd be surprised how many drunks turn violent in the morning and attack an officer of the law." The cop smiled when he said it, but the smile did not make it up to his eyes. Dexter heard the warning.

"I'm slow, Officer, but not stupid. I'll take whatever you have to kill my bear." He expected the usual battery acid coffee. Instead the cop handed him a quart bottle of water.

"Drink this," he said.

"Water? You've got to be kidding."

"Alcohol dehydrates. Your brain is ischemic, that's why it hurts."

"Ischemic?"

"Lacks fluid in the intercellular spaces. I read a book."

"And if I drink the water, it fills up the spaces?"

"Something like that."

"Well, this is a first. I usually get a bad cup of coffee."

"Worst thing for you. It's a dehydrator, too, and will play hell with your stomach. You need to rehydrate and rest. Give your body a break. This afternoon, take a walk. Eat a sensible meal. Take it easy, and get off the booze. You're killing yourself."

"I mistook you for the wrong TV character before. You aren't Andy's deputy, you're who? Doctor somebody."

"Nope, just a guy who used to be just like you."

"Like me? I don't think so. How, like me?"

"I used to be a drunk, son. Here, take this." He handed Dexter a leaflet.

"AA? You think I should join AA? Doc, I appreciate the thought but the last thing on this earth I want to do is lose my right to drink myself into oblivion."

The cop shrugged his shoulders.

At the booking counter, Dexter got back his belt and shoelaces. He signed for the manila envelope containing the rest of his possessions.

"I had a coat," he said.

"Not when you checked in here, you didn't. You must have lost it."

Dexter did not figure the cops stole it. It would be a thing only to be coveted by a very select group, bums and the homeless. He relaced his shoes, slipped his belt through the pant loops, missing two, and dumped the envelope's contents on the desk. Not much there. His wallet, fourteen dollars in bills, twenty-seven cents in change, his round-trip ticket stub for the metro, a Timex that looked like a Rolex, and her picture. He pocketed the change and put the bills, picture, and ticket in his wallet.

"Who's the picture?" the cop asked. "Your wife, girlfriend?"

Dexter shoved the wallet in his hip pocket. The water seemed to be working.

"Nobody," he said.

"Okay, Mr. Light, you can go. Think about what I told you. It's one day at a—"

"—time, right. Thanks, but no thanks, Officer. Now, if you would just point me in the direction of the nearest metro station, I'll get out of your hair."

He'd missed his train. The next one that went from out in the county all the way downtown and across to the east side would not be along for a half hour. He walked a block, found a McDonald's, and ordered a breakfast platter of soggy pancakes, sausage, and eggs. Well, they were supposed to be eggs. They were yellow and looked vaguely like eggs. The little plastic fork bent when he poked them. He pushed the sausage patty out of its puddle of grease and sipped his water. Eat sensibly, the cop said. Right. One day at a time. Right. He wondered if his stomach was up to the swaying and lurching of the metro. He wondered if he went back to Scott, would he find his coat. After all, he didn't have a lot on his agenda today. He drank more water. He skipped the sausage and eggs and ate the pancakes. The sugar in the syrup seemed to revive him. Carbs—the quicker picker upper. He'd go back to the school, retrieve his coat, and then maybe…

THE LAST REMNANTS OF THE reunion weekend lay in untidy piles and bundles, stacked on the grass beside the quadrangle. Boxes and tables, their legs folded modestly beneath them, sat ready to be loaded into vans. A few workmen milled around. He didn't see any students. But then there weren't as many boarders nowadays. Dexter pivoted around in a complete circle, taking in the buildings, the trees. Sunlight glinted off rooftops. He could smell trampled grass and a hint of honeysuckle. Did he imagine it? He couldn't see any honeysuckle in the area. Honeysuckle grew thick in Old Oak Woods. Honeysuckle and wild forsythia.

He looked for the cannons. There used to be two vintage World War I cannons in front of Main Building, but now they were gone, casualties of the demilitarizing of the country in the seventies. When he thought about it, which he rarely did, he believed the worst thing that ever happened to the country was the Vietnam War. A whole way of life disappeared. But then, his father said the same thing about Korea, so there you are. Somewhere in his genealogical tree, he guessed someone probably said it about World War I, the Spanish American War, and the Civil War. His stint in the army had been between conflicts, free of even the hint of war. Like many men who missed out on combat, he sometimes wondered how he would have performed under fire. He hoped he would have been brave. Then he thought about his present state and realized he didn't have the courage to face a day without alcohol. God only knew what he would do in a real crisis.

He made his way across the quadrangle to the spot on the grass where twenty-five years before, he'd called the student body to attention. He closed his eyes and saw it all. Companies of boys in West Point blue-gray, ranging in age from six to eighteen, standing in platoons of twenty or so, three platoons to a company, eight companies, all of them waiting for the corps commander, for him, to give them their orders. He felt tears stream down his cheeks. He caught his breath. Sobriety did that to you, he thought, filled your head with useless memories and reminded you of lost things, lost loves, lost lives. He bowed his head and walked back into the shade. He needed a drink. He needed a drink in the worst way. He sipped from his water bottle instead.

He found his coat balled up on a bench. It was badly wrinkled and reeked of stale beer and cigarette smoke. He had a dim recollection of sitting there the night before and talking to someone about the boys, but he couldn't remember who or why. Something to do with that writer with a woman's name…somebody Smith? And there were other people, too, or did that happen earlier? He had a nagging feeling it would be important to remember, but he couldn't think why. He had the uneasy feeling he'd made an ass of himself, but then realized he always made an ass of himself at parties and most folks had come to expect him to. They'd be disappointed if he didn't. He wondered how long he'd been lying to himself like that and then pushed that thought aside. That way led to madness. He'd stay with being a drunk.

He wandered over to the chapel and sat on its granite steps. The carillon groaned and ran through the Westminster chimes sequence for the three-quarter hour. His head did not pound with each note as he expected. Have to give the cop some credit. Who'd have thought water would do the trick? The chapel's dark oak doors were not fastened—at least that had not changed. He pushed his way in and sat in a back pew. Light filtered through stained glass windows. The chapel had its own distinct scent, a mixture of wet marble and furniture wax. His classmates said, facetiously, it was the aroma of righteousness. He began to feel uncomfortable in its presence.

He weighed his options. If he walked down the hill one way, he'd go back to the metro stop and eventually home. If he went down the other side, he would end up in Old Oak Woods. The first choice he found depressing, the second frightening. He stepped outside, pulling the doors closed, and walked a few paces, considering. He finished the bottle of water and started to throw it away, then changed his mind and refilled it at a drinking fountain. That was new, too. In his day, there were no such luxuries, conveniently placed water fountains outside the buildings. The only fountains he'd known were in the buildings and you required permission to use them. Now the school had fountains, vending machines…he closed his eyes. He suddenly realized he was sounding like the alumni he'd ridiculed the night before, like an old man. He put on his jacket, shoved the bottle in one of its pockets, and headed downhill.

EIGHTEEN

"SHE'S DEAD, BARBARA. What else do you want me to say? In any case like this, the prime, no, the only suspect the police consider is the 'nearest and dearest.' They have been after me for years, asking the same questions over and over again, so much I sometimes wake up in the middle of the night and think, 'Did I do that?' I almost drank myself to death. I had to get rid of all the booze in the house. I threw my gun away...my *gun,* the one the studio gave me out in Hollywood when they shot the twenty-sixth episode of *Collars.* And you, my own daughter..." Anger, frustration, and the pain of years of nagging doubt drove the words from him, hammered at her. She staggered, clasped the back of a chair, and stood, mouth agape. She started to cry again. Frank let her. He was out of napkins and out of patience. What did she think he would say? At least Rosemary had the decency to let it lie.

"I don't want to believe you did anything," she sobbed, "but I need to know. The police must have a reason...."

He sighed and sat down. "What can I possibly say to you that will help? No matter what comes out, you will always wonder, don't you see? When the police made the allegation, they poisoned the well, and left me with nothing to say to anyone, one way or the other."

"You could say if you did it or not."

"Yes, I could, but I won't. Your mother disappeared four years ago. She went for a walk and never came back. That's it. There is nothing I can add to that. Not now, maybe later."

"Later? What can happen later that can't happen now?"

"The police can do their job. If they do that, I may have something to say then, but not until."

"Dad, I'm your daughter!"

"And I'm your father, damn it," he shouted. They stared at each other, two broken hearts with nowhere to go to fix them.

"You might have asked about her, you know," he said, this time softly.

"Ask about her? What do you mean, ask about her?"

"She had cancer, Barbara, ovarian cancer. You know about that?" *Déjà vu*, he thought.

"I didn't know. Why didn't you say something?"

"Your mother wanted it that way. She wanted to be remembered as she used to be, not as a sick, dying old lady. The pain, the real pain, had just started. Walking seemed to help take her mind off it. You remember how she was when you were little?"

His daughter wiped her eyes with the back of her sleeve. Her mascara smeared across her face, making her look like a depressed raccoon. "Oh, my," she said, her words barely audible. "She taught me to play tennis. I never went to summer camp, but Mom made up for that. She could do anything…dance… sing…she even played the ukulele. She was always so full of… you don't think that she—"

Frank shrugged his shoulders.

"I don't know what to say," she said. But the look still lurked behind her eyes. A dark idea forming in her mind, a new possibility? The old doubts shifted over to different paths and scenarios, about him, about a violent death. They insinuated themselves into her mind. Did she? If she didn't, then…what?

Frank watched as her thoughts flitted behind her eyes like bats at twilight. He wondered if killing Sergeant Ledezma could be considered justifiable homicide, if not in the eyes of the law, at least in the eyes of God. A clear case of self-defense if ever there was.

HIS YOUNGEST GRANDCHILD bore his name. They'd started by calling him Frank Two, one generation removed from becoming a junior, sort of. He did not have the correct surname, but who cared? His older brother, made aware of the procession of generations and the proper way of designating them, Junior, the third, fourth, etc., and of royalty and their tidy enumeration, dubbed him Frank the Twoth, which quickly became Frank the Tooth and finally just Tooth. Barbara hated the nickname, but Tooth thought it the best name ever and happily introduced himself to all her friends that way.

"Tooth," Frank called, "where's your brother? It's time to go to the game."

"I'll get him." Tooth scampered out the kitchen door to the backyard. Barbara, face washed and looking slightly better after an hour's nap, but still red eyed and drawn, slipped in behind him.

"I'm sorry, Dad," she said, her voice hoarse. "I won't bring it up again."

"No," he said, but he didn't believe her. She was like a dog worrying a bone. She would chew on it forever. Doubts and distrust would be a wall that would separate them until one of them died. He hoped it would be him. Once the dogs are let out, there's no getting them back until they'd hunted and killed.

Tooth skipped across the lawn toward them, his brother, Jesse, ten paces behind. Jesse carried his lacrosse stick, working it back and forth, keeping the ball low in its pocket. In the springtime in Baltimore, lacrosse sticks become a permanent part of a boy's anatomy. No self-respecting kid living north of Thirty-third Street would be caught dead at a college lacrosse game without his stick. Tooth would grab his before they left, as well.

"Hey, Tooth," his brother shouted, "catch." With that, and before Tooth could turn, Jesse cradled the ball in the stick's webbing and hurled it at his brother. The hard rubber ball caught him square in the back of his head and, propelled at the thirty or so miles an hour the leverage of the stick provided, knocked him off his feet.

"Jesse!" his mother screamed. Frank burst through the door and down the steps from the small back porch. Tooth lay face-down in the grass. Frank touched him but thought it best not to move him.

"Tooth," he said, "are you okay?" The boy rolled over and sat up. He looked at his brother, screwed up his face, and burst into tears. Frank put his arms around him. Barbara lit into her oldest son.

"What on earth were you thinking about, Jesse? You could have killed your brother."

Jesse looked stricken. "I don't know," he said.

"Why, Jesse? Why did you do that?"

"I don't know, I—"

Barbara rattled off a laundry list of dire consequences that might have accrued had the ball hit Tooth sooner, later, in another place. Blindness, paralysis, orthodontic catastrophes filled the air. All Jesse could do was hang his head and repeat his *mea culpa*.

"I'm sorry," he said again and again, interspersed with, "I don't *know* why, Mom."

Finally, when her fear subsided and her anger seemed slaked, she turned back to Tooth.

"Are you all right, sweetie pie?" she crooned.

Tooth could manage most motherly approaches, but he had to be really sick to respond to *sweetie pie*. He stopped crying immediately and leaped to his feet.

"I'll get you for that, Jess," he yelped and ran at his brother, ball in hand. Jesse took off down the yard, zigzagging until Tooth managed to bounce the ball off his retreating backside.

"Ow," he said, less in pain than out of contrition.

Tooth, satisfied he had exacted appropriate retribution, ran back to his grandfather.

"Come on, Grandpa, we'll be late."

"Go wash your face and comb your hair," his mother said. "And tuck in your shirt!"

Jesse, eyes lowered, slipped past them into the house. "I'll just wash up and...um...tuck in my shirt, too," he said. The screen door slapped shut behind him.

"What was that all about?" Barbara said.

"People do stupid things for no apparent reason," Frank replied. "It's impulsive behavior. With kids it's often physical, a push or shove. Most of the time nothing bad happens. Once in a while someone gets hurt. When they get older it can be more serious, particularly if they're behind the wheel of a car or playing around with a gun. Adults do it, too, but it usually involves relationships or spending money foolishly."

"But he could have hurt Frankie."

"He didn't think about that, Barbara. He just threw the ball—impulse. A split second after he let it fly he realized what a stupid thing he'd done but, of course, by then it was too late. Irresistible impulse."

"What?"

"Wonderful book by Robert Traver, *Anatomy of a Murder,* they made a movie of it, too. Jimmy Stewart, Ben Gazzara, Lee Remick—"

"*Anatomy of a* what?"

"Sorry. The lawyer in the book, and the movie, presented to the judge a defense based on 'irresistible impulse,' his client's inability to stop himself from killing the bartender who allegedly raped his wife, something like that. From time to time we all yield to pressures, do stupid or cruel things, and then spend the rest of our lives regretting them."

"—*of a Murder?* You did say murder?" Barbara's expression shifted from a mixture of mild curiosity and confusion to thoughtful consideration and finally to questioning. He shook his head sadly. He would not volunteer an answer to her unasked question.

"Grandpa," Tooth called, "let's go." He had his lacrosse stick in his hand, but his shirttail was still not tucked.

NINETEEN

DEXTER WALKED ALONG THE perimeter road until he found an opening in the thick underbrush. He left the shoulder and pushed into the woods. The path that used to lead from the main gate should be to his left. The copse he sought would be to the right. He couldn't be sure. Nothing looked the same. He smiled. For some reason, people think their memories of places will always endure, that they can go back to their hometown, or school, or battlefield and it will be exactly as they remembered it, that the passage of years, decades even, will not affect the shape of things. Then, they are shocked at the change. Now strangers lived in their house, strangers with very bad taste. The streets were wider or missing or renamed. He turned right and left, hoping to find a landmark, anything that would tell him which way to go. But twenty-five years is a long time. Trees die, new ones grow up in their place, and streams change their courses. Nothing ever stays the same. That is the lesson of sobriety, he thought. Intoxication, on the other hand, allowed one to believe that nothing changed, to live in a time warp where problems could be held at bay and relationships remain in any state one wished. But today, sober and very thirsty, Dexter surveyed his woods and his life. He did not recognize either.

He moved a few yards deeper into the forest until he spotted the bole of an old black walnut. The limbs were stripped of their foliage and the bark had begun to flake away from the trunk. No dark, finger-staining fruit lay on the ground, only a few ancient husks lay scattered about. But he knew the tree. It once had blue panicles festooned from its limbs, the promise of fruit. Nuts to keep the population of gray squirrels through the winter. He took a breath and turned to his right. The copse should be just ahead, if it still existed. Twenty-five years. The underbrush was thicker than he remembered. He almost needed a machete.

It was the forsythia that first caught his eye. Their yellow blossoms beckoned him forward. In twenty-five years, they had spread, and he had no idea if the original circle with its center clearing still existed, but he needed to find out. The honeysuckle presented an almost insurmountable barrier. In the old days there had been two or three gaps in the wall formed from its tendrils. He stopped, looking for a way in, if there was one. He was sure the clearing he sought was closer to the road back then. The privacy it afforded depended on thick brush to screen them. He worked his way back toward the road. Finally he found a gap. A small one, but passable. He twisted to his right and wriggled through. The clearing appeared smaller and the grass in its center rougher and higher. A tree had fallen sometime back and bisected the clearing, its limbs all but obscuring the space. But he could pick out the old perimeter and remembered it as it once was.

He sat on the tree trunk, took the water bottle from his pocket, and drank. The cloying scent of honeysuckle hung in the air. Honeybees worked its thousands of blossoms. He scanned every inch of the clearing looking for signs of life, for signs the place had been used recently. There were none. The copse and its secrets had been lost to this generation of students. He wondered if other places and secrets existed nearby or if other students over the century and a half of the school's history had constructed their own lairs and hideouts like this one, had used them and then forgotten them. He wondered if other students or faculty had come to this very place or one like it to meet, to talk, or to lie in the grass on a thin blanket and make love on a soft Saturday afternoon in May. He felt a wave of sadness wash over him.

"What did you expect?" he said. "That she'd pop out of the bushes unchanged and ready to start again? She'd be in her mid-fifties now. And the child, he'd be what, twenty-four, twenty-five?" Who would have guessed it would turn out this way?

"Excuse me, Mrs. Gardiner?"

"Yes, Mr. Light." Mrs. Gardiner never called any of the students by their first name, insisting on the formal *Mr.* And while Mrs. Parker, her assistant in the library, was known to the students as "Hot Pants," Mrs. Gardiner soldiered on as "Iron Pants."

"Yes, ma'am…um…I need to see Mrs. Parker about something. Is she around?"

"No, she isn't."

"Oh. Do you know when she will be?"

"She is gone, Mr. Light."

"Gone? When will she be back?"

"I do not think she will be back, Mr. Light. Not now, not ever."

"I don't understand. She's not here?"

"Mr. Light, let me give you some advice." Mrs. Gardiner lowered her voice and looked at him with something approaching compassion. "She is gone. She has left the campus. It is highly unusual and Headmaster is very upset. He made it clear it is not a situation to be discussed with or among the students. Headmaster Daigle was quite adamant about that, but…" She paused and led him back toward the end of the checkout counter. "Because of what I presume to be the situation between you and Mrs. Parker, I will tell you this. She and her husband are separated. He supposed she may have been unfaithful to him. I do not know if that is the case or not. The reasons are not important. In any event, the best thing for you, Mr. Light, is to say nothing, know nothing, and believe me when I say this, it is the best thing to have happened to you."

Dexter felt cold fingers clutch at his heart, half dismay, half panic.

"Ma'am?"

"I may seem a dried-up old bag to you and your generation," she continued quietly, "but I feel like you do, only with the experience that comes with age. When I say it is the best thing to have happened to you, I mean both the before and now, the after."

He stared at her, confused. She pulled herself up and sighed. Dexter had never really looked at Mrs. Gardiner before. The only object worth viewing in the library was the now departed Mrs. Parker—for Dexter and all the students who attended the school during the six years she worked there.

"Everyone falls in love, Mr. Light," she said softly. A hint of a smile crossed her face. "At your age it comes fast and hard. You find yourself saying and doing foolish things, even rash and stupid things. You act on impulses driven by new moons and hormones, but it goes away. When you get older, say Mrs. Parker's age, that rashness and impulsiveness often lead to tragedy. Hold on to your memories, but forget your love. Do you understand what I am saying?"

He nodded, not convinced.

"I have nothing more to add, Mr. Light. I've said too much already. Here, she left you this." She shoved an envelope across the desk at him and walked away.

The note was written in Luella Mae's schoolgirl scrawl, half printing, half cursive, the distinctive trademark of an all-girls'-school alumna.

THEY'D MET ONLY ONCE after that. She sought him out in his first year at the Naval Academy. He had to go over the wall to meet her. He'd been caught on that first offense. Later, when it was compounded with the heavy drinking that started shortly thereafter, it resulted in his dismissal during his second year. His parents were devastated and cut him loose. Four years in the army as an enlisted man did not straighten him out as his father had hoped, and after his discharge, he slid downhill, moving from job to job, each a little less remunerative, a little less prestigious than the last. And now he sat on a fallen tree trunk in the middle of Old Oak Woods in a place he had not seen in two and a half decades, wondering where all the years had gone.

A long time ago, she'd left him there. "Give me five minutes," she'd said. He remembered her scent, the feel of her skin, the… all of it. He felt tears again. He took the picture from his wallet and stared at it as if seeing it for the first time. In it she remained a perpetual thirty-two. She smiled at the camera, standing in front of an antique car, and held the baby in her arms.

"Who's your daddy?" he said softly, and tore up the picture, letting the pieces fall on the spot where, a quarter of a century before, he had known her for the last time.

TWENTY

THE GAME HAD BEEN CLOSE and Loyola lost to the University of Maryland by one goal in the last five seconds. His grandchildren were alternately bummed and elated. Tooth rooted for the Terps and cheered the win. Jesse, whose Greyhounds let a midfielder through to score, returned home glum.

"Your guys were just lucky," he grumbled.

"Better team." Tooth grinned, showing new incisors that Frank swore were far too big for his mouth. They argued all the way home.

Barbara had not said a word to him since he left with the kids for the game. He didn't know if she harbored some residual anger or was embarrassed by the drift their conversation had taken. Either way, he thought it best to make his exit with Rosemary as unobtrusively as possible. He showered and dressed, timing his actions so that he would be downstairs and ready to leave at precisely six-thirty, the time Rosemary said she'd pick him up. He hoped she would be prompt. He really did not want to deal with what he supposed would be Barbara's reaction to Rosemary.

"You look nice," Barbara said as he stepped into the foyer. She reached over and adjusted his collar. "No anonymous golf club blazer, I see." Cool, very cool. So much for careful planning.

"No, not tonight. I managed to find enough gray cells to sort through my clothes this evening, but I did come close to wearing that coat." He kept his gaze fixed on the street outside. He saw the car round the corner, hesitate, and then pull into the driveway.

"Here's my ride." He opened the front door and waved. "Well, goodbye, don't wait up."

"I wouldn't think of it." Barbara followed him down the steps to the driveway. Rosemary opened the driver's side door and got out to greet him.

"Hi, Frank," Rosemary greeted him with a huge smile, a smile much too broad, much too personal to be gifted to someone categorized as just an old friend. It was a smile with a secret. Frank winced. "Would you like to drive, or shall I?" she asked and then, without waiting for an answer, turned to Barbara. "Hello, I'm Rosemary Mitchell. Your dad and I go back a long ways—a very long ways."

"Yes? Well…how do you do?" Barbara seemed taken aback.

"You drive, it's your car." Frank moved toward the passenger side door.

"It's nice to meet you," Barbara and Rosemary said in unison.

Frank stood anxiously to one side watching the scene play out, like a theater critic unsure how the drama would end, and at the same time nearing panic for fear his daughter would drop any pretense at civility and grill Rosemary.

"Is the party nearby?" Barbara's tone ranged somewhere between icy and arctic. She knew full well where the party was.

"No, it's out in the county. Don't worry, I'll take care of your father."

"I'm sure you will."

Rosemary studied Barbara for a second and then smiled. "Well. Let's go, Frank."

"Here's Bob," Frank said, before Barbara could reply. Her husband drove up and paused in the street, his turn signal winking at the driveway. Frank waved and hustled Rosemary into the car and climbed in on the opposite side. "Let's get out of here."

Rosemary backed out of the driveway and they pulled away as Bob took her place.

"Look in the rearview mirror. What are they doing?"

"Who?"

"Barbara and Bob, what are they doing?"

"I can't tell. Talking, I think."

"Do they look angry?"

"Frank, we're a block away now. I can't make out what they're doing. Is there a problem?"

"I don't know, maybe. Probably. It's another mystery for me to solve, I guess."

"You want to tell me, or is it a family thing?"

"No, I don't suppose it would hurt. I could use a woman's point of view."

He filled her in on Barbara's suspicions and fears. She waited until he finished. She had a habit, when she thought hard about things, of squinting her right eye and pulling the same side of her mouth up. It made her look a little like Popeye.

"You know, Frank, women value security over position, and men hold to the reverse, so your daughter is afraid of losing her place, her nest, if you will. Her husband has a wholly different set of worries. If he can't provide for her, what does that do to his self-image?"

"But she's afraid he's seeing another woman."

"It's not the other woman that has her worried as much as the thought of losing him to her. You see?"

He didn't.

"Either way, Frank, they are adults and they need to solve their problems themselves. And you need to stay out of it, but be prepared to pick up the pieces, if any."

"I said I'd check around."

"Not a good idea."

"How come you know so much about this stuff?"

"I read books, take courses, and I've been there." She gunned the car onto the expressway.

THE PARTY WENT WELL. The host had piled two tables with hors d'oeuvres. One table featured Chesapeake Bay cuisine, including small crab cakes and jumbo shrimp. The other end held the usual array of meatballs, cheese squares, and sausages. Another table had sensible food—salads, raw vegetables, and fruit. Nobody seemed interested in it.

Frank managed to avoid Bill Powers and spent a relatively pleasant evening reminiscing with the remnant of his class. Rosemary moved more easily among them than he did. She had been a part of their meetings for years; he had avoided all contact with them for fifty.

By ten-thirty, he had listened to all the stories he cared to, put names to faces, and stuffed himself with crabmeat. He did not want to talk about his books, hear any more stories about his father, and suffer through the embarrassed silences that followed an accidental mention of his brother's name. Rosemary slipped up beside him.

"Are we having fun yet?"

"I am done—cooked. You?"

"I have eaten too much, drunk too much, and my feet are killing me."

"Let's blow this joint."

"Would you mind driving? My night vision isn't very good anymore."

"I'm not sure mine's any better. Maybe between the two of us we can navigate our way back."

He made his way through the labyrinth of suburban streets to the beltway. Once on it he turned to her.

"Where to?"

"You mean like, 'your place or mine?'"

"Can't be mine, I don't think. We could stop somewhere."

"You have a problem with my house all of a sudden?"

"No, I just don't want to—"

"Well, I do. You okay with that?"

"I'm okay."

The drive back to Ruxton took a bit longer than the trip out. He drove much more carefully at night and the streets were not familiar to him.

He parked her car in the driveway.

"Do you have nosy neighbors?" he asked.

"Probably."

"You're not worried about what they might say?"

"Should I be?"

Inside, she shed her jacket and he loosened his tie. Arizona is not a venue for tie wearing and he no longer felt comfortable with one. He had had to search the closet in his guest room, where he stored his "Back East" clothes to find a tie. She fixed them drinks and then fetched another thick envelope from the little green desk.

"Now what?"

"While you've been amusing yourself with sports and games, I've been working. This is four hours on the Internet searching for anything I could find out about the missing boys. There are printouts from *The Baltimore Sun* and the now defunct *News-Post,* sorry, *American.* I can never remember which is correct. Anyway, they cover the three weeks following the disappearance, as well. There's a squib from *Newsweek* and some bits and pieces from sites that I thought you might find useful. One says martians picked them up."

"That's useful?"

"Actually, it is. It defines the investigation's dead-end. The disappearance was so absolute, they might as well have been kidnapped by aliens. You see?"

"Okay." He leafed through the stack of papers. "Did anything in here strike you?"

"No, not yet, but I want to read through them again."

"We should visit Elizabeth Roulx, I think."

"Who?"

"She teaches English at Scott and is the school's archivist. There may be something in the archives that will help."

"More than what we have already?" Rosemary looked doubtful.

"You never know, and we will want to read the police reports, witness statements, too, if they'll let us."

"Why wouldn't they?"

"Well, the police are not that keen on amateurs poking around in their files. That's in the first place. Then there is the problem I pose."

"You?"

"They will check me out with the police back home and then 'hell will freeze over,' so to speak."

"Then, I will ask for the reports. I will say I am writing a book or something, but what good will having the police reports do? They have gone over them again and again. What can we find that they can't?"

"We will play *what if.*"

"What if?"

"Look, we know those boys weren't beamed up into a UFO and whisked off to the galaxy of Andromeda. They walked into those woods and vanished. Whatever happened to them, you can be sure neither magic nor extraterrestrial abductions played any role in it. Somewhere in those reports there's a detail, some small thing someone said or saw that didn't seem important at the time but will solve this thing. So we play *what if.*"

"I still don't see."

"Okay. Let's say someone claims to be sleeping at the time and couldn't have done this or that. We say, *what if* he wasn't asleep, or *what if* he wasn't in Detroit or taking a bath. Will the dominos fall a different way then? The whole story might change."

"How will we know if we found the right *what if?*"

"People who were not thought of as significant at the time become important, things like that—dates, times, sequence. At least we should try."

"I'll see about the police reports. I have a friend who's a county judge and his father is a retired county cop."

"It's nice to be connected." He picked up the papers. "Now tell me about these."

"Now? It's pretty late. What about Barbara?"

"You told me it wasn't my problem."

"Right, but—"

"Past your bedtime?"

"You should know me better than that by now. Where do you want me to start?"

TWENTY-ONE

DEXTER PUSHED OPEN THE DOOR to his apartment and switched on the light. He looked at the clock on the bedside table and shook his head. Seventeen hours without a drink. That is a modern-era record, he thought. He stepped over clothes scattered on the floor and made his way to the corner that served as a kitchenette, a badly scratched Formica-topped counter with a double hot plate, a tiny sink, and a mini-refrigerator beneath. He kept a bottle of scotch under the sink and it sang a love song to him. He bent over and pulled at the cabinet door, then stopped and stepped back. From harm's way, he thought. He sat heavily on the edge of his bed. It had taken him hours to navigate his way home and his feet burned from too much walking. He glared at the cabinet door, daring it to open.

"Tomorrow. I am going to uncork and finish you. Tomorrow will be a head buster, but not today. I am going to complete one sober day, if only to see if I can."

He stood and retraced his steps to the door, kicked it shut, and contemplated the mess on the floor. Clothing, newspapers, and brown paper bags, the long thin kind designed to hold fifth- and quart-sized bottles—the kind that come filled from liquor stores. A half dozen were strewn about the thin carpet like fallen leaves on an October lawn. One by one he picked up his clothes and stuffed them in a laundry bag. He collected papers, bags, and cartons and crammed them into a trash bag, which he then deposited in the hallway outside his door. He found a rag, moistened it at the sink, averting his eyes from the cabinet door below, and wiped down counters, walls, windowsills, and his cramped bathroom. He made up the bed with clean sheets. He kept at his housecleaning for hours, working furiously, straightening, scrubbing, and sorting. Finally his mania gave way to exhaustion and he collapsed on his bed. He fell asleep before he could turn off the light.

BARBARA THOMAS SAT UP and gathered the blankets around her.

"He's not back yet." Her husband moaned and rolled over.

"Bob," she said, her volume increasing with each word, "Dad has not come in yet."

"What time is it?" he mumbled and tried to make out the numbers on the alarm clock. Without his glasses the LED images blurred together.

"Two o'clock." Her voice was edged equally with anger and fear.

"He's probably out with his old buddies, Barb—big reunion, *auld lang syne,* and all that. Go back to sleep."

"I can't go *back* to sleep. I never got to sleep in the first place. He's not with buddies, Bob, he's with that woman."

"Okay, he's with a woman. What's the problem?"

"What's the problem? Bob, what about my mother? He can't just forget her. We don't know what happened to her, and he could… What's that woman want with him, anyway?"

"What any woman wants, I expect."

"Men, it's all you think about. Women aren't like that. Dad might want to, you know…whatever. But she's got something else on her mind, I'm telling you. Besides, they're both pushing seventy."

"It's none of our business, Barb."

"It is my business. He's my father and he's old and easily duped by any flashy woman with an eye to get his money or whatever she's after."

"Barb, be sensible. Your father is perfectly capable of taking care of himself. He's not suffering from dementia and has never, in my experience, done anything rash or foolish, and I don't think I'd describe Rosemary Mitchell as flashy."

"It's the boys' money, Bob. That's what she wants. They will need it for college when he dies. What if she gets her hooks into him? Women do that, you know."

"Women? I thought it was only one woman. My guess is she probably has money of her own. I know George Mitchell's accountant and I think he left her pretty well-off. Go to sleep."

"But—"

"Barb, listen to me. It's not the boys' money and it's not your money. It's his. He earned it over fifty long years. If he wants to squander it, that's his privilege."

She got out of bed and turned on him. "How can you say that? Do you think you will ever earn enough to take care of your family? No, you have to disappear every whipstitch to go to 'work.' Do you want them to go to public school? You think the state university system is going to get them to the top? Well, I won't let that happen. You can roll over and watch your children's future slip away, but not me."

"I'm doing my best, Barbara, and I could use some help here, instead of this constant harping."

"Your best isn't enough, is it?"

She flounced out the door. He heard the guest room door slam shut. Any hope he had of a decent night's sleep was caught up in the silence that followed.

BRAD STARK HAD HAD A BAD day and when it didn't look like it could get any worse, Felix Darnell had called him in. Judith had kept him jumping around like a puppet on a string most of the day, alternately teasing and excoriating him. She would coo and purr like a Persian cat and just when he thought their relationship had returned to some resemblance of normalcy, she unsheathed her claws and left him hurt and bleeding. As if that weren't enough, that night he had to hop from one reunion class party to another. He missed most of the people he wanted to speak to, and the ones he did manage to buttonhole put him off with vague smiles and "Send me something in writing, Brad."

He turned and studied his wife. She'd insisted they make love when they got home, although what transpired seemed more contest than connubial. Now, she lay on the bed, sprawled across its width like a child, face as innocent as a baby. But twenty minutes ago that same face had been contorted with excitement. She loomed over him, teeth bared, hair damp and flying wildly, as she shook her head back and forth and spat out commands like a mad drill sergeant.

That had been the characteristic that attracted him to her when they first met. Her willingness to take risks and the ferocity of her lovemaking intoxicated him. He felt they lived on the sexual edge. But now, settled in a community like Scott, where everyone's life was an open book, the very thing that once possessed him like a narcotic now frightened him. The thrill had been numbed with the passage of time. He wondered if she didn't need some sort of psychological help. The sheets had fallen off the bed. He pulled them up and covered her. She hadn't bothered to put her nightgown back on. He stepped out onto his mini-porch and dug out his last cigarette. What to do?

Darnell had thrown Meredith Smith up at him—that and Brad's poor performance on that project to date. He had not closed the deal. He had not even put the deal on the table. In fact, he'd missed Smith completely. And Smith planned to leave for Arizona the next day. What was Brad going to do about that, Darnell wanted to know.

He told Darnell he managed to persuade Smith to stay over a few days. He said he'd personally convinced him to study the mystery of the missing boys and perhaps write another book with that as its theme. Naturally he, Brad, would be with him and there would be time to work on the gift. Smith, he'd declared, would not commit to a donation as big as the one they were after unless he had time to think. But, by demonstrating the school's support for his work, etc., etc… Of course, Brad made most of it up, but Darnell couldn't know about that.

"Are you sure it's wise to pursue the missing boys mystery, Stark?" Darnell had sounded worried. "That tragic chapter is closed. Do we really want to open it up again? It would mean the press, all those reporters, TV. It can't do us any good. Think of the families of those poor boys."

"Well, Dr. Darnell, you're quite right, as usual." Brad began to backpedal. "I'll just make it my business to see that he doesn't succeed. In the end, there will be no story. The past is the past." Yes, indeed. The last thing Brad needed was for that business to come back and haunt him—haunt them all. Now there would be no resolution. Not now, not ever.

And, if it turned out Smith did, in fact, leave for Arizona on Sunday, well, he couldn't be held responsible for that. These old guys were not exactly the most reliable people, after all. But to be on the safe side, he'd have to get hold of Smith first thing in the morning and convince him to make good on his promise to look into the disappearance. At least long enough for him to make a pitch.

Judith rolled over, spilling the sheets back on the floor. He thought he saw her eyelids flicker. He decided to sleep in the guest room.

ROSEMARY STOPPED TALKING when she realized Frank's breathing had become much too regular. She placed the paper in her hand on the coffee table and turned to him. His head had slumped forward. Eyes closed, he dozed peacefully at the end of the couch.

Poor baby. He's had a big day.

"What do I do now?"

Put him to bed?

"Hush."

She yawned, stretched, and considered her options. Should she wake him? And if so, should she do it now or later? And if later, how much later? She decided to let him doze for a while. She stood, adjusted a pillow so that he could lean back.

"Frank?" she said softly and shook his shoulder. "Frank." Louder. His eyes snapped open.

"I'm okay. What were you saying?"

"You were asleep."

"No, just drifted off there for a second."

"You were dead to the world, my friend. Now you have two choices. Since I don't like to drive late at night, you can take my car and go back to your daughter's, or you can spend the night here. Either way, I'm beat and going to bed."

What are you up to, lady? This will be three nights in a row for the two of you here in the house.

"I know what I'm doing."

"I'm sure you do," he said, sleepily, confused.

"Actually, I wasn't talking to you," she said.

He sat up and looked around. "There's someone else here?"

"In a way. I'll tell you about it some other day. Your decision." She dropped the car keys on the table. Frank yawned and his eyelids crashed again. She found an afghan, put his feet up on the couch, and covered him. She watched him for another minute and then, certain he would not awaken, at least not soon, she put out the lights, and disappeared into the shadows at the foot of the stairs.

TWENTY-TWO

"LEDEZMA?"

"Yeah, who's this?" he rasped. The clock read 6:00 a.m.

"It's Barnett. You know, I work the eleven to seven shift at the medical examiner's office."

"Right, okay. Sorry, Barnett, it's Sunday and I'm not quite awake yet. What's up?"

"You still working the Smith case, the one where the old lady—?"

"Yeah, for now, anyway. That could change in a week, though."

"No kidding? I guess the brass wants to put the old files on ice, right?"

"Something like that. So what've you got?"

"Maybe nothing, maybe you caught a break. You said I should call if anything turned up, you know. So when I get the paperwork, I'm thinking of you right away."

"Right, thanks. What paperwork?"

"What we have here is a body. Well, not a body, a skeleton mostly, but it's a woman for sure, and the doc says fifty to seventy years old and in the desert at least three years. Could be your dame."

Ledezma slipped out of bed and started dressing. This could be it, he thought. Finally, a break. "How'd she die?"

"Somebody put a bullet right through the old brain box."

"Bingo. Don't do a thing until I get there."

"No problem, Sergeant. You don't, by any chance, have a copy of her dental records, do you? The doc says we're stuck

until Monday because the dentist's office is closed and we don't
have a warrant anyway."

"I've got them. By the way, where did they find her?"

"Out with the saguaros and the snakes."

"I'll be there in an hour."

LEDEZMA DID NOT LIKE the morgue. The place gave him the creeps.
It smelled of chemicals and other things he didn't want to identify. He recognized formaldehyde from his days in biology lab,
and the clove oil. When things got really ripe, they'd use clove
oil to cover the scent. He tried not to think about the sweet, rot-
ting odor that served as a kind of olfactory pedal point to the
rest. He considered himself a pretty tough guy. He'd seen his
share of gore and body parts in various stages of decay in his
time, but the morgue always threw him. Somehow, to collect all
that human garbage in one place seemed obscene.

He looked around the room. McMicken used a morgue set
up in an old building next to the county medical examiner. The
town struggled to keep up with the explosive growth and coinci-
dent increase in the homicide rate, so they expanded as best they
could. There wasn't much to see. The room had the predictable
white tiles on the walls and tiers of refrigerated drawers to hold
the bodies, each with its identifying card slot. He'd pulled one
of those drawers once and vowed he'd never do it again. He had
just joined the force then. His squad sent him to the morgue to
identify a body. What he didn't know was one of the officers
had been put in the drawer and covered with a sheet. When he
opened the drawer, the cop sat up and moaned. He cleared the
morgue and the building in something like four seconds flat.

Bones were laid out on a stainless steel table. A steel bucket
was positioned on the floor at one end. Someone, the medical
examiner probably, had begun to arrange them in order. He
would count them first to make sure they were all there. Then
he would try to retrieve some DNA to confirm the ID. He'd arrange the bones this way and that to make up a story about how
the person had died. Ledezma shivered, not just from the chill

air—they kept the temperature down, like working in a refrigerator—but because he secretly feared the place.

Barnett, the ghoul who helped the ME, stood a few paces away, waiting. He was a messy man wearing a stained tan lab coat over an equally stained T-shirt. He had hair that had started out as a widow's peak but male pattern baldness sent his forehead up and back. Only the peak remained, a thin, greasy brown smear of hair clinging to his forehead like a drowning rat. Ledezma contemplated with distaste Barnett's large, pitted nose, his slouching stance, and wary, sly expression. He felt about him in the same way as he felt about the room; he didn't like either of them for the same reasons. But Barnett served a purpose. Ledezma peeled a twenty off his roll and put it in Barnett's palm. He got a yellow crooked-toothed grin by way of thanks. Ledezma turned back to the body, or what was left of it.

Bits of fabric and metal had been stuffed into plastic bags. Ledezma picked one up and peered through the plastic, a buckle of some sort, too small to be from a belt. He didn't recognize much else, khaki that might have come from a pair of shorts or slacks, some denim, and coins. He sifted through the pile looking for personal belongings. Nothing. Curious.

"What's this?" he said, pointing to a pile of bleached canvas on the next table.

"That's what covered her, probably why they never spotted her on the flyovers. It was the same color as the ground, see?"

He flipped a corner of the material, noted the bit of white trim on one edge, and then turned his attention back to the bones. Forensics he left to others, but he knew a bullet hole when he saw one. He moved to the head and inspected the skull. He took a new pencil from his pocket and inserted it in the eye socket, then rolled the skull on its side. He peered at the shattered bone at the back, then at the larger hole in the front. If he remembered right, the entry wound indicated she took the shot in the back of the head, like an execution, almost. He frowned. That didn't fit, but he'd wait for the ME to fill him in.

"Where's her wedding band?" he asked.

Barnett shrugged. "None came in, so I guess the crime scene guys who picked up the body didn't find one, or they decided that since she was dead she didn't need it anymore."

"No ring, no jewelry at all?"

"Nada."

He rolled the skull back in place. The ME did not like people tinkering with his work-ups. Ledezma scanned the rest of the skeleton, looking for breaks, anything out of the ordinary.

"Healthy sixty, plus-minus, female," the ME boomed from the door. "Don't touch."

The medical examiner was a big man. He stood something over six-seven, probably went three hundred and fifty pounds, and had one of those voices you expect to hear on an opera stage. He didn't talk, he projected. Ledezma jerked his hand away from the skeleton like a kid caught with his hand in a cookie jar.

"Are you Ledezma?" the ME intoned, a little *recitative* before the big aria.

"Yeah, Sergeant Ledezma."

"Your case, isn't it?"

Ledezma resisted the impulse to sing. "Yes, it is."

"You have the dental records?"

"I do." He handed the papers to the ME, who looked at them briefly, then, Hamlet-like, picked up the skull and stared at its teeth.

"Need dental forensics in here for the official determination, but I'd say this is your woman. The amalgam filling is the clue, see...." He pointed to a molar. "Hardly anybody does amalgams unless they don't show or their dental plan is a bad one. It's an old one and in the right place. And there is a gold crown in the back. Yep, this is your woman."

Ledezma nodded his head. Now it begins.

"How'd she die?" he asked. He knew, but he wanted the ME to have the privilege of telling him. The ME snapped on a pair of latex gloves.

"Big bullet in the base of the skull just above the occipital foramen, see?" He held the skull so that Ledezma could look at the hole again. "Then it comes out here in the frontal bone right where it joins with the parietals."

"That means she got popped in the back of the head," Barnett volunteered. The ME shot him a withering look and Barnett shrunk an inch or two and skulked away.

"Shot in the back of the head, as our Deaner says, in the nape of the neck, bullet comes out through her forehead. Poses an interesting problem. I wish I'd been there at the scene."

"What kind of problem?" Ledezma did not want a problem. He wanted a nice clean homicide. Shoot and drop.

"Well. It means that to figure out the who, see, I need to know the how. Your suspect—the husband—describe him. He's not a dwarf, is he, or a jockey, a short guy?"

"No, average build, for an old guy, five-eleven—"

"See, there's the problem."

"I don't see."

"She took the bullet here," he said, pointing to the back of his own head with his left forefinger, "and it came out here." Right forefinger high on his forehead. "Now, she would stand five-six or five-seven, so if he shoots her he has to be kneeling on the ground or she has to be standing on a stepladder, you see?"

"No. Why on a stepladder?"

The ME picked up the skull again and, taking the pencil from Ledezma's pocket, ran it through the two openings. He held the skull level and Ledezma saw the angle it made. The pencil pointed at the ceiling. A man Smith's height would have shot level or down.

"He's sitting on the ground."

"Possible, but think about it. If you're going to shoot someone, are you going to sit down and shoot her in the back of the head or are you going to stand and take careful aim?"

"Stand, I guess." Ledezma's heart sank. "Suicide?"

"No, rule that out. There's no way someone can twist their arm around and shoot themselves in the back of the head like that. Why would they even try?"

"So Smith is out, too?"

"Oh, no, it's just the bullet holes present a problem. Problems are what we specialize in here, Sergeant. No, of course she wasn't on a ladder. Silly idea. I just mention that to show the difficulty of shooting her standing up and getting this wound track."

"Doc, I appreciate the lecture, but could we get to the punch line?"

"Patience, Ledezma, patience. See, if you really want to nail your man, you need to go through this with me. Otherwise some smart lawyer will shred you on the stand."

"Sorry. So show me."

"Right. We have two possibilities. First, the shooter has the gun in his hand and presses it flat against the back of her neck like this." He made a pistol with his hand and pressed it against Ledezma's neck. "Then, bang. But it's not a natural way of holding a gun. Now, if the victim was lying on the ground, then you could get this track. Say she's lying on her stomach, face in the sand. He's at her feet." The ME took a position at the foot of the steel table, pointed at the skull with his forefinger, and cocked his thumb and fired. "Bang."

"So you think that's it?"

"It works, but I don't think so."

"Why not?" Ledezma shifted from foot to foot. His low tolerance for the morgue and its aroma began to creep up on him. In a minute or two, he'd have to leave. Leave or heave. He wanted the ME to stop showing off and get on with it.

"Well, let's consider the normal reaction one has lying face-down in the sand. Do you stick your nose in it or do you turn your head to one side or the other?"

"Turn my head."

"Right again, so the track would be behind one ear and out through the temporal or opposite parietal. Not the case here."

"Finish this for me, Doc, I'm fading fast here."

"Okay. Here's how it must have happened. She is kneeling. Look at these photographs." He pulled a sheaf of pictures from an envelope. "This is how they found her. Her knees are together and turned a little to the left, legs angled out a little. See that? And her arms are under her, hands together."

"Look, you're the expert, but if she's kneeling and he shoots her from behind, the bullet would go in high and come out low, the opposite of what we have here."

"Very good. So what conclusion do you draw from that?"

"I don't know. Just tell me."

"Okay. She's kneeling. Look at the picture. Hands together, no sign of them being tied, and—this is the good part—she has her head bowed. She's praying. Bang, bullet in here, out there."

"She's praying?"

"That's what it looks like. For mercy, for release, for her killer perhaps."

Praying, for God's sake—yes, for God's sake, indeed. That ought to pop loose some resources. The scenario worked. It had to be. A poor woman kneeling and praying to her god and he blows her away, the son of a... "Get me the confirmation on the ID," Ledezma snapped, "pronto. And give me your best guess on the caliber of the gun."

Ledezma almost ran to the door, his cell phone out and to his ear.

"I need a team of divers," he said. "Yes, today. Okay, tomorrow. And metal detectors, the kind that work under water." The door's glass rattled dangerously as it banged shut behind him.

"He didn't ask me about the canvas," the ME said. He frowned and moved the bones forming the left ring finger over to the right. "He should have asked me about the canvas."

TWENTY-THREE

FRANK WOKE UP FEELING like Conan the Barbarian spent the night rampaging around in his skull. He still wore his slacks. He'd shed his coat, shirt, and tie and they lay in a heap on the floor. He shook his head and sat up. Somewhere downstairs he heard his grandchildren arguing. The aroma of bacon and coffee filled the room. Sunday morning breakfast, the meal that surviving the week made worthwhile. The trick this morning was to survive waking up. He pulled on a sweater, made a quick trip to the bathroom, and went downstairs. His daughter looked at him like he was three-day-old fish.

"Good morning," he said, ignoring the look. She mumbled something he couldn't make out.

"What are we going to do today?" Tooth asked.

"You're not supposed to ask," his brother said and punched him on the arm.

"Ow. Mom, Jesse punched me."

"Jesse, stop punching your brother." A mother's reflex.

"Can you take us to the ball game?" Tooth asked and this time managed to avoid his brother's fist.

"What time?" Frank asked. A ball game might be just the thing. Would Rosemary go? Why did he care if she did or didn't?

"Three o'clock."

"Let me make a call first, but yeah, we can go to the game."

"Yay," Tooth cheered.

"Not so fast," his mother said. Her tone sounded ominous. "I need to talk to your grandfather first."

Tooth scowled. "But—"

"No buts. Go get ready for church—now."

The kids scuffled out of the room, leaving the field clear for whatever major engagement their mother had in mind.

"Dad, it's none of my business, but where were you last night?"

"You're right, it's none of your business. Look, if I'm in your way here, I'll move out. The plan was for me to leave today, anyway. I can still do that. Solving the school's mystery can be left to someone else. Or, I can move into a motel." His head still throbbed. If it hadn't, he might have been a little more civil. But he was beginning to resent his daughter's insistence he be treated like a naughty boy.

"Or move in with Mrs. Mitchell?"

Frank studied his daughter. He supposed she had a right to be upset, what with her mother's whereabouts still in limbo, but she should also know her limits.

"I don't have any plans to cohabit with Mrs. Mitchell," he said, his voice hovering on the thin edge of anger. "If I had, I wouldn't have come home last night at all, if you must know. I'll get a motel room. That way, you won't have to worry about what time I go to bed."

"Or with whom."

It was his turn to give her a look. Their eyes locked for a moment and then, feeling foolish, he started to leave the room.

"You haven't eaten your breakfast," she said.

"No. Thanks, anyway. I'll be out of your hair in an hour or so." He left.

"Grandpa, are we going to the game?"

"Not this trip, guys. Sorry."

Frank went to his room and rummaged in his coat pocket for his cell phone, retrieved it, and called Rosemary. Sometime during the past two days her number had made it into his speed dial program.

"Hi. I seem to have your car in my daughter's driveway."

"No problem. I hoped you'd take it. I worry about you."

"I'm flattered but I'm fine. Look, I need to get the car back to you and then I want to book into a motel while I work on this project for Scott."

"We."

"What?"

"While *we* work on the project for Scott. Nick and Nora, remember? And why a motel? Why aren't you staying with your daughter?"

"Long story. How about I pick you up—"

"And take me to church and to lunch afterward?"

"Ah...well, why not. In an hour?"

"Yes."

He hung up and called his home number, entered his code, and listened to the messages in his voice mail. The fifth and last changed the expression of bored attention to concentration. He frowned, pushed the appropriate button, and listened again.

Important I speak to you as soon as possible. There's been a development. Call me.

Frank knew the number but hesitated. What kind of development? What had Ledezma turned up now? No need to get panicky, at least not yet. They didn't know where he was, and until he knew what had developed, they wouldn't. He snapped the phone shut and began making a pile of his clothes on the bed.

"Dad?" Barbara stood in the door, hands clasped, face worried. "I'm sorry. I spoke out of turn. I didn't want to upset you. I...please don't feel you have to go."

"It's for the best, Barbara. I love you, but you and I are not going to stay friends very much longer if I remain here. And anyway, there is a hotel near Scott. Then I won't need a car, see. I can walk to the school to ask my questions. It's near the metro, too, so I can get downtown if I have to, and I have a ride if I need one." He saw the momentary flash in her eyes and realized he should have skipped the last part.

She sighed and nodded. "You don't have to, you know. Really, I feel bad about this...the ball game—"

"I'd still like to take them, if that's okay," he said.

She nodded again, searched his face, and then retreated back into the hall. He listened until her footsteps faded out of earshot. He redialed Rosemary.

"Church, lunch, then to the ballpark with not one, not two, but three handsome men—one old coot and two rather dashing youths. Suit you?"

"It'll be like a tea dance at the Naval Academy, so many men, so little time."

SUNDAY. AGAINST HIS BETTER judgment Brad made up his mind to go to the woods. He reckoned nobody would be around, at least not in the morning. He hadn't set foot in the woods since his return to Scott, but now it called to him, tugged at him, sirens singing from the rocks on some mythic shore. He tried to remember his mythology. Who were the sirens and who called whom? Jason and the Argonauts? What happened to them? He thought he remembered something about earwax but couldn't be sure. Or maybe it was Odysseus.

He showered and dressed. Judith still lay sprawled across their bed in the same position he'd left her the night before. He watched as a fly landed on her shoulder and started a pilgrimage across her chest. She brushed it away without waking. He rearranged the sheets again. In the raw morning light, she didn't look quite as alluring, quite as desirable.

He made himself a cup of instant coffee and two slices of toast, slathering a glob of peanut butter on each. He stalled, picked up the Sunday paper, thought about reading. He stared at the wall, drummed his fingers. Then he realized if he didn't go soon, before his wife woke, he wouldn't go at all. He swallowed the last of his coffee, made a face, walked down the steps to the basement, and slipped out the sliding glass door.

It took him ten minutes to walk down the hill and into the woods. Ten minutes in real time, a quarter of a century in his mind. He hesitated and then plunged in, afraid he might be sick, afraid of what he might remember, but mostly, just afraid.

THE ME STARED AT THE skeleton spread out on the table. He had a clipboard in his hand and checked off items as he counted. Early desert sunlight filled the dingy room, etching the peeling iron rafters with unforgiving light. He needed to be absolutely sure. In his world, every detail counted. Now cops, he thought, cops would skip over things. "Not important," they'd say, "just give me the big picture," they'd say, and then they would miss one small thing and some bad guy would stay on the street to kill again. This guy, Ledezma, impulsive, always in a hurry, can't wait. Like some TV cop, "Just the facts, ma'am." And he never asked the right questions.

He scratched his bald spot with latex-gloved fingers, pulled his eyebrows together to squint at the bones again. Only three bones, some phalanges, interested him now. Left or right ring finger? He picked them up, one by one, and replaced them. He checked the articular facets of the adjoining carpel bone just to be sure. Definitely the right hand. He would check with the state's forensic anthropologist to be sure, but he felt absolutely certain he had it right.

"I guess she wasn't praying after all," he said and made a note on the clipboard.

TWENTY-FOUR

ROSEMARY SWUNG THE CAR into the hotel's portico. No eager bell-man leapt to open the door or handle luggage. Frank had spent the trip from the ballpark looking at her out of the corner of his eye. He thought she looked tired. The lines on her face were deepened with fatigue. Her face had also started to turn pink from the sun—except around her eyes where she'd worn sun-glasses. The heretofore missing freckles had finally surfaced. In an hour she would look like a reversed-out panda. "Frank, is it okay if I just drop you off? I am exhausted. Too much fresh air, too many hot dogs, and too much fun for this old lady to take in, in one day."

"Not old, Rosemary. Old is like—for castles. Old is for sea tortoises, old is for Methuselah. Do you know how they describe a used Mercedes in my part of the world? *Experienced*, not used, not old, but experienced. That's us. We're not old, we're just experienced."

"Well, this extremely experienced woman of indeterminate age is experiencing the effects of severe exhaustion."

Frank got out, removed his bags from the trunk, and was surprised to see what he assumed must be a bellman. Hotels, in his experience, did not usually provide such frills. He handed his bags to the man, who, shirt unbuttoned and worrying a tooth-pick in the corner of his mouth, accepted Frank's dollar tip with a grunt and disappeared into the hotel carrying only one of the two bags. Frank walked around to the driver's side door.

"Tomorrow," he said, "I'll check with Elizabeth Roulx in the archives. That will take most of the morning. How about you work your charms on your connected people and see if you can get your hands on the police reports?"

She nodded and then wagged her finger at him, to come closer. "Thank you for a wonderful day. I think your grandchildren are adorable. Do you think they liked me?"

"They thought you were spectacular. Tooth wanted to know where you got your hair dyed white. He said he'd like to have his dyed that way, too. I think he wants to be a trendsetter."

"What did you tell him?" she said, grinning.

"That he'd have to wait until he was older. He pouted for a while. Apparently that's the answer he gets for everything he wants to do—from skydiving to scuba. Jesse told him he was dumb. That you didn't have your hair dyed, you just had 'old hair.'"

"Experienced hair. Well, I'm flattered, but if I could exchange this mop for his chestnut curls, I'd do it in a heartbeat. Okay, I've got to go." She leaned toward the open window. He hesitated, smiled, and kissed her. She kissed him back.

"Tomorrow. We'll meet back here for lunch and swap information."

"What time tomorrow? Never mind, call me." She drove off.

Frank watched her roll down the ramp and onto the street, picked up his remaining suitcase, walked into the lobby, and checked in. The clerk took his credit card, fussed with the computer keyboard, and frowned. Frank hoped that didn't mean anything. Clerks have a habit of studying their computer monitors like they're on the brink of discovering the unified theory of the universe. The clerk raised his eyes, head nodding like a bobble-head doll, and assigned him a room. When Frank asked, he assured him that they did indeed have a business center where he could use a computer. Instructions on how to use his key card to access it, the faxes, and the Internet were printed on the inside of the key folder which he handed Frank. There would be a charge, of course. He raised his eyebrows slightly when Frank asked for two key cards, but swiped them without asking any questions.

Rooms in motels and hotels, particularly chains, have a predictable sameness that for travelers on the road for long periods can sometimes cause clinical depression. A hotel can be a Sheraton one year and a Ramada the next as its owner plays franchise checkers, but that fact will go largely unnoticed by his guests, unless they prefer one shampoo choice over another. Frank inspected his room. He found it unremarkable from dozens he'd stayed in before. It had two double beds, a television set on cable with pay-per-view movies, a small refrigerator, a coffeemaker, and a safe. He figured they all might come in handy. He would give Rosemary a shopping list and stock up on goodies. He might save time and a little money eating in once in a while.

He dug his phone charger out of his bag and plugged it in. He opened the phone. A phone call might just shake something loose. Could they trace a cell phone call? He couldn't remember. He wrote about that in one of his books, *Lying Distance,* and at the time, you couldn't, but time changes things. He unpacked and flopped full-length on the bed and immediately fell asleep.

The phone woke him.

"You're in and settled?" Rosemary, sounding a little fresher.

He cleared his throat and tried to sound wide awake. "I'm good," he said. The clock read nine-thirty. He hadn't had dinner and his stomach sent him angry messages about it. "I'm just going out to get a bite to eat. Sorry you can't join me."

"I'm still working on those hot dogs, thank you. I may be at it all night. Next time you decide to invite me to one of your Boy Scout outings, remind me to pack a lunch."

He chuckled. "Everybody needs a stadium dog at least once a year. They are a metaphor for life in the twenty-first century. They taste wonderful, you're sure you can manage any and all on your plate, and five hours later, you have heartburn for decisions made without reflection."

"Deep, very deep. Who knew how my life would be enriched when I met the famous author? But if it's all the same with you, I'll skip the metaphors for the nonce and say goodnight. See you tomorrow."

The hotel did not have a restaurant but it did offer a conti-

nental breakfast. Otherwise, guests were on their own, to drive
to the mall a half mile away, or to any of the several eateries in
the area, or use the chain restaurant next door. Frank hoped it
was still open. The thought of eating out of vending machines
did not appeal to him.

It wasn't.

He managed to extract a limp Danish packaged in a cello-
phane wrapper from a vending machine, made a pot of in-room
coffee, and washed it down without cream. He sighed, realizing
that with the caffeine and the hours he'd slept since he checked
in, the likelihood he'd go to sleep was remote. He took the elevator to the lobby and found the business center.

The computer beeped to life after he swiped his key card in
the slot on its monitor. He stared at the screen and then found a
search engine that would take him to the Arizona newspapers.
He tried the latest editions of several. None mentioned anything
about him or Sandy. The development must have been too recent,
he thought, to make the Sunday edition. He'd have to try the
next day. He remembered Rosemary's complete set of printouts
about the missing boys. She said she got them off the Internet.
He probed the *Arizona Republic* Web site for an hour, trying
to find a way into their archives without any success. How did
she do it? He thought about calling her. Half past ten, too late.
He'd have to ask her tomorrow.

Back in his room he spread the reports she'd downloaded
on the bed. He arranged them in chronological order and began
to read. He concentrated on the pages for two hours, stopping
only to visit the vending machines for more drinks and crack-
ers. From time to time he jotted a note, a short sentence, con-
structing a rough outline of the events that afternoon long ago.
At midnight, he pulled the papers back into a single pile, folded
them, and put them in the shallow safe with his notes.

Somewhere in the thousands of words he'd read there had
to be a clue, something that would steer him in the right direction. He turned on the television, keeping the volume low, and
switched to the headline news channel. He noticed that as he

grew older, the news seemed to have become repetitive. Politicians postured and pointed fingers. People were shot, robbed, raped, and abused. Folks wrecked their cars or other people's cars. They did so because they were drunk, too old to be driving, too young to be driving, or just plain stupid. He wished the newscast would run a stupidity index with stories instead of attempting to make them into an investigative exposé. A man nearly killed himself diving off an eighty-foot rock ledge into a lake somewhere. The ledge stood at least twenty feet back from the water's edge, another ten from water deep enough to dive in. Clearly, a candidate for a Darwin award. Guys like that couldn't be good for the gene pool.

The international news included a report from some polling company indicating the popularity of the United States had waned significantly in France. Nothing new there—Freedom Fries, that's the answer. Frank watched with glazed eyes, feeling sleepy but still hungry.

The carefully coifed and smiling anchorman reported on the results of the latest government study which showed that one quarter of the United States population suffered from mental illness at some level. Frank snorted. "That," he said to the TV screen, "is six-dollar bullshit. It is the inevitable outcome of a self-absorbed society wallowing in self-diagnosis and excuse making. Fifty years ago…" He stopped in mid-rant. Old age speaking. When would he learn that this generation did not care what happened fifty years, thirty years, even ten years ago? History held no meaning for them—that was then, this is now—the mantra for a generation who, Frank believed, would be well-advised to learn Chinese.

The talking head, expression earnest, smile sincere, went on to declare that in Elkhart, Indiana, two boys were nearly killed when some scaffolding they were climbing on collapsed and left them dangling fifty feet in the air. They'd broken into a deserted construction site and saw the rigging as a huge jungle gym. Only the quick thinking of a third boy, who called 9-1-1 on his cell phone, kept the incident from becoming a tragedy. Frank had been eight years old before his family had a telephone at all, and it was a party line at that. But this kid had his own cell phone? What kind of society thinks it needs to equip a nine-year-old with a cell phone? I am getting old, he thought, old and bitter. I need to lighten up. The effects of an afternoon in the sun finally hit him. He stabbed the remote at the television to turn it off and went to sleep.

TWENTY-FIVE

FELIX DARNELL AND BRAD STARK met Frank outside the building that housed the school's archives. Since he hadn't told anyone except Elizabeth Roulx he intended to do some research, he guessed she must have given them a heads-up. Darnell wore a smile that could have deep-fried a bushel of potatoes. Stark, on the other hand, showed no expression at all. His eyes were on Darnell, not Frank.

A pair of sharks, Frank thought, circling an old white whale. Moby Dick, that's me, Ahab's nemesis—or maybe Ledezma's—or maybe I have it backward. Does Ledezma have the harpoon or do I? Hard to say who's pursuing whom. We are two fencers, thrusting and parrying, each after the same thing but unwilling to help the other get it. Capone and Ness…stop! That's way too many metaphors for one paragraph. A writer's curse, he thought. He smiled at his hosts and shook their hands.

"Dr. Darnell, nice of you to come. Not necessary, of course. I only want to sit for a few hours and read through some of your news clippings, yearbooks, that sort of thing."

Darnell maintained his smile, but his words came out cool, sober. "I hope," he said, "that you understand the seriousness of this project. Scott is known for its academic excellence and the care we provide our students. I would hate to think of what might happen to the school and to the families involved if this were all to be dragged out into the open again." He reconfigured his face to an appropriate seriousness.

"The gist of what you are not quite saying is—you don't want me to write a book about whatever I find, is that right?"

"Well, of course, the decision to do something like that is

entirely yours, and I would not want to give the appearance of influencing it, but—"

"I'll tell you what. I'll change the name of the school."

"Well…" Darnell looked doubtful. Evidently his attorney told him any attempt to stop a book or sue subsequently for damages to the school's reputation would be a stretch. He should try persuasion instead. "Could you put us, that is, this fictional school, in another state?"

"I could do that. On the other hand, it might work better if readers were left to guess." No sense letting the guy off the hook too easily.

"If you don't figure this out," Stark cut in, "what then? I mean, a lot of people have come through here trying to untangle this mystery and none have ever succeeded. These were professional people, real detectives, not… But it doesn't stop people from trying. We've even been on television—unsolved mysteries, cold case files, that sort of thing. So what are your chances?"

"Listen, would it matter so much if I didn't? I write fiction. The mystery of the missing boys is a great plot device whether I figure this one out or not. I don't have to solve it to write about it, and the truth of the matter? I am not very sanguine about sorting this one out, frankly. It's been twenty-five years and, as you say, better minds than mine have tried and failed. But I am intrigued by its possibilities, and as a mystery junkie, I think, however remotely, it's possible. So there we are."

Darnell's face collapsed into worry. Stark, on the other hand, looked relieved. Relieved about what? Frank wondered. That the book might not be written after all? Not likely. That the mystery wouldn't be solved? Why would that be good news to him? He's their fundraiser and public relations flack, of course. Frank realized he would need to come back to Brad Stark and his peculiar take on solving the mystery—a challenge he had been party to in the first place.

"How about this. If I write the book and name Scott, I'll assign fifty percent of the royalties to the school." Now he had them. Like the Godfather, he'd made them an offer they couldn't refuse. If they had any ethical sense, they could. But he guessed they had none. He'd put the bloody horse's head in their bed.

Darnell cleared his throat. He'd developed a tic in his right eye. "Well, in that case…" His voice trailed off. Stark paled. Frank turned and descended the steps into the basement.

The Scott Academy archives were located in the lower level of the Upper School girl's dormitory. Elizabeth Roulx met him in the small space that served as a work area. Darnell excused himself, claiming the press of business. He left Stark to oversee Frank's studies. The room, or more properly, the basement, smelled of damp and old paper. A small gray steel desk, the sort you see in government offices, sat in one corner. Frank pulled up a chair and arranged his legal pad with a handful of pencils neatly in its center. Stark settled in a chair across the desk from Frank. Elizabeth Roulx took Frank's itemized list from him and went to search for the items he'd requested. Stark spent the next hour interrupting all Frank's efforts to read. Finally, in exasperation, Frank asked him to leave. Stark looked genuinely startled and started to protest. Elizabeth Roulx, who witnessed it all, assured him she'd be happy to stay with Frank. Stark's face reddened with embarrassment or anger, Frank couldn't be sure which, and he huffed out.

He thanked her and she winked. "They want something from you, you know."

"Well, I did make them an offer, but if it's real money they're after, they may have to wait."

He turned his attention to a small stack of clippings. They were the same stories Rosemary had pulled from the Internet, except for the pictures. He studied the grainy likenesses, four boys, three age twelve, one age eleven. He wondered about their parents, how they must have felt in that awful moment when the realization their sons were gone for good finally hit them. How they must have felt then, and perhaps even now, knowing there would be no body, no closure—ever. He knew something about that. Without a body, you just never know. Somewhere, some mother or father may still be harboring hopes that…what were their names?…that Teddy or Ned or Tom or Bobby would come walking through the door—knowing it wouldn't happen but hoping anyway. He pushed away a vision of Sandy Smith. She wouldn't be coming through his door, either.

"Are the parents of any of these boys still around?"

"The father of one is. Aaron Sands teaches music in the middle school."

"Mrs. Sands?"

"She couldn't take it, apparently. She left him. I think she lives in Towson. I don't think she remarried and so she should be easy to find. I will tell you now, Aaron will not discuss this—period."

"Anyone else on the faculty then still here?"

"Marvin Parker. His wife left him that year. Nobody knows why. I don't think there is any connection, but you never know. There were rumors about an affair, but no facts. And to answer your question, no, we don't have her address. He might know where his wife went, though, if you need to speak to her."

"I doubt it. I'd like to talk to him and to Sands, though. Can that be arranged?"

She said she'd try, and Frank returned to his clippings. He found nothing new or interesting in them and turned to the yearbook. Scott produced an impressive annual, paid for in large part by businesses owned by the students' parents. He leafed through its pages. Each class had a group picture. Young men—boys in blue-gray woolen dress uniforms and those awful choker collars he remembered—picture day. They were seated or standing in neat rows on bleachers set up for the occasion. He read the names of the sixth-grade students, Robert Sands, Thomas Richardson, and Edward Sparks. The fourth boy he found on the previous page with the fifth graders, Theodore Krantz—Bobby, Tommy, Ned, and Ted. He picked up the next year's book. Same pictures, same bleachers, same smiles. But new boys with different names had taken their places.

Frank thought about his brother. How the yearbook put together the year after he died must have looked—short one smiling face. No mention of his death. No indication he'd ever existed. He resisted the temptation to find his yearbook and look for Jack. Enough was enough. He opened the first book again and studied the fifth and sixth grades, flipping the pages back and forth, reading names, studying faces. It took him three tries with the sixth-grade picture before he found it. Bradford Stark with a brooding, familiar face stood at one end of the third tier.

"Stark never told me he knew these boys."

Elizabeth looked up from her papers. "Stark? Yes, I guess he must have. I never really thought about it, but yes, his father taught here for a while and he would have known the boys. I gather there was a pack of them—all campus kids. You should talk to Stark."

A pack of them. Frank had run in a pack when he was their age. George and Kim and Mike were his pack. And Jack.

"Yes, I will. I wonder what else he would rather I didn't know." Frank leafed through the remainder of the book. He set it aside and then pulled it back. Another picture had caught his eye as the book fell shut. Senior pictures. Dexter Light.

"My, my, now there's an irony."

"How's that?"

"This boy, Dexter Light, BMOC as we used to say. Corps commander, president of his class, bound for the Naval Academy, captain of…good Lord, was there anything he wasn't the captain of? Isn't he the rather dissolute forty-something who brought this whole thing up? What happened between then and now, I wonder?"

"Nobody knows. He's an embarrassment to the school. They, that is, Darnell and the pooh-bahs in the admin offices, wish he'd just go away, but he pops up every year at the reunion to demonstrate that you can be a Scott graduate and a failure."

Frank put all the material aside and thanked her. She said the addresses of anyone he might want to contact would be in the alumni office or with Stark, if they were anywhere. He looked at his watch. Eleven-thirty. He'd call Rosemary and set up lunch.

"You wouldn't know how to access newspapers archives,

would you? I tried the papers' Web sites but couldn't find the door in."

"You have to go directly to the papers, most of the time," she said. "There's too much material for them to post. Your best bet is either a local library, or a general search. You'd be surprised what obsesses people and they dump on the Internet."

"Library, of course. Thanks."

He stopped at the alumni office and jotted down several addresses. The human resources office gave him three more and the names of the few people still on the staff in some capacity, who had also been employed twenty-five years before. He did not visit Stark's office. He wanted to save him for later.

TWENTY-SIX

ROSEMARY FOLLOWED THE hostess to a booth. The restaurant had the requisite number of artifacts and signs suspended from the ceiling and attached to the walls. This outlet, because it stood on what used to be a working farm twenty or thirty years before, had been decorated with implements, tractor parts, and feed advertisements. She surveyed the lot of them, testing herself to see if she could identify any. Rosemary knew a bit about farm life. Scott once boasted a working farm, but it had never really interested her. She thought of herself as a city girl. She recognized a scythe but only because it figured in images of death, the grim reaper. She also recognized a rake but did not give herself credit for that. Rakes were everywhere. She wondered whatever happened to restaurants that were just that, a place to eat, whose owners did not feel the need to evoke some geographical area, some sociological theme or historic era. If she wanted to eat in a New Orleans restaurant, she'd fly to Louisiana.

Grumpy, grumpy. What's got into you this afternoon?

"Be still. I don't need you now."

"Pardon me?" Her waiter hovered over her, a confused look on his face. She hadn't noticed his arrival. He couldn't be more than sixteen.

Eighteen. You have to be at least eighteen to wait tables in a restaurant that serves spirits. Or is it twenty-one?

"I'm sorry, I was daydreaming," she said and smiled at the boy/man. "I'll have an iced tea. I am waiting for someone to join me. We'll order when he comes."

"Certainly. Will that be sweetened or unsweetened?"

"Oh, ah…sweetened, I guess."

"Raspberry, mango, or strawberry?"

"What? Just plain, please."

"We don't have sweetened plain iced tea."

"Then bring me unsweetened iced tea, and something to sweeten it with."

"Sweeteners, sugar, and sugar substitutes are on the table," he announced and swept away to attend to his other customers.

She glanced at her watch. She'd arrived early. She rooted through her purse for a mirror, positioned it a foot or so from her face, and inspected her makeup. She did not wear much—enough to cover Frank's remembered freckles, a little blush, some eyeliner, and lipstick. She sighed at the lines around her eyes. Crow's feet. They looked more like turkey's feet, maybe Big Bird's feet.

We're not buying into the "you're not old" business, are we?

"Why do you always have to yank the fun out of everything?"

Somebody has to keep you from making a fool of yourself.

"No, that's wrong. You are the manifestation of my loneliness, that's all. And that could end soon."

He could be a murderer.

"I don't care."

Her tea arrived. The server gave her an odd look and hustled away.

Frank appeared in the entryway. She waved to him. He waved back, said something to the hostess, and made his way to the booth. He slid in beside her and before she could react, kissed her on the cheek.

"I hope PDAs don't embarrass you," he said and smiled.

"Sorry? PD whats?"

"Isn't that what they were called in your school? They were in mine—public displays of affection, PDAs."

"Oh, those. I'd forgotten. Oh, my, yes. Big trouble from head-mistresses and chaperones for that. My goodness, how quaint we must seem to younger people now. My son is already worried about my granddaughter. He wants her on some contraceptive regimen. She's only twelve, for goodness' sake, but he tells me the whole group of them are sexually active and he can't think how else to protect her."

"What did you say to that?"

"I told him to teach his children to respect themselves and their families, to say no, and to wait until the experience held some meaning. He just rolled his eyes and said, 'That's easy for you to say, Mom,' and changed the subject."

"My daughter told me one of her neighbors' teenage girls was bugging her for breast implants. She said all the other girls were getting them for graduation presents."

"No. What did the mother say?"

"She said, and I am here quoting my daughter, but I cannot reproduce the tone of her voice, she said, 'Only if you get a B+ average.'"

Rosemary felt herself blushing as he spoke. She never did get used to talking about sex. Not because she had a problem with it. Three months into her marriage she discovered the exhilaration, the sheer exuberance of it. That was not something either her mother or her "health classes" had prepared her for. However much her friends may have thought of her as prim or prudish, she and George knew how to give and receive pleasure. But talking about it still challenged her.

"You're blushing," he said.

"Too much sun yesterday. What did you learn at the school?" She needed to change the subject fast or she might start thinking about him in other ways.

Carnal thoughts?

"Ah, quite a lot, actually. For example, the director of development, Stark—you remember the shortish man with the tallish wife?"

"Everybody knows Stark," she said. "Remember, I saved you from him at the dinner?"

"Right, I forgot. I assumed everyone is as dense about who's who as I am. I forget you have been in the flow for years and I have not. Anyway, he lived on the campus and played with those boys, in the same class with three of them. In different circumstances, he might have disappeared, too. Funny thing, though, he never mentioned it. Then, the father of one of the missing boys is still on the faculty. His wife lives in Towson. Elizabeth Roulx says the father won't talk, but the mother might. We can check her out tomorrow. There are some other people who were there at the time who we can talk to, as well. Let's see, including a bus driver, the daughter of the then head librarian, and another English teacher. What did you get from your contacts at the police?"

"From them, nothing. Even my friend the judge couldn't spring the reports. But, the retired cop came through for us. He had his own copies. He told me he never liked the way the investigation went and he's been digging through the case on and off ever since."

"He's working it as a cold case, I guess. Does he have a theory?"

"No, that's the problem. He said he looked into every conceivable angle—pedophiles, drug dealers, serial killers, you name it. He's scoured the Internet, contacted other jurisdictions—his word. I guess he meant other police departments and—nothing. When I talked to him all he could do is shake his head. He made me copies of everything he had. We can read through them this afternoon. He said if we came up with something, to call him. He's lived this mystery for a quarter of a century and wants an answer as badly as the parents, I think."

They ordered. While they waited, Frank shuffled through the stack of papers she handed him. He held his reading glasses up to the light, squinted at them, then polished them with his necktie. Men, she thought, never seem to have the equipment they need with them in spite of all their pockets. Women were severely limited when it came to pockets—at least women of her generation were. She remembered seeing a young girl at the mall wearing cargo shorts and envied her. The problem with men seemed to be they couldn't remember to shift the contents of their pockets from one jacket to another. They ought to give up their macho ways and start carrying purses. The only man she'd ever met who seemed adequately supplied with whatever he needed was an artist she dated briefly right out of college who wore the same jacket every day. It smelled of turpentine and linseed oil. She couldn't remember him in any other. He daubed Impressionist-like landscapes but didn't sell much, and she lost touch with him when she met George Mitchell.

She nibbled at her sandwich and sipped iced tea. Frank put down the papers and attacked his lunch. They ate in silence. On two occasions, she looked up and caught him staring at her. On the third, she put her glass down and stared back.

"What?" he said.

"You were studying me, I think."

"No, I—"

"You were. You were sizing me up like a stamp collector trying to decide whether to invest a huge sum on a particular bit of used postage. Or would it be experienced postage?"

"For stamps, used would be correct, and I wasn't."

"Then what were you doing? I saw you, Frank. Not an ogle, not a glance, either. You were giving me the once-over."

"Okay, if you must know, I was trying to remember what you looked like when we were kids. I could have done that a few days ago. I hadn't seen you for years and so my memories were locked in time. But now that I've had the pleasure of your company for a few days, the new data, so to speak, has displaced the old. So I'm studying this face so I won't forget it later."

"That's a very pretty speech and I don't believe a word of it. I'm a stamp and you are a philatelist, admit it."

"What do you call someone who collects butterflies? I'm one of those if I must be anything. You are much too beautiful to be a stamp."

"A lepto…something…lepidopterist?"

"The very word."

She examined his face in turn. Nothing butterfly-like about him. He looked weathered and—and what? Experienced. It fit him. And behind the eyes, buried deep down in there somewhere, she saw pain.

"Are you collecting?" she asked.

He sat back and laughed. "Well, maybe I am, at that."

You're falling for this guy. Doesn't the missing wife worry you?

"You know what? I'm okay with that."

TWENTY-SEVEN

MARIA GUTIERREZ TAPPED ON Phelps' door. "Excuse me, Lieutenant, but you said you wanted to see any reports Ledezma ordered before I put them in his box." She held a manila envelope in her hand. "It's the ME's preliminary report on the body they found in the desert." She read the label on the front. "Saundra Smith, missing since May…four years ago."

Fresh from the police academy, Maria had been assigned as an intern to Homicide, the first of her rotations through the department's various sections and divisions. This month she was assigned to Phelps. What she really wanted was to ride right seat in a patrol car.

"Thanks. Now, here's what I want you to do. Make me a copy of the report and then take the original to Ledezma. Then, get on the computer and pull all the incident reports for anything that happened within two miles of where that lady lived on the day she disappeared. No, make that three miles. We have to assume she was moderately healthy and could do a long walk. Put those in one group. And then, do the same thing for up to three months before and afterward."

He read the question on her face. He leaned back in his chair and smiled. It wasn't much of a smile. Homicide seemed to reduce the smile quotient among its members. He could joke with the squad. It wasn't that they didn't say funny, usually ironic things, but the response lacked the easy laughter of ordinary society. Homicide was about death. Its first victim, for those newly assigned to it, was laughter.

"I want to see if there is any pattern in the area—any activity that might point to a reason the woman disappeared."

He saw she still didn't get it.

"Suppose other people walked away and weren't found. This guy lived out near a retirement community. Do you have any idea how many old people walk away from home and get lost out there every year? It's Alzheimer City. Is there any reason to suppose this is anything else?"

Gutierrez nodded. Whether she understood or not he could not tell, but it would be her first lesson in routine digging. She needed to learn it now and from him, not the seat-of-the-pants detective work she'd learn later.

"Go through them and cull out any that aren't relevant."

"How will I know which are relevant and which aren't?"

"Well, we are tracking a missing woman, so missing cats, bicycles, loud parties, that kind of thing, won't apply. Domestic disturbances, ditto. When you're done, copy them all and bring them to me."

"Copies to Ledezma and Pastorella?"

"No, they should have already seen them."

"Sir, when I'm done with that, can you get me a ride?"

"You don't want to learn detective work?"

"Well, yes, but…"

"We'll see how well you do on this project, Gutierrez. Then, maybe."

"Yes, sir. Anything else?"

"Get me Dave Fowler on the phone." He saw a cloud cross her eyes. "He's the dive team leader. He left me a message to call him. That's it for now."

Three minutes after she left, his phone rang.

"Fowler, sir," she said.

"Thanks. What line?"

"Three, sir."

He punched the third red button. "Dave, what's up?"

"I wanted to ask you the same thing. One of your guys had my crew tied up all Monday afternoon. I thought we were after a sinker but it's not the way it went down."

"Who tied you up?"

"Ledezma. He had us out in a lake on a golf course in the West Valley. He said he wanted to find a gun."

"Did you?"

"Yeah. We found two, as a matter of fact, a nickel-plated 1911 Colt .45 and a newer .38 caliber S&W. The .45 looked like a presentation piece and had been in the water for a long time, the .38 maybe a month or less."

"So what's the problem? You found at least one piece."

"Ledezma kept us out there for three more hours searching for anything else we could find. Artifacts, he called them. What the hell is an artifact?"

"No idea. Did you find anything else?"

"Yeah, a golf club. Looks like some guy missed a hundred dollar putt and tossed the thing in the lake."

"What kind of putter?"

"I don't know, from golf, Marty. It had a funny, short name. Not a name I'd recognize."

"Cleveland, Taylor Made?"

"No, short, like a sound."

"Ping?"

"Yeah, that's it. You want it? I have it right here."

"Sure."

"And that's the lot. Two guns and a putter. Five hours, three men at time and a half, plus air tanks, setup. It could bust your budget, Marty."

"Thanks, Dave. I'll talk to Ledezma. The next time someone over here calls, give me a heads-up, will you? Oh, by the way, where are the guns?"

"Crime lab."

He hung up and drummed his fingers and dialed the lab. Saul Levinson answered after ten rings.

"You got two guns last Monday or Tuesday early from either Dave Fowler or Manny Ledezma. What can you tell me?"

"The .45 is in bad shape, Lieutenant. Been in the water a long time. We lifted the serial number. Registered to a Frank Smith."

"What about the .38?"

"Number's filed off. We were able to fire it and get a good slug, nice lands and grooves. We put the image in the computer and we're running it for a match for anything local. We are dabbing the filed part with acid to lift the serial number. We'll send it to the FBI later."

Phelps hung up a second time and continued his drumming. So, they found the gun, but nothing else. Unless Smith had a second piece. What did Ledezma think he'd find in that pond besides a gun? The trouble with big-city cops who move to small municipalities like this one, he thought, is they have no patience with grunt work. They're used to umpteen shootings a day and so focus on the nearest suspects and grind them until they nail them or lose them. Ledezma needed to learn detective work all over again, Phelps style.

"Maria," he shouted, "how are you coming with those reports?"

"Here, this is for you." Frank slid the key card still in its paper envelope toward her.

"What's this?"

"Key to the room at the motel or hotel. I'm not sure what to call it. It has a bellman, but a bad one—that makes it a hotel in my book, but there's no restaurant, so it's a motel."

"Does it make a difference?"

"No, I suppose not. Anyway, here's the key to the room."
Well, at least he didn't say my *room.*

"Is that important? That I have a key, I mean."

"Not important. I just thought it might be convenient for you if I'm not around and you have something to put in the safe or want to rest or—"

Or fool around?

"Not likely. Well, maybe…to put things in the safe, I mean." She took the key card and slipped it in her purse. He cocked his head to one side and stared at her quizzically. She took a deep breath.

"Frank, I have a confession to make. I hear voices. Well, not voices, a voice, and I talk to it."

He leaned forward as if he wanted to sample her perfume.

"Who?" he said softly.

"Who, what?"

"Who do you talk to, that who."

"Oh. Me, I talk to myself, but not really. This is confusing, but I need to tell you because our waiter thinks I'm rude and the server, the little round girl with the ponytail, thinks I'm crazy. I thought if you knew, you could sort of help."

"Right. I'll just point at my temple and circle my finger and wink at them while I tilt my head your way. The woman's nuts but not to worry."

"No. That's not it at all. I shouldn't have said anything." Rosemary's face reddened again, but not from blushing.

"I'm sorry. It's not something to joke about, is it?"

"No."

"How long have you been having these chats with yourself?"

"Not myself completely. A part of me…an alter ego, I guess. She taunts me, dares me, you know? No, you don't. Well, anyway, this other me pops up in my head and says things and before I know it I answer, lately, out loud."

"And sometimes the out loud part is misunderstood by waiters and servers—"

"And sales clerks and friends and—"

"This has been going on just lately or for a while?"

"I think I always did. It was a way to think. You have conversations with yourself or made-up people and work it out. I expect if everyone were honest, they'd say the same thing. Then, a year after George died and all my friends stopped dancing attendance on me, unless they needed a chair filled at dinner or a fourth for bridge, I found myself with lots of time on my hands. It seemed like my entire life had become solipsistic. There's a difference between being alone and being lonely. I guess this is the way I keep from being lonely. You probably know about that, too."

"I do."

"I just wanted you to know, so that when I say something apropos of nothing, I'm probably arguing with my other self. You should not be alarmed or confused."

"So when you answer a question and the answer is a little eccentric—"

"I'm probably talking to me and then trying to make the comment fit the conversation I'm having with you, yes."

"Well, for what it's worth, I've been there, done that, too. Not to myself, though—talking I mean."

"To your wife?"

His expression changed just for a split second, but in that second she saw the accumulated pain, fear, and anxiety—the overwhelming burdens he carried. She reached across the table and laid her hand on his.

"Tell me about her, tell me the rest," she said.

Are you sure you want to know?

"Are you sure you want to know?"

She smiled. "Yes, I'm sure."

TWENTY-EIGHT

THE FIRST TIME HE EVER laid eyes on Saundra Halliwell, she was stark naked, hands flying about trying to cover up and at the same time pull her window shade back down. He'd taken a short-cut through the parking lot behind the women's dorm on his way to the library. The sound of the shade slapping against its roller and her gasp caused him to look to his left and there she was, a brunette Venus. Her mouth formed a perfect O. He stood transfixed. In the seconds that passed before she managed to pull the shade back down, he fell in love. He often wondered if he would have anyway, if he hadn't caught her at that precise moment.

His problem after that was to find out who she was without revealing how he knew her, in a manner of speaking. It took him three weeks of hanging around outside the dormitory door and watching its inhabitants come and go before he spotted her. It was not an easy task. It is one thing to recognize a face in normal circumstances, quite another when the fit impression includes a whole lot more skin than a face. He supposed that in this day and age, it wouldn't make much difference. Nudity, frank discussions of sex, *Sex and the City* had changed the world, and it didn't include him or his generation. He guessed his parents felt the same way when they were his age.

When he finally approached her, she almost screamed. Apparently, he'd been noticed lurking, her word, around the dorm, and the women in it had come to the conclusion he was some sort of pervert. *Stalker* had not entered the lexicon then.

His difficulty came in convincing her he wanted to meet her and no one else, and he had to do that without telling her why.

They had no classes together, ate in separate cafeterias, and had absolutely nothing in common. It would make for a good match.

He didn't tell her about the window shade until much later— on their honeymoon. After that, when she would see a secret smile on his face, she would say, "window shade," and he'd nod. He still smiled that way once in a while, but now it hurt.

"WE MET IN COLLEGE. SHE WAS an undergraduate and I was in graduate school. We were married a week after she graduated. I'd finished my graduate work the same year and we moved to Chicago. I taught a few years on the North Side, then we drifted to Omaha and finally to Phoenix."

"Did she work, have a career of her own?" Rosemary asked.

"At first she worked a variety of jobs. She was a French major in college, not the best choice to establish a career path. She thought she might be a translator at the UN or something like that."

"And?"

"And...we were happy, had two kids, nothing unusual or unique."

Rosemary waited. For a man who could write two dozen books, Frank Smith had very little to say.

"I'm sorry," he said. "I will never see her again. Talking about her this way does not make it any easier. It's enough to say we loved, we had a good marriage, and now she's gone."

She sat watching him, trying to read his expression. "You said two children? I know about your daughter. What about the other?"

"My son, Francis...we aren't speaking at the moment."

"What happened between the two of you?"

"He, like Scott Academy, thinks I have money. The fact we lived modestly did not dissuade him from that notion. He just thought I was cheap. Anyway, he invented or wrote...I'm never sure which is correct...a software program that he claimed could accurately predict the stock market. He wanted me to provide the risk capital to market it."

"Could it predict the market?"

"No idea. I don't think so."

"Why not?"

"Well, if it could, he wouldn't need me to front end the financing and, more importantly, Francis didn't know anything about the market. He was a math and computer science major in college, the two years he actually attended. He was guessing."

"So you turned him down cold."

"Not cold. I said, 'Come back with a business plan and some other investors and I will contribute toward the project.' He got angry. Said I never trusted him, and so on."

"That's it?"

"Pretty much. I think my wife sent him money from time to time but…"

She waited. Clearly, Frank had nothing more to say.

"I lost track of your family when they moved away. What—?"

"My father bought a house in South Carolina near the coast. Not in one of the fashionable towns but very nice. Any hopes he had for a peaceful retirement went out the window when my mother developed Alzheimer's. She died after a money-draining, soul-scarring eight years. My father just gave up and died the next year. That disease takes its toll on everybody around it."

"On you, too?"

"Oh, yeah. You think, what if it's genetic, what if I'm next?"

"Are you?"

"I don't know, but I live with that fear every day. It rummages around in my subconscious, pulling up reminders of my slipping mental faculties. Every time I forget a name, misplace my keys, or can't recognize a familiar street…I think, here we go. It's awful."

He told her about the backlog of books on his hard drive. "Sandy would just have to pop out a book a year, let an editor fix it up, and there'd be money in the bank. Frank Smith may have to go to that big mystery-writers conference in the sky, but Meredith Smith could live on forever."

"Do you still work that way?"

"Yes, but now it's just a habit. My kids will be responsible for sending them in, I guess. You know the worst of it? When you disassociate."

"How's that?"

"It's hard to explain. You find yourself rejoining a conversation but you have no recollection of having drifted away. Most people have had that happen—mind wanders and then you hear someone repeat a question or look at you funny and you say, 'Sorry, just wandered away for a moment.' But with disassociation, you don't remember going anywhere, only coming back. You wonder, 'How long was I gone? A nanosecond, a full second, a minute, and when will the day come when I don't come back at all?' It scares the hell out of you."

"I'm sorry. It must be awful to have something like that hanging over your head." She'd never thought about it before, losing one's mind and drifting, or perhaps speeding would be more accurate, into senility. "Is there some way doctors can predict if you…have it?"

"I think so. I'm not sure. Even if they can, I don't want to know…would you?"

She guessed she wouldn't. They sat in silence after that. Rosemary sipped her tea and scanned the room. Frank picked up the reports and began to read.

An older couple sat across from them. The husband, it had to be a husband, seemed agitated. He twisted and turned in his chair, searching, it seemed, for his server. He rubbed the check between his fingers as if it was currency and he needed to be sure it wasn't counterfeit. He wigwagged at his waitress and held up the bill.

"Two dollars and eighty cents for coffee?" he said, glaring at her.

"Yes, sir, two coffees at—"

"I've never paid that much for coffee." He patted the carafe in front of him.

"Sir, the coffee was for two cups and we leave the carafe for your convenience—"

"It's highway robbery," he said, shaking his head. His wife kept her eyes fixed on the back wall, not looking at either her husband or the waitress.

"This is highway robbery," he repeated and glared some more. "I'm telling all my friends not to eat here."

"Sir, if you'd like to speak to the manager—"

"No, thanks. What can he do except make up some lame excuse? My friends will never eat here. This is outrageous." As he rose, Rosemary thought she caught a fleeting look in his eye, the briefest hint of confusion, as if it flashed through his mind he might be wrong and was making a fool of himself. It faded just as quickly and he stomped away to the cashier's station.

The waitress didn't move as she watched him pull out his wallet and start in on the cashier about the cost of coffee. The cashier comped him the coffee. He didn't seem satisfied even then. His wife shifted around in her chair.

"I'm sorry," she said to the waitress. "Sometimes he forgets."

"It's okay. He probably had a bad day."

Rosemary suspected the wife had spent the last forty or fifty years apologizing for hundreds of small misunderstandings on his part. Her husband returned, face still red. He helped her to her feet and gently slid the walker in front of her.

Then the truth hit Rosemary so hard she wanted to cry.

"That couple has been married forever," she said. "They had an arrangement that worked all those years. He did the business end of the marriage, she did the domestic. Now, she is crippled and can't keep up her end. She can't cook for him, so they eat out. He probably never learned to do anything more complicated than boil an egg."

Frank stirred but still concentrated on his papers.

"My guess is she prays daily that she dies before he does.

She has no idea where the money is, how they live…anything.
She'd be completely lost without him."

"What?" Frank said finally, lifting his eyes from the papers.

"Getting old is a bitch."

TWENTY-NINE

THEY TRUDGED UP THE SMALL rise from the restaurant toward the hotel. Rosemary inhaled. The air carried the aroma of new-mown grass and deep frying. She laid her hand on his sleeve. "Are you sure about this?"

He looked up and sniffed. "Sure about what?"

"Doing this search, investigation, whatever it is we're up to."

"You're having doubts?"

"Maybe. Some, I think."

He sighed. "Do you think they're right?"

"Who?"

"The youth of America, or in this case, the sleek young people who snookered us into doing this. Are they right to discount us? I'm not sure how much of my willingness to pursue this is professional curiosity and how much is annoyance at a generation that assumes we're all dotty."

"It doesn't do any good to rail about being discounted as old and marginalized, Frank. As far as the general population is concerned, that's what we are. It doesn't matter that many of us stay in reasonably good shape, vote intelligently, and take care of our health...you name it. We are routinely patronized by the culture that sees us as fragile, quirky, and foolish. Wrinklies, they call us. We are the butt of jokes on late-night television and the target of every scam artist in the country."

"But why?"

"Because for every one of us who is normal and stylish, if you will, there are a half dozen who, God love them, wear black knee socks with their plaid shorts, striped shirts, and too-white sneakers with Velcro closers."

"And dorky sunglasses. Don't forget them, the ones that fit over your regular glasses."

"And talk too much about the old days, make right turns from the left turn lane, and complain about the noise in the neighborhood after nine o'clock at night. The truth is, Frank, there are two kinds of old folks, those like you and me, who resent the stereotype, and the rest who *are* the stereotype. And here's the bad news, you and I are about ten years away from joining the latter. A walker with yellow tennis balls on the back legs beckons even now."

"This has got to be the most depressing conversation we've ever had."

They sat in silence for a moment.

"Do you want to know something else?" he said. "Those sunglasses really work. I don't care how silly they look. Back where I come from, where the sun can be unremitting, they are the only thing I ever found that really protects my eyes. They block the UV rays front and side."

"And there are days when I would die for a pair of Velcro closure shoes," she said. "You see how it is? At some point we surrender to comfort and what works and toss style and what other people think about us out the window. On that day, we become the very thing for which senior citizens are ridiculed."

"Yeah, but the good news is, we will soon outnumber all the other age groups and will be the trendsetters. Soon teenyboppers…are they still called that? Soon they will wear clunky sunglasses and ridiculous shoes and shirts that don't match, shorts that don't fit, and…wait a minute…they already do! It's only their parents that don't fit in."

"Why don't I feel reassured?"

THEY TRIED READING IN THE lobby. Frank thought she might be reluctant to go to the room. It might have worked, but just then a convention of noisy medical technologists arrived and filled the area with happy chatter. Frank sent Rosemary up to the room while he had one more try at the Internet. Nothing in the papers caught his eye. He retrieved his home phone messages. Nothing new there, either. He called his daughter; got her answering machine. He didn't leave a message. He joined Rosemary in the room. Rosemary sat calm and composed at the desk. Whatever old-fashioned misgivings he might have had about being alone with her in a hotel room seemed not to be shared.

Lunch caught up with Frank an hour after they began to read. His eyelids gained five pounds. Tryptophan, he thought. I shouldn't have had the turkey club. He put the report down and stretched. Rosemary had the yearbook open in her lap.

"I need some fresh air, or coffee," he said, "or a nap."

"Well, there's a bed handy," she said. "As long as you don't snore, it's okay by me."

"I'm going to settle for coffee." He fixed the coffeemaker next to the sink and turned it on. The room had one chair at the small desk, and another in the corner. Since there didn't seem to be any light for that one, they had to settle for Rosemary at the desk and Frank on one of the beds next to the nightstand.

The room filled with the aroma of freshly brewed coffee. He loved it but it masked her perfume, a loss, he reckoned. He had not enjoyed a woman's perfume for four years. His daughter rarely used it.

"Coffee smells wonderful," she said. "Your notes say that one of the people still on campus is a Marvin Parker. There's no separate picture of him, but in the library spread, there's a Luella Mae Parker. Were they related?"

He poured two cups and gave her one. "Ms. Roulx said they were married but she left that year, divorce or something. Anyway, we can talk to him tomorrow. What kind of name is Luella Mae, anyway?"

"Southern, honeychile. You won't find any Luella Maes north of the Mason-Dixon line. She's from South Carolina, Alabama, someplace like that. She was quite a looker."

Frank looked over her shoulder at the woman on the page. Even in black and white, she was a knockout.

"Wow. I bet the library did a booming business. Can you imagine what adolescent testosterone and this woman could create?"

Leaning close to her this way, he could smell her perfume again. Scents and colors were not his forte. Sandy used to kid him about both. She said she could douse herself in apple cider and wear a trash bag for a dress and he wouldn't know the difference. He would have. He might not be able to identify the scent but he knew what he liked, and he liked whatever Rosemary wore.

Rosemary looked at the picture again. "Assuming the worst about this woman, and we have no reason to do so, she could cause a heap of trouble, especially when you throw in one of those Southern accents dripping magnolias."

They found several more pictures of Luella Mae scattered through the book. A very popular woman, it seemed. There were no pictures of her husband except in the faculty group shot. Bow tie askew, he peered myopically at the camera, through unfashionably large, horn-rimmed glasses.

"The owl and the pussy cat." He returned to his corner of the bed and picked up the reports. They worked quietly for the next hour, only occasionally exchanging a comment. The coffee had only a marginal effect on his sleepiness.

"Here's the picture of that man, Dexter Light," she said. She had been reading his notes, writing some of her own, and referring to the book. "He was a nice-looking boy then, and important, Corps Commander, no less."

"Went to the Naval Academy but bilged out, I gather."

"Here's his page. My word, captain of two teams, clubs, and voted Teacher's Pet. I'm not sure I would want that honorific if I were a boy. It says, 'Dex is bound to succeed. All that time in the library stacks has got to pay off.' What do you suppose that means?"

"Either he had a reputation as a bookworm, or he, like most of his classmates, hung around the pulchritudinous Mrs. Parker like drones around the queen bee. Given his status, I expect his droning seemed more obvious than, say, the nerdy-looking guy on the next page."

She flipped the page and smiled. "This guy is the CEO of one of the biggest dot-coms in the country. I read about him in the alumni magazine last year. Don't you remember?"

"I don't read the magazine. Never have."

She looked up and shrugged. Frank shuffled his reports again and put them back in chronological order.

"We should write an outline of what happened and then see how we can fit these people into it as we go along."

"You dictate. I'll write."

"Okay, but if you think I'm off, or have something to add, jump in." He waited until she had a fresh sheet of paper in front of her and began. He dictated slowly, referring to the reports and notes from time to time. It was like writing a book backward. When he wrote a book, he knew the story and created the crime. Now he had the crime and needed to write the story.

When he finished, she read it back to him. The details were the same as the news reports. They hadn't found anything new, but writing it out helped them to focus. She paused in mid-sentence and reread one line.

"A group of boys, four or five, were seen entering Old Oak Woods at two in the afternoon." She paused, a frown line appearing between her brows. "Four or five, the reports say. At least two witnesses say something like that. One says there may have been as many as six."

"Right. Apparently there were a group of campus kids who ran together—"

"I know, but that's not what caught my eye. It's the number thing."

"The number thing? I don't follow."

"It's the way people perceive them." She walked to the window and stared down. "Come here for a minute, I'll show you." He went to the window and stood beside her.

"Look over there in the parking lot, in that corner. How many cars do you see?"

"Three."

"Okay, now over against the wall, how many?"

"Four."

"Good. Now right below us, how many?"

"Um…there are six."

"Right. Do you see what I mean?"

"No. Did I miss something?"

"When I asked about the first group you said three. No hesitation, no doubt, three you said. Same with the second, four, but when you got to the third group you had to pause. You were counting, one, two, three, four, five, six. It's the number thing."

"I still don't get it."

She sat down at her desk again. "Most people can identify numbers up to four without counting. You see one person, it's one. You don't stop to count. One is one. Same holds with two, three, and a group of four. But five, for most people a group of five requires a quick check. Maybe a count. And six and up… you see what I mean?"

"Not yet."

"The reports, the witnesses, all but one, say four or five, even six. That means they weren't sure, didn't count, just saw a group of boys larger than four. Four they would have known, would have recognized with a fair degree of certainty. We now know four went missing, not five. You said we were to play *what if*. Well, here is mine. What if five, not four boys, went into the woods at two o'clock?"

"It would mean that someone might know what happened to the other four and isn't talking. That's a maybe, of course. It requires five boys and it requires the fifth one to stay with the other four and not go home for a dentist's appointment or something."

"But it's a good what if?"

"An excellent what if. You are very good at this. I should hire you as a story consultant."

"I work cheap."

"Okay. *What if* number one: five not four." He wrote it down.

"Two's company, three's a crowd, four's a given, five's a... count?" she chanted.

"Very good. Anything else strike you?"

"Only that one of the witnesses who saw the boys go in the woods was our lovely Luella Mae. She said...let me see." Rosemary glanced at the notes. "'I had just gone for my walk, it was such a beautiful day....' Can't you just hear her? Police must have had their tongues hanging out. 'And I remember distinctly hearing the chapel bells toll the hour.' Too bad we can't interview her. I wonder what she looks like now."

"The rest of the reports are vague about the time, aren't they? So if she made a mistake about the time, we have another *what if*," he said.

"How so?"

"If the boys went into those woods at one or one thirty, all sorts of other people need to account for their whereabouts, drivers, other hikers, other boys. Remember, the boarding students would be around and possibly in the woods at an earlier hour." He looked at his watch. "It's late. I've kept you too long. Let me buy you dinner and let you go home."

"After that lunch, restaurant food doesn't appeal. How about I cook you dinner at my house?"

"I can't ask you to drive me all the way back out here."

"You could stay over."

Frank inhaled the last of her perfume and guessed as he did so that she was deep into another conversation with herself.

"What did she say?" he asked.

"She thinks you are dangerous. Are you?"

"Very."

THIRTY

"THIS GUY WRITES CRAP," Ledezma said, and tossed his copy of *Monkey See, Monkey Don't* on the desk. Pastorella looked up from his magazine.

"Who writes crap?"

"Smith. He's like all those mystery story writers—except Connelly, of course—they don't have a clue how real crime works. Take this book." He pointed to the book on the desk. "The eyewitness to an animal trainer's murder is a chimpanzee that's been taught sign language. Do you believe that? Then his detective takes two hundred pages and two more murders to figure that out, get a signer in to talk to the ape, and then get the bad guy, who, of course, can't be prosecuted because a monkey's evidence isn't admissible in court. How many monkey murders do you get a year, Dom?"

Pastorella grinned. "Jeez, no more than a half dozen.... You're kidding about the book, right?"

"Read it. That's the story. And the lieutenant wants to know why I think he's our guy. See, these writer types think they're smarter than people. They think because they write about murder, they can get away with it."

"I never read that stuff," Pastorella said. "Waste of my time." He resumed the perusal of his copy of *Hot Rod* magazine. Ledezma picked up the envelope Maria Gutierrez left earlier. He looked at the label, lifted the flap, and peered inside at the sheaf of papers. He tossed it on the desk next to the book.

"The ME's preliminary," he said. "It ought to convince Phelps once and for all."

"You read it?"

"No need to. I already talked to the doc in person. The Smith dame took a slug in the back of her head while she knelt and prayed for mercy. Can you see it, Dom? She's praying for him not to shoot and he blows her away. I want to nail that bastard, Dom. I want his butt on the frying pan. Lethal injection is too good for him."

"We'll get him." Dom didn't sound convinced, but Ledezma put that down to inexperience. Some things you could only learn when you worked a city like L.A., things that didn't translate to McMicken, Arizona. He'd have to teach Pastorella detective work, L.A. style.

"When do we notify Smith about finding his wife's body?"

"Not yet. We don't have to until it's official, and I want Smith to think he's in the clear a little longer. I want to check out one or two more things, and if he doesn't know, well, he won't be on guard, will he? By the way, where's our intern with the big knockers?"

"Gutierrez? Boss gave her the rest of the day off so she could ride right seat with Bobby Abramowitz."

"Great. Barbie Goes on Patrol with Ken—coming soon to better toy stores near you. Patrol car sold separately."

DEXTER LIGHT'S EARS BURNED. His grandmother used to say that meant someone was talking about him. Somehow, he had managed to navigate past the Scylla and Charybdis of The Ironman and Cal's and the other half dozen bars that lined his route home. He bought food, a novelty for him. The checkout clerk asked if he just moved into the neighborhood. He smiled at her and allowed, in a way, he had.

He'd just spent the longest Monday in his life—no, the second longest, trying desperately to stay focused, make his quota, sell something. The longest was that Monday in the library with Mrs. Gardiner. He'd been a good telemarketer before today. You had to be on something—in his case, slightly drunk—to sell some of the dreck they put on your desk. He made his call quota, but

hadn't sold much. Chalk up another for sobriety. He'd spared
the public from buying more crap.

Somehow he made it to his apartment, flipped on his tiny
window air conditioner, and collapsed on the bed. The unit rattled and moaned. A little cool air settled on his forehead. The
bottle of scotch began to sing to him again. He considered pour-
ing it down the drain. He had not done it yet. As long as that
bottle sat under the sink, he could fix his world. If he got rid
of it and needed to restore the haze that shielded him from his
guilt, it meant buying another. Also, if he did manage to stay
sober, the presence of the booze so close certified his change.
He could take it or leave it. Not the course recommended by the
experts, but the one he needed. He either had character or he
didn't. He fell asleep.

The telephone's ringing caromed around his skull, hit the
backs of his eyes, and knocked them open. His phone never rang
except when he overslept and Janetta called to get him moving.
This would not be Janetta.

"Yeah?" His voice sounded like he'd gargled with sand.

"Dexter Light?"

"Yeah, I'm Light."

"Are you the Dexter Light that attended the Scott Academy
in—?"

"That's me. Who am I talking to?"

"I am Harlan Mosley. I am an attorney representing the estate of Mrs. Mae Farragut."

"Who?"

"You probably remember her as Luella Mae—Luella Mae
Parker?"

Dexter sat up and reached across the few feet to the sink. He
jerked the cabinet door open and reached for the bottle.

"Mr. Light? Are you still there?"

He uncorked the bottle and poured two inches into his tooth-
brush glass.

"I'm here."

"Well, Mrs. Farragut specified in her will that certain documents should be forwarded to you in the event of her death. I will need you to personally pick them up at the office or, if that is not convenient, I will need some sort of authentication that you are the person to whom these documents were intended."

Dexter gazed into the golden liquid like Merlin pondering King Arthur's future in his crystal ball.

"Your office. Where might that be?"

"Spartanburg, South Carolina."

"It will not be convenient. Can't you just tell me what the documents are and then I can tell you if I want them?"

"That would be very convenient, but, unfortunately, I don't know the contents. The envelope is sealed and I am prohibited from opening it."

"How did she die?" he asked. He didn't know why. Except for the note and picture, he had not been in touch with her for how long? He scratched his head. Why now?

"Massive cardiac failure, I believe, unusual for someone her age, but then, Mrs. Farragut was an unusual person, as you probably know."

"Yes, she was. What do you need from me, exactly?" Dexter put the still-filled glass down and squeezed his eyes shut.

"I think a notarized statement establishing your identity would do. Send it to me and I will mail the documents to you."

"If I gave you a power of attorney in addition, could you open the envelope and tell me the contents over the phone? Then, if I want them, you could mail them to me."

"I suppose I could do that, yes. Are you sure that's what you want to do?"

"It's what I want," Dexter said. He jotted down Mosley's address and hung up. He lifted the glass of scotch up to the light. "How many more lives must I destroy before I'm allowed to forget?" he asked. Neither the scotch nor the glass had anything to say in return. He decanted the liquor back into the bottle and replaced it under the sink. He didn't spill a drop.

"Now ADMIT IT, THIS IS better than a restaurant."

Frank sat opposite Rosemary at a mahogany dining room table that would be too big for a dozen people. She had prepared a simple meal, but the atmosphere and, he supposed, the company made it special. His mother used to talk about houses like Rosemary's, usually with a hint of envy in her voice. Rosemary lived in Ruxton on what might be the last eight-acre lot in the area. The dining room had, in addition to the table, a large sideboard, wall sconces, and molded plaster filigree that marched across the walls a few inches from the ceiling. Two silver candelabra provided most of the light.

The living room, he knew, was at least twice the size of this room. Oriental carpets on inlaid oak floors throughout, antiques and reproductions all tastefully arranged, polished, and expensive. George Mitchell had done very well indeed. He figured if she kept half an acre with the house and subdivided the rest, she would clear at least two million dollars on the lots alone. Rosemary did not have to worry about where her next meal might come from. He pushed back his plate and folded his napkin.

"Can I ask you a personal question?"

"It's a little late to worry about that, isn't it?"

"You think? Anyway, it's okay, right?" She nodded and returned his smile.

"What scent are you wearing? Is that the right word? Do you say scent or perfume?"

"I don't know or, for that matter, care. I think people say scent now because perfume, good perfume, costs so much, and so a lot of women use cologne."

"You?"

"I grew up with perfume. Haven't changed. It's Shalimar today, by the way."

Frank inhaled noisily and grinned. She shook her head.

"Coffee on the patio," she said, "unless you want something stronger." They filled coffee cups in the kitchen and she led him through French doors onto a screened porch and then outside through a screen door that slapped shut behind them. They descended four steps to the patio, made with bricks set in concentric circles. A table and four chairs stood at the center. Azaleas formed a low hedge around the area, broken only where brick paths entered or exited. In the half light, he couldn't tell if the azaleas were white or pink.

"This is very nice," he said and stretched out his legs.

"It's nice now. Spring is the best season. We can sit out here. It's not too cool and there are no bugs yet. In the summer we have to sit on the screened porch or the mosquitoes will eat you alive. What's it like in Arizona?"

"McMicken is one of the new municipalities in the West Valley. Surprise, Goodyear, and Buckeye are growing so fast you can't leave for a week and not have trouble recognizing your street when you return. They are rolling up the desert, citrus farms, and cotton fields and building thousands of houses. Roads that were two lanes into the country are now six lanes of divided highway and crowded. Autoplexes, cinemas…you name it, we either have it or will soon. The weather is hot, most of the time, very hot by East Coast standards. That's in the valley. In the high country, Flagstaff and places like that, the climate is more like it is here. Snow, rain…seasons. But down in the valley, hot is the word. No mosquitoes to speak of. No screened porches as a rule."

"No pests at all?"

"I didn't say that. We have scorpions, snakes, coyotes, and rabbits destroying the lantana. It's the law of compensation. Ease in one area is always balanced by hardship in another." They fell silent again. Then she sat forward, put down her cup, and folded her hands.

"What comes next? About the mystery, I mean." Was she blushing? He caught the fading scent of her Shalimar.

"Tomorrow, we'll start interviewing. I'll call people in the morning. We'll use the hotel as our base, so if we lose touch, that's where we'll hook up again."

"Are we going to talk to them together or separately?"

"I don't know. What do you think would work best?"

"I think I should do the women, you do the men, and we do the families together—if there are any."

"I want to talk to Dexter Light sometime. He lives downtown. We'll have to do him late in the afternoon, I think. He works, but the alumni office didn't know where."

"Try him tomorrow evening. You can take the car to wherever and I'll make dinner again. When you are finished, call me. If he's downtown, that is to say, way downtown, you will be twenty minutes from me. That way I can time the meal."

"You're sure about the cooking and…everything?"

"I'm sure."

THIRTY-ONE

THREE THINGS HAPPENED in the morning, and one of them would change Frank's life forever. Dexter Light mailed off his documentation and power of attorney to Harlan Mosley—next-day express. Rosemary Mitchell slipped her engagement ring and wedding band from her hand and put them away in her jewelry box, and Fletcher Brent, a fourteen-year-old eighth-grade student at John F. Kennedy Middle School, threw a three-pound rock onto I-95. He watched in fascinated horror as the stone arced into the middle lane and shattered the windshield of a late-model Volvo. The driver, momentarily stunned by rock and glass imploding in his face, swerved into a bridge abutment and hit it head-on at sixty-five miles an hour. All of the occupants of the car, which included the driver's wife and his two young children, were killed instantly. Fletcher ran all the way home. He would never tell anyone what he'd done.

Frank only knew about Fletcher's madness when he heard the story on the morning news. He made a point of not commenting on the missing rings, and would have no idea of what Light had done for at least another twenty-four hours, if ever.

Rosemary handed him a fresh cup of coffee and sat next to him on the edge of the bed. They'd eaten a quick breakfast of bagels and cream cheese and gone to the hotel room to make their calls.

"That's awful," she said as the newscaster reported the accident. "Who would do such a terrible thing?"

"Impulse," he said. "People do things like that without contemplating the consequences. Then, they either own up or, more often than not, run. If there are no witnesses, whoever tossed the rock will never be found unless or until his conscience moves him."

"Not a her?"

"No, probably not." He patted her hand. Not a her. Girls, women, act impulsively, but usually in different ways. A boy would toss a rock onto a busy highway; a girl would make up some awful gossip. Either could be lethal.

He shut off the TV and laid index cards out on the desk. Each had a name and a telephone number. He opened his cell phone and punched in the first number.

"Who're you calling?"

Frank held up his hand. She shook her head and looked at the cards remaining on the desk.

"Mr. Parker? Frank Smith, one of the alumni in for the weekend. I'm sorry to disturb you so early, but I wonder if you would have time to meet with me for an hour or so this morning. What? Yes, you're right, most of us have left, but Dr. Darnell asked me to talk to the few faculty members left on the staff who were here twenty-five years ago when—"

He listened for a moment. Rosemary lifted her eyebrows into parentheses.

"Yes, I know, but if you wouldn't mind doing it one more time… Yes, I do write books and yes, it is possible I might write one about this mystery, but I assure you if I do, names, dates, and so on will be fictionalized…. I see, you don't care. You want your ex-wife to be exposed and would I do that? I, ah, well, I'm not sure how that fits into the story, but I suppose I could…. Is there some reason I… Certainly, you'll tell me at ten this morning. Thank you, yes, goodbye."

"What was that all about?"

"Hell hath no fury like a schoolteacher scorned? I don't know. Apparently he's still angry about a wife who walked out on him twenty-five years ago. The chance to see her excoriated in a book, even if fictionalized, is just too good an opportunity to be missed. He said he could tell me things no one ever heard before."

She printed *MARVIN PARKER, 10:00 A.M.* on the schedule sheet. He picked up another card. For the next twenty minutes, he made calls. They filled the sheet for the morning. They kept an hour clear at noon, even though some of the appointments would have been easier to make had it been on the lunch hour. But, since they'd be operating separately, they would need time to compare stories.

"No luck with Dexter Light?"

"No. He works, I don't know where, and I suppose he's gone there for the day. We'll try again in the evening."

HARLAN MOSLEY CONSIDERED himself an ethical man. He served two terms as President of the County Bar Association. His practice, while not large by some standards, earned him a comfortable living. Trent Farragut provided a substantial portion of his legal work. Farragut lived ten miles outside Spartanburg on a restored antebellum plantation. He owned seventeen automobile dealerships in four states and was arguably the richest man in the state, undoubtedly in the county. Harlan owed him, as they say. The question he wrestled with this morning had to do with the contents of Dexter Light's envelope. He had not been entirely forthcoming with Light. He knew exactly what the contents of the envelope were. He'd put them in it himself when Luella Mae Parker approached him years before.

Harlan grew up with Luella Mae. They both came from what used to be considered the wrong side of town. Both of them had bootstrapped their way out, managed a college education, and moved on with their lives, never looking back, never returning to the old neighborhood. She'd married a man from Maryland, but that hadn't worked out. She'd returned to Spartanburg, pregnant and broke. She had not lost any of her beauty, and three months after the birth of her son, she snagged Trent Farragut. They were married; he adopted the boy, and she dropped Luella from her name. Mae Farragut.

That spring she'd brought him the documents and made her

will. Just in case, she'd said. For old times' sake, and by way of payment for his legal services, she introduced him to her husband and persuaded the latter to engage Harlan as his attorney. He owed her, too, big-time.

Trent Farragut had called and wanted to know if there was anything in Mae's will that he should know about. Harlan struggled with that all morning. He picked up the phone and called Farragut. He had just left for Atlanta, his secretary said, and asked if it was important.

"No, nothing that can't wait until next week," he said and relaxed. Light would probably call before Farragut got back, and then it wouldn't make any difference if he disclosed the contents or not. He removed the documents one by one. A birth certificate for Dexter Light Parker, four bearer bonds which at the time she bought them were worth twenty-five hundred dollars but were now worth nearly fifty thousand, and photographs—scenes of Luella Mae and a young boy. He fingered the bearer bonds and contemplated his ethical dilemma.

"MY WIFE MAY HAVE LIED in her statement to the police," Parker said. "She had a reason for not being in those woods before two o'clock."

Frank made a note on the pad in his lap. He didn't know where this line would take him, but he decided he'd let the little schoolteacher talk, tell his story. Then he would ask questions.

"See, she had this problem. She couldn't seem to get enough, ah…in the physical relations area."

"She was oversexed?"

"Yes, that's one way to put it. Anyway, I finally had to say to her, enough. You know…every day and night…well, it interfered with my studies. I was enrolled in the Master's Degree in Teaching program at Hopkins and I needed time to prepare for my classes, not just the graduate work, but the classes I taught here at Scott. Well, you can see how that must have been."

Parker sat in an Eames chair, his legs crossed, knee over knee, and fingered his paisley bow tie. He wore a brown shirt, blue slacks, and black loafers with short, gold-colored socks. Frank did not consider himself a style maven, but he knew Marvin Parker could be a candidate in anyone's contest for worst dressed, either that or he was color-blind. Parker loaded an onyx cigarette holder with a filter tip and lit it, exhaling a plume of smoke at the ceiling.

"The thing is, I believe…no, I know…she was having an affair. The sex thing, you see. And I think she met someone that afternoon when the boys disappeared."

"Why would she lie about the time?"

"Well, if the person she met needed to be protected or something, she could do that by changing the time, you see."

"But you don't know if she did, in fact, meet someone."

"No, not for a certainty, but—"

"But what?" Frank wondered if he hadn't just wasted an hour of his time.

Parker brushed cigarette ash from the front of his slacks. He jerked his head up and leaned forward, thrusting his face toward Frank. His relative calm replaced with an expression of fury.

"The little slut," he spat. "She seduced students. She didn't think I knew, but I did. Everybody knew. How do you think that made me feel? Every upper schoolboy knew about it. I could hear them sniggering behind my back. For all I knew, any one of them or the entire graduating class might have been in bed with her."

Frank said nothing. He had met women like this man's ex-wife. Not many but a few, most of them in Hollywood when he went to watch the filming of his TV series. Either their husbands wallowed in their infidelities, divorced them, or killed them, often enough, the last.

"Well, you may wonder how I know all this. I'm not paranoid, you know. Mrs. Gardiner told me a little. She said I was better off. She was the head librarian, Luella Mae's boss at the time. Then there was the doctor's report she tried to hide from me. But I found it."

Frank waited while Parker stubbed out his cigarette and patted his lips with a handkerchief.

"We weren't planning on children, you see. Not until I finished my doctorate. We agreed on that. But I think she decided to go ahead anyway. She would throw her pills away, one at a time. She didn't think I'd notice. But I knew, so I took care of the prevention business myself. But with the activity she engaged in, it was just a matter of time."

"She got pregnant?"

Parker looked away. Frank thought he saw a tear.

"I showed her the report. She cried and said the baby was mine, that nothing is one hundred percent sure, you know. We had a row. The next day she emptied our savings account and left. I don't know where she went."

"You never tried to locate her?"

"No."

"She said the child was yours?"

"Yes, that's what she said. I didn't believe her."

"Any idea who the father was if it wasn't you?"

"No. I'll never know. Sometimes I wonder if she told me the truth and by driving her away, I lost my child. I would like to have had a son."

THIRTY-TWO

ROSEMARY SNEAKED A PEEK at her watch. Susan Banks rambled. It didn't seem to matter what question Rosemary asked, she insisted on talking about her difficulties with a lazy husband and two insolent teenagers. Rosemary would ask about the missing boys and she would puff, "Boys. Let me tell you about boys…." and launch into a ten-minute detailed monologue about her sons, their shortcomings and most recent scrapes with the law. She did the same for every topic. She only once mentioned anything even remotely interesting; the belief her mother held that her assistant, Mrs. Parker, was in a scandalous relationship with a senior student whose name she could not recall.

"Now, you know, we lived on the campus only that one year," she said. "My mother disliked the regimen living here imposed on the family. But I knew those five boys very well. Pottymouthed nasty little things, they were."

"Five? You said five but there were only four, Mrs. Banks."

"Four, five, it didn't matter, they were like peas in a pod. Could hardly tell them apart. Now, you take that Bradford Stark. He turned out all right but the rest of them, well…"

"But the others are dead."

"Yes, that's so."

"Why did you say five?"

"Well, Muffy and me…that's Myrtle Daigle…she hated that name…she was the headmaster's daughter and my best friend at the time. We drifted apart after we moved off campus…we used to go down the hill toward the woods to pick wild strawberries in May and we saw them go in. Five of them."

"But there is no statement from you in the police records about that."

"Of course not. They never asked me, and Mother said it probably wasn't important."

"Who was the fifth boy?"

"I already told you. You weren't listening. That's the trouble with society today. Nobody listens to a word you say."

"I'm sorry. Who did you say the fifth boy was?"

"Bradford Stark. He works at the Academy now, doesn't he?"

"Now you know it's a funny thing about that. See, I been driving that there run for maybe seven years back then. Drive downtown took a hour. Load up the order and drive back. Seems like I always got to the front gate at one-thirty, one-forty at the latest. But they say, 'No, you must have got it wrong, Sam, 'cause someone done fixed the time at two on the dot.' Well, I don't argue, see. I didn't have no watch on me that day, so I say, 'Okay, two it is.'"

Frank shook his head. Sam Littlefield sat hunched on a stool in the back room of the school's garage. He seemed ageless. The sun struggled through a begrimed window high up on the wall and lighted his brown face and startlingly white teeth.

"I remember your daddy. Not you. You was gone time I come to work here, but your father, I knew."

"Really?"

"Oh, yeah. Fine man. Some folks said he was a little hard but he treated me good."

Sam had been driving school buses and vans since he was eighteen and had refused retirement twice already. Not an educated man but an intelligent one, and certainly not one given to making mistakes. If he said one-thirty, that's the time Frank would use. He guessed that since the two o'clock figure came from a faculty member, and a white one at that, the police had ignored Sam's timing.

"My husband does not want to talk to anyone about it." Mavis Sands looked tired and worn. Some people arrived at fifty trim

and alert, like they just stepped off a luxury liner. Others, like
Mrs. Sands, staggered in like they'd spent the entire voyage in
steerage, dowdy, old, and bitter.

"I understand," Rosemary said, hoping to soothe the feelings
of a woman she feared could very easily dissolve into tears or
erupt into anger at any moment. "It can't be easy for you, even
now."

Mavis Sands' lower lip began to quiver. "You people," she
whimpered, "come here dragging this all up. I just want an end
to it. Can you make an end to it, or are you and that writer fellow just here to exploit us like all the others? It cost me my marriage."

"Frank Smith is a good and decent man," she said and realized the moment she said it, she believed it. She smiled at the
revelation. The smile seemed to reassure Mrs. Sands and she
relaxed, her lip steadied, and she sat back in her overstuffed
chair.

"We never got to an end, you know. It's like all those men
who are missing in action back there in the jungle. Where are
they? My cousin from Des Moines, he would be much older than
me, went missing in Vietnam. They think he was sent to China
and then, who knows. My aunt died never knowing. They never
buried him. And then, our Bobby…there's never an end to it."

Rosemary handed her a tissue and waited while she blew her
nose and collected herself.

"If you and Mr. Smith could just do that," she said.

"If it can be done, we will do it."

"They went out to play, the way they always did on a Saturday, Bobby and Edward, Teddy, Thomas, and Bradford, the
Starks' boy. The wonderful thing about living on the campus
then was they had nearly nine hundred acres of woods and fields
to play in. We never worried about them. Every Saturday, Bobby
would do his chores. He took the trash out, cleaned up his room,
you know how boys are, and off they'd go."

"You said five boys."

"Well, four or five, maybe six. It depended on who could get
away. I never noticed that day. I wish I had. I don't know why,

but as I thought on it over the years, it seems to me that it might be important to know."

"Bradford Stark is working at the school now. Have you ever asked him?"

"Well, I've thought about it but, you know, he couldn't have been with them that day because of the DISH."

"Excuse me, the what?"

"DISH. That's what they called Detention Study Hall. Boys who received delinquency reports were required to report to the study hall on Saturday afternoon. Bradford spent more than a few Saturdays in that place, I can tell you."

"So he wasn't with Bobby that day?"

"No, he couldn't have been. That's why it must have been four. Jack Blazek was part of that gang, he might have been with them, too, but his mother said he went to the doctor's office that day. I don't know if she told the truth. I never trusted that woman. She could be covering up for him. If he knows anything...."

Rosemary wrote *Jack Blazek?* in her notebook.

"Did your son ever say anything about what they did in the woods?"

"What do you mean?" Mrs. Sands' expression quickly turned stormy. Rosemary backed away.

"Oh, nothing really. I just wondered if it were possible they might have told everyone they were in the woods, but they could have exited out on the backside and met someone or gone someplace they didn't want you to know about. You know how boys are." She sounded like Susan Banks.

Mavis Sands' brows knit together. "You know, I never thought of that. Boys do things like that, don't they? And they'd never tell us because if they did, they'd be in trouble. Boys are so secretive sometimes."

"Girls can be, too."

They exchanged smiles. Oh, yes, girls, too.

FRANK'S CELL PHONE BEGAN to break up in the middle of the interview. Jack Blazek lived in Chicago and worked at the Merchandise Mart making a risky living dealing in corn futures. It took them nearly five minutes to establish who Frank was and why he had called. Once done, Blazek continually broke off the conversation to answer another phone or shout to someone nearby.

"Sorry, you were saying?"

"I wanted to know what you can remember about the day your friends disappeared into Old Oak Woods."

"You a policeman or something? I already went through this with them, and with one of the networks, and some retired cop from the county a dozen times."

"No, I am not a cop. The headmaster asked me to look into the mystery, I guess, one last time. Put it to bed, so to speak."

"Well, I'm not the guy you want to talk to. I had a doctor's appointment that afternoon. Really frosted me at the time. We had plans to do some exploring, that's what we called it, crashing through the woods like jungle hunters. Ned Sparks told me he found something he wanted to show us, something important."

"What was that?"

"He didn't say, just looked mysterious and said, 'Like, wait and see.' I said, 'Come on, Ned, you can tell me.' But he wouldn't. Then they all disappeared and I never did find out."

"Any guesses?"

"With Ned it could have been anything, anything from a fox's den to a dead horse. Actually, we did find a dead horse one time. Big day for us."

Frank heard the static on the phone begin to stretch into longer intervals and knew he would lose Blazek any moment. He thanked him and hung up. He looked at his watch. He had ten minutes to meet Rosemary for lunch.

THIRTY-THREE

Frank met Rosemary on the parking lot. It had turned warm and his shirt clung to his back. He had to walk from the campus to the restaurant. She drove. They took a booth in the corner and ordered.

"Anything?" he asked.

She removed a notebook from her purse and flipped through its pages. "The number five keeps coming up. Never four and that's significant. Even after twenty-five years and the fact that only four boys went missing, people involved still say four or five."

"Anything else?"

"Susan Banks is the daughter of a Mrs. Gardiner, the former librarian, who believed that our Luella Mae, the woman with the movie starlet body, and probably proclivities, might have been involved sexually with one of the senior students. I gather she would know if anybody did."

"That jibes with what the ex-husband said, only he thought there may have been multiple affairs. I think he has an image of his wife as a latter day Marlene Dietrich and the Scott Academy Upper School as the Eighty-Second Airborne."

Rosemary raised her eyebrows. "The what?"

"Sorry, guy stuff. The stories coming out of the Second World War had it that the movie star started with the commanding general of the Eighty-Second, Gavin, I think, and worked her way through the entire division, or nearly so. All exaggerated, of course."

"Exaggerated or not true?"

Frank shrugged.

"Men," she muttered.

"There seems to be a strong feeling that if five, not four, boys went into the woods, Brad Stark was one of them."

"Susan Banks said as much, as well."

"The other thing that bothers me is the time. Sam Littlefield drove a van into Baltimore and back every Saturday during the school year and had the run timed almost to the minute. He says the boys went into the woods at one-thirty or one thirty-five at the latest. I'm inclined to believe him and not Luella Mae. And her husband says the same thing. He thinks she set the time at two to protect someone, but he didn't know who. She was pregnant, by the way."

"My, my, the plot thickens. That's what writers say, isn't it?"

"Not if we can help it."

"Did you know about the DISH?"

"Say again."

"Detention Study Hall—DISH. Apparently students in trouble had to go to this study hall on Saturday. Stark had to."

"Never heard of it. When I was a student, if you received demerits you went out to the school on Saturday and worked, shoveling coal, raking leaves—things like that. What time did the DISH start?"

"I don't know, but it would be important to find out." Frank shuffled through his notes. Their lunch arrived and they ate.

"We said there were two what ifs," she said. "So, what if the time set at two could be earlier and what if there were more than four boys in the woods? It looks like that is exactly what we need to explore." She cocked her head. "Oh, golly, you know, my heart goes out to the families. That poor Mrs. Sands, all she wants is some kind of closure. She is so afraid all we will do is stir up everything again and leave her with her hurt."

He nodded. "Okay," he said. "Here's what we need to do. This afternoon I'm scheduled to interview Stark. Instead of asking him what he remembers, I will go after him. You can go back to the archives and find out whatever you can on the DISH. Do they have old rosters? I doubt it, but you never know—things like that."

"I can, but I can't help you much past late afternoon. I'm expected home. Previous engagement...."

"No home cooked meal after all."

"I'm afraid not."

He hadn't expected this. He was beginning to be comfortable with their relationship. He couldn't complain, of course, he had no call on her, but he wondered. Had he said something? Did she resent the Marlene Dietrich remark? He didn't know why, but he felt disappointed. He pursed his lips and cocked his head and waited for an explanation. None came. She smiled and squeezed his hand and they left together.

"Tomorrow, ten o'clock?"

"I'll call."

"Call the hotel, and if I'm out, leave me a message. My cell phone is acting up. I'm going to turn it off and tonight I'll try recharging the battery."

She waved and drove away. He watched the car disappear.

"THE ID IS OFFICIAL," Phelps said. "You get hold of Smith and tell him."

"Lieutenant, I don't think we should do that. Once he knows we have a body, he'll start covering his tracks."

"Ledezma, he's had four years to cover his tracks. What's left to cover?"

"Look, I know this guy. He thinks he's pulled it off. He thinks we don't have his wife and can't prove anything, no *corpus delicti,* but if he knows we do, and can match the bullet hole to his gun, well, he's off to Brazil."

"He's not going anywhere and there is no way we can positively match the hole in that skull with his gun and you know it. Go tell him and then see what he does. That will tell us a whole lot more than saying nothing."

Ledezma slouched out of the lieutenant's office. "Let's go," he said to Pastorella.

"Go where?"

"Smith's house. Lieutenant says we have to tell him his wife's body's in the morgue."

There was no answer at Frank's house. The two men walked around to the back and peered in the windows. Nothing. They went next door and rang the bell. A pretty woman Ledezma remembered from his previous trips to the neighborhood answered the bell. He vaguely recalled her as being a retired church organist. She did not look like one at the moment. She wore a bikini top and a towel around her middle that he supposed covered a matching bottom. She looked to be about fifty and in very good shape. She told him Frank Smith left town for the weekend.

"Weekend ended Sunday, he's not back?" Now he understood why Smith hadn't reacted to the diving crew Monday. He'd halfway expected him to come out and watch, but then figured Smith might hunker down and wait for him to come to the door. He wouldn't give him the satisfaction, only now it turned out it didn't matter after all.

"No," she said, "he called and said he'd been delayed and would have to stay over."

"Stay over? Where is he?"

"He went to Baltimore for a high school reunion."

"So he hasn't answered his phone or anything since last Friday?"

"Wednesday, I think. He left early to visit his daughter."

"You don't have a phone number where he can be reached, do you?"

The woman looked at him suspiciously. Ledezma showed her his badge.

"Oh, now I recognize you, you're that policeman who's investigating Sandy's disappearance. Are you any closer to solving that mystery?"

"Yes, ma'am, we are," he said. "The phone number?"

"I've got it right here. I called him." She looked embarrassed. "When you all were dragging the lake or whatever it was you were doing."

"He call back?"

"Nooo.... That surprised me a little, you know. He's a wonderful man and, well, I guess he was busy with his friends." She went inside to retrieve the number.

"You hear that, Pastorella?"

"No, what?"

"She called him about the gun in the lake."

"So?"

"So, we should check her out. Maybe she is more than just a friend."

"You think Smith and her was—"

"Shhh...."

The woman returned with a Post-it note with Frank's cell phone number on it. He thanked her and they walked to the car.

"Lucky break," he said. "Smith is out of town. He went to Baltimore for a reunion or something. We can't tell him anything."

"You got a number."

"I got a cell phone number, but the lieutenant doesn't know that." Ledezma felt very pleased with himself. Let the bastard squirm, he thought. "First thing tomorrow, we check out this woman. With a body like that, you have to suspect something at least. It's going down, Dom."

When they got back to the office and Ledezma left to use the lavatory, Pastorella retrieved the slip of paper with the phone number on it from the trash can where Ledezma had dropped it. He put it in his pocket. He liked his partner, but he liked his chances of staying on the force as a detective better if he played ball with the lieutenant. If the lieutenant wanted Smith to know about his wife's body, then he would see to it that he did. He looked over his shoulder at the restroom door and dialed the number.

THIRTY-FOUR

IN A DISORGANIZED WORLD, Rosemary valued order above almost everything else. That is why she immediately liked Elizabeth Roulx. Elizabeth showed her how the files were arranged, how the photographs and documents were cross-indexed, and the ease with which she could retrieve information.

"Mr. Smith said something about how you might be working on his project." Rosemary let the *his* go. "I found these, since he stopped by." She pulled some yellowed newspaper clippings from a folder. "It seems someone had this folder checked out on Monday. I wonder who." She consulted her computer screen. "Ah, Judith Stark had it. What do you suppose she wanted with it? Anyway, it's a complete account of the story for the week following the boys' disappearance."

Rosemary gingerly opened the brittle newsprint and read. She did not find anything new in the earlier reports. She had missed the part about the heavy rain that fell the night of the disappearances, which explained why dogs were unable to turn up anything the next day. By the second week, investigators seemed to have gotten desperate and called in a psychic. The woman, who called herself Sister Rosanne, would only say, "The earth just swallowed them up." No news there.

"Tell me about DISH," she said.

"Detention Study Hall. What do you need to know?"

"How did it work? Who ran it? When did it start? Anything."

"Well, it replaced work parties. The school's lawyers told the administration that their liability insurance probably would not cover any damages that might be awarded if a student were injured in one of those work sessions, or the premiums would skyrocket. Either way, we didn't need the publicity attendant on a lawsuit like that, and we would have gotten one. It's a litigious society now. So we ended the practice of putting the kids to work and substituted a study hall. Not as punishing, but it did cost them a Saturday. We still run it."

"I know it's asking a lot, but by any chance are there any documents, rosters, things like that in the archives? We'd like to know who had DISH duty that day."

"You know, you're in luck. Normally we don't save that sort of thing, but the man who started collating the material that eventually became our archives thought that day so important he saved everything, at least everything surrounding the event. I think he thought he might write a book. That's an irony, isn't it? He won't, but Meredith Smith will."

"Might. That's not been established. He's concerned about the families having to relive the pain and the publicity." Rosemary said the words knowing full well that she and Frank had never discussed the idea of the book one way or another. She wondered when she had started thinking of herself as his confidante and partner.

Elizabeth Roulx put a stack of documents in front of her. She sorted through them. The roster for Detention Study Hall, entered in pencil, had faded significantly, but she could make out most of them. She only recognized two, but those two made a huge difference in the way she and Frank needed to think about their next steps. She tried calling Frank on his cell phone, then remembered he'd turned it off. She left a message in his voice mail anyway, just in case, and called the hotel. She left him the same message and asked him to call her when he could. There didn't seem to be anything more for her to do at the archives. She thanked her host and left. She had some unfinished business to attend to in town.

PASTORELLA TRIED THE NUMBER a second time with the same results. "Leave a message at the tone," an electronic voice dictated.

Ledezma would emerge from his afternoon routine at any moment. He left the message. If the lieutenant asked, he could always say he did his best.

BRAD AND JUDITH STARK sat on a damask-covered sofa across from Frank. He had not planned on interviewing both of them and wondered whose idea it had been for them to make it a joint meeting. Surely Judith Stark couldn't add much. As far as he knew, Judith Stark had no direct information to offer at all. He soon found out why she joined her husband. The moment he began pressing Stark on whether he had in fact been with the other boys that day, she quickly interrupted with a question of her own.

"Are you intending writing this in a book? If so, you will need releases from all the persons named in it. Brad and I may not grant you one."

"Releases? You're a bit premature on that, Mrs. Stark. But yes, I know about the need to cover my publisher's reluctance to pay for lawsuits. If I need them I will certainly be back for them, or I shall so completely fictionalize the events that there can't be any. Now—"

"I just thought I'd let you know that, Mr. Smith. Even fictionalized might draw a lawsuit. That could be costly to you personally, couldn't it?"

"No, not really, Mrs. Stark. Unless the person suing decided to be particularly difficult. But I don't anticipate—"

"I understand some authors pay their sources for their information and their release."

So there it was. The cunning Mrs. Stark had a pecuniary mind-set. He looked around the small apartment, at the clutter of too many people living in close quarters, and wondered what she had sacrificed to enable her husband to take the job at Scott. She stared at him with cat's eyes, the smallest hint of a smile on her face.

"Brad has very important new information that he can give you, don't you, dear?"

Stark twisted around in his seat. "What are you talking about? I've told this story a hundred times. It's a matter of public record. There's no 'important new information.'"

"That's right, dear. He'll have to pay for what we have."

Frank did not know where this was leading, but he knew he'd lost control of the conversation. "We now know that there were five boys who went into the woods that day and you were one of them."

"I already told the cops and anyone else that would listen. Yes, I was with Bobby, Ned, Tommy, and Ted. We were playing near the woods. I had to leave and go to Detention Study Hall. The chapel clock struck two when they went in. Read the reports, read Mrs. Parker's statement. At two o'clock I was sitting in a desk in Main, in the study hall."

"We have information that Mrs. Parker lied."

"Mrs. Parker lied all the time. But not about that."

"Why do you say she lied all the time?"

"Oh, now, that's a whole other story. Mrs. Hot Pants Parker cheated on her husband with the older boys. Everybody knew about it. She had a different favorite every year. Boy toy. That year, it was Mr. Wonderful, the once but no longer heroic Dexter Light. She was with him in the woods that afternoon."

"And that relates to the time change how?"

"I don't know. Who cares, anyway? They're all gone. My friends, Light, Hot Pants, everybody, all gone and forgotten, or should be. You should let this go, Smith. Hundreds of people have tried to figure out what happened back then and can't. You think that your experience as a writer gives you some edge over professionals, but it doesn't. Fiction isn't reality. And then there is your age. I mean with your memory... Anyway, I think you're wasting your time here. I have nothing to add to what I've already said."

"That's right, dear. Wait until he comes up with an offer. We're thinking mid-six figures," Judith Stark said and tossed her head, her smile now a Cheshire grin.

"I hate to disappoint you, Mrs. Stark, but there isn't going to be any payday, now or ever, on this case." Frank stood to leave.

"Very well, but you might want to think it over. If Brad ever does talk, someone could get very rich."

"Judith, what the hell are you talking about?" Frank thought Stark seemed genuinely confused. Apparently, Judith Stark liked to play games. He guessed she could be a very dangerous person in the wrong circumstances. He let himself out and descended the steps to the ground level. He could hear them shouting at each other but could not make out what they said. He stopped at the apartment building's entrance and listened. He thought he heard her say something like, don't be stupid.

Good advice.

THIRTY-FIVE

ROSEMARY SHUT OFF THE ignition. The Buick's new-car smell had faded into something she thought of as "Early Frank." She sat behind the wheel, biting her lower lip and studying the brightly striped awning shading the restaurant's entrance. She'd spent more time in eateries in the last few days than she had in the last three years. So much change in so little time. She rubbed the now vacant place on her left ring finger. That would take some getting used to as well, but she had to start sometime. Now she needed to take the next step, which meant shedding herself of a major portion of her old life. Bart would be in there, waiting. Would she be able to do it? They were old friends. He'd understand.

Are you sure about this?

"I don't know. Yes, I think so. Am I being foolish?"

It had to happen sometime, you know. The kids are gone and not likely to come back to the area. That life is over. Time to move on.

"Yes, but it's a big step. He'll be upset."

Well, don't tell him about Frank. He won't understand that part. Just say it's a decision you came to on your own.

"Okay, here we go." She exited the car, locked it, and walked toward the double doors. Barton, she thought, he would understand—wouldn't he?

FRANK THOUGHT HE SHOULD have rented a car. He puffed up the rise to the hotel. The clerk greeted him and checked for messages. Just two, on the phone. He'd wait until he got to the room, he said. The room seemed stuffy. Before he switched on the air conditioner, he tested the air, hoping for a trace of her scent. He imagined he caught it and smiled. The cooling unit hummed to life and he sat.

The message button on the phone winked at him. He picked up and listened to Rosemary's report of her session with Elizabeth Roulx. He already knew Stark had DISH that day. He did not know Light did, too. So, if Stark had told him the truth about Luella Mae and Light, it would explain why she insisted the time the boys were in the woods was two o'clock. It would remove any possibility that she and Light were in the woods together. Not that it would have mattered in the long run. Everybody seemed to know what they were up to. He smiled at the psychic's pronouncement. You had to hand it to Sister Rosanne. No way would she be caught off base on that one.

His daughter had left the second message. She wanted him to come to dinner. The children wanted to see him and Robert asked if he would take a moment to talk to him. He called her back. Robert would pick him up and why didn't he just check out of the hotel and come back? It was silly and she was sorry. He considered it but refused. Not because it didn't make sense—it did—but because he had all his papers and notes in the room and he didn't want to gather them up and then have to spread them out on her dining room table.

Now, if Rosemary had made the offer...

"You're sure about this, Rosie?" Barton Flagg insisted on calling her Rosie. Rosemary had hinted repeatedly she did not like the name. She never had, but he seemed impervious to subtlety. He leaned forward, earnest. She pulled back, his aftershave or cologne had nearly caused her to choke. Musk, subtle like a rhinoceros. Well, this would pretty much be the end to their relationship. She wondered if, as a friend and because she would not be seeing him again any time soon, she should say something about his cologne. She supposed that should be his wife's job.

"I'm sure, Barton. Look, the house is too big for me. Alice lives in Houston with her oil man. George Jr. is in Denver and settled. His wife's parents live there and there's no way they'll

ever move back east. I don't need four thousand square feet of
house and eight acres of lawn to mow and leaves to rake. The
heating bills alone are out of sight. It was George's place, not
mine. Look, George already had the land rezoned. There are
fifteen half-acre building lots, plus the one the house is on. I
want to sell the house, its lot, and two adjacent lots. The last
time George had an appraisal made, that bit priced out at seven
hundred and fifty thousand. That would be eight years ago. You
value it any way you like, but that's what I want to walk away
with. That's my bottom line."

"But where will you live?"

"I'll put most of the furniture in an auction house, some of
the smaller pieces and the ones I have some feeling for, in stor-
age. I plan to move around."

"Gee. I don't know, Rosie—"

"Bart, I've never said this to you before, but now is as good
a time as any. Please don't call me Rosie. I hate it."

He looked stunned. He'd called her Rosie for three decades.
"I had no idea. Sorry. You're sure about all this?" She nodded.

"Okay, then." He pushed a standard real estate representa-
tion contract across the table toward her. She read the contract
carefully and signed it. In turn she pushed plat maps across to
him and marked the lots she wished to sell.

"What about the others?" he asked.

"I'm holding those. My brother is well-off in his own right.
My grandchildren are going to the colleges of their choice, not
the state school because it's all they can afford. And if they don't
need it, well, maybe I'll throw a party."

"Hell of a party. What I meant was, if I find a buyer and he
wants to negotiate for more or perhaps a different lot or lots—"

"Then call me and we will see. Are you okay with that?"

"Yes, that'll be fine. Where will you go, Rosie…Rosemary?"

"I don't know. I'll vacation this summer, maybe travel, take
a cruise, and then decide. I'm thinking Arizona. I've never been
to the Southwest. What's the Grand Canyon really look like?
You know, I've never seen it, never seen Arizona." There, she
said it.

"It's hot."

"So I've heard, dry and no bugs, only coyotes and rabbits that...never mind."

Boy, talk about burning your bridges.

"That's it, I guess," she said. "Now you can buy me dinner, Barton. With the commission you'll make on this sale you can afford it."

"CAN I TALK TO YOU, FRANK?" Robert kept his eyes on the road. They were in the middle of rush hour, but luckily they were headed toward town while the traffic made its frenetic evening migration to the suburbs in the opposite direction.

"Certainly. What's up?"

"I don't know what Barbara's been telling you about us, about me, and I wanted to clear the air."

"Sure. Clear away. She thinks you're fooling around, by the way. Are you? It's not that I don't care about you, you understand. I've always liked you, Robert, but blood, as they say, is thicker than water." He flinched a little at that.

"No, Frank, I am not. Why would she say that?"

"Well, I gather you spend a lot of time away from home claiming to be at work, only a call to your office reveals you aren't there. Woman's intuition, Robert. If a man says he's at work and he is not at work, he's seeing another woman. Not intuition, really—eighty-five percent of the men who tell their wives that story are, in fact, cheating. And you've lost weight—another tell, as they say in Las Vegas."

"Count me in the remaining fifteen percent, then."

"Okay, so what are you doing and with whom?"

Robert clenched his teeth. The muscles on the side of his jaw bunched up like he'd swallowed a fist. He glared out the windshield.

"I'm working three jobs, Frank. I have two part-time positions."

"Why?"

"Barbara. I know she's your daughter, but somewhere along the way she acquired expensive tastes. She spends more than I make. And now she's on about Scott Academy. I can't send the boys to Scott. I can barely manage the parochial school where they are now."

"So you work the other jobs to do what? Earn tuition for Scott?"

"If that's what it takes to keep her happy, yes."

"You'll burn out, Robert. You will explode. You won't live long enough to see them graduate. I hope you have plenty of life insurance. Why haven't you told Barbara? You don't need her thinking you're playing around."

"Because if she finds out how much money I'm pulling in, she'll spend that, too. She'll find something else we absolutely have to have—she's already mentioned a bigger house. What the hell do we need a bigger house for? I'll be right back where I was, only working three times as hard."

"Greater love has no man than he lay down his life for his kids' tuition. What about college? It gets even worse then."

"I don't know. I guess I'll cross that bridge when I get to it."

"Robert, you don't have to do this. Barbara will have to get used to it."

"She thinks you are going to pay for it. She's afraid Mrs. Mitchell is after your money."

Frank burst out laughing. "Rosemary Mitchell is probably worth three or four million dollars. What would she want with my not even close to a million dollar net worth? I'll talk to her, Robert. In the meantime, consider some family counseling. You two are killing each other. Spouses aren't supposed to do that."

Robert gave him a sharp look but said nothing.

THIRTY-SIX

THE TALK WITH BARBARA did not go well. At first she did not want her husband in the room at the same time. Then she insisted she did not have a spending problem. Robert had an earning problem. When he pointed out to her that Robert's income put them in the top ten percent of wage earners, she laughed out loud. No one in their right mind, she declared, would believe that. Finally, Frank made her a deal. He would subsidize the boys' tuition—he laid heavy emphasis on the word *subsidize*—but only on the condition that she and Robert enter family therapy. She practically screamed at him then. Why? she wanted to know. They didn't need some phony-baloney shrink poking his nose into their lives. Frank explained that they needed it because, one, they did not communicate with one another at even an elementary level, and two, if they didn't get help, the deal was off. If she had been a cartoon, lightning would have flashed out of her eyes and smoke from her ears. Hell hath no fury...

Dinner began in icy silence. The boys' eyes flicked back and forth between their parents. Frank guessed many mealtimes were characterized this way. Finally, Tooth grew tired of adult-imposed penance and turned his attention to his grandfather.

"How's Miss Rosemary?"

"Mrs. Mitchell," his mother corrected, her face screwed up like she had been sucking lemons.

"Why, she's just jim-dandy," Frank said and smiled.

"What's Jim Dandy? Is it like hunky-dory? Paula's granddad always says hunky-dory. Do all old people say stuff like that?"

"They do, Tooth, and you know what? Someday some smart little sprat is going to ask you the same question."

"What's a sprat?"

"Shut up, Tooth," Jesse said. "Grandpa, will you help us build a tree house?"

"No tree houses," his mother said, "and we don't say shut up."

"Sorry. Why not build a tree house?"

"Why? For one thing, you don't have a tree big enough to hold one."

"We could build it in the park. They wouldn't mind." They, Frank assumed, would be the city government. He shook his head.

"Come visit me in Arizona. We'll build one there."

"Dad, you don't have any trees at all."

"We'll build the tree first."

"Did you have a tree house when you were little?" Tooth asked.

"Oh, my, yes. Your great-uncle Jack and I built one behind the house where we lived, and we had hiding places all over the campus. Back in the woods we found these big growths of honeysuckle. We'd crawl into the middle and trample down the center bushes. That would make a bushy circle with an open space in the middle, like a doughnut. We could sit in there and people could walk by not ten feet away and never know we were there. We built forts out of fallen trees and once we dug a cave."

"Cool. Can we see them?"

"You mean the forts and hideouts?"

"Yeah, all that stuff."

"Oh, they'd be long gone by now. Oh, my…" Frank paused. A memory jumped up at him. Jack…

"What, 'oh my,' Grandpa?"

"Sorry, I was about to repeat myself—bad habit."

"Old guys do that a lot, don't they?" Tooth volunteered. "Paula's granddad tells me the same story every time he sees me. He says, 'Hey, you look just like Macaroon. I was in a movie with him one time.' And then he tells me about an old movie he was in when he was little, where kids sang and danced and saved some old guy's business or something. What's a macaroon?"

"I think he said Mickey Rooney."

"Is that anything like a Jim Dandy?"

"Almost exactly."

"Mr. Light, this is Harlan Mosley. You wrote that this time would be the best to call you. I hope I am not too late."

"No, this time is fine." Dexter had no plans. Any other night he would be nursing shooters at the Ironman Tap, but not to-night.

"Very well. I have opened the envelope and the contents are as follows a short, typed letter addressed to you, several photos of Mrs. Farragut holding a small child, and two bearer bonds valued at roughly twenty-five thousand dollars."

"Read the letter."

"It's personal—are you sure?"

Dexter grunted his assent.

Mosley read.

Dexter, dearest,
If you are reading this, it means I am dead. For a long time, I've wanted to tell you I'm sorry. That time I found you in Annapolis I didn't know how to tell you what had happened. I shouldn't have called you....

The phone call had come after dinner. She said she just wanted to find out how he was doing. He'd have known her voice anywhere.

"Are you all right, Dex?"

"Where are you?"

"Here…I mean, in Annapolis. I—"

"I'll meet you. Give me a half hour."

"Dex, I can't. I'm with people and you aren't supposed to—"

"At the bridge near the yacht club. Someone can tell you where that is."

"I know where it is. We're staying at the hotel down the street, but—"

"Thirty minutes."

"Dex, this is not a good idea."

He hung up and persuaded his roommates to cover for him. Slipping off campus had not been easy, but to see her one more time… She waited for him on the bridge and he drew her into the relative darkness at one end. She looked small and forlorn. Her hands were cold.

"I'm to be married," she said, sounding like a heroine in a gothic romance. "I was pregnant and a man I met took me in." His heart rose and sank. Pregnant?

> *I married a man from my hometown. He is wealthy and kind and took care of me. I really didn't have much choice back then. He adopted the baby as his own. The baby has been well cared for so you don't have anything to worry about….*

"He's yours."

"Marry me, then," he said. "I'll quit the Academy and we—"

"Dex, honey, it would never work…but, oh my, I am tempted—"

"Then say yes."

"No, I can't, I…"

She turned from him. Her scent, soap and lilacs, he thought, competed with the briny aroma of the incoming tide. A cold December breeze whipped her hair back from her forehead.

"I am almost old enough to be your mother, did you know that? I am nearly twice your age. How will that work? In ten years or so, what will we be like?"

"I don't care. I love you. And you're not that old."

"You're nineteen. I'm thirty-two, Dex, going on thirty-three! And what would you do…what would we do? How would we live?"

"I'll get a job. I heard about these guys who left the Academy and they are making big money in Norfolk."

Tears streamed down her cheeks. "I can't, Dex. You have your whole life in front of you. You are going to do wonderful things. I am...I am not what you want or need." He started to protest. "No, no, it's true. You have to let it go, darlin'...for my sake, let it go...please."

It was very cruel of me to meet you that night. I guess I just couldn't help myself. Was I so awful? Please forgive me. As for the boy, do not try to find him. He has a wonderful future and an adoptive father who dotes on him.

Keep the memories, let the rest go.
Luella Mae

She reached out and pressed his right palm to her breast and kissed him one last time. His hand fell empty to his side and he heard her scurry off into the darkness. He didn't remember how he made his way back to Bancroft Hall.

The picture came in the mail two months later. No return address.

"THAT'S IT, MR. LIGHT." Mosley's Southern drawl brought him forward twenty-five years. "Mr. Light, are you there?"

"Sorry. I slipped away for a moment. So many memories, I... sorry, you were saying?"

"There is a birth certificate naming the baby Dexter Light Parker. His surname, however, has been changed pursuant the adoption. What would you like me to do with these papers?"

"Mr. Mosley, do you have a shredder?"

"I do."

"Then send me the bonds, certified mail, and destroy the rest, shred everything else."

He put down the phone and stared at the wall, not seeing the faded wallpaper and ragged posters. He gazed back a quarter of a century to a time filled with light and promise. As he did so, the images finally began to fade. First the forsythia that crowded the honeysuckle in their hiding place...gone to gray, all gone…sounds, scents, her voice, and the kids he'd heard that afternoon—the kids. She'd gone to join the missing boys.

"LIGHT?" FRANK ASKED, unsure if he had the correct phone number.

"This is Dexter Light."

"Good. Frank Smith here, I'd like to talk to you."

"What about?"

"Over the weekend, you and some of your friends challenged me to solve the mystery of the missing boys. I need to speak to you about that day."

"I'm on record—"

"The record is horse manure, Mr. Light. Horse manure piled so high it's buried the truth. You can help dig it out, once and for all, if you're up to it. What do you say I buy you breakfast tomorrow?"

"I have to work tomorrow."

"Call in sick. I expect you've done that once or twice before."

"Listen—"

"No, you listen. You and your friends started all this and now we have to finish it. Something awful happened in those woods twenty-five years ago and you were a part of it. At the very least, you are a material witness, a probable perjurer, and I'm guessing maybe even more than that. Meet me at seven o'clock at the restaurant next to the hotel near the school. You know it? It's near the metro. I won't keep you long. What the police will do is another matter."

Light hesitated but agreed to meet him. He hoped that by the morning, Light would be more agreeable. His next call was to Rosemary.

"Will I see you tomorrow? All your appointments cleared? Good." Rosemary sounded cheerful—a good sign. Whatever distracted her earlier seemed to have been resolved.

"Meet me at the hotel at ten. I have an appointment with Dexter Light for breakfast first. Oh, and wear or bring some sensible shoes and slacks. We're going for a walk in the woods."

THIRTY-SEVEN

"GUTIERREZ," PHELPS SHOUTED through the open door, "where are you?" He looked at his watch—a little after five. It would be past eight on the East Coast. Ledezma said Smith went east for a meeting or something. Phelps told Ledezma to find him and get him back.

"You wanted me, Lieutenant?"

"Yeah, I want you to do a little detective work for me." Gutierrez's eyes lit up. "You see these two reports here?" She nodded and tried to read them upside-down on his desk. "I want you to check out this Ms. or Mrs. Kindernecht. I want you to go over to her house and ask her to repeat what she told the uniforms that worked the INS raid in this other report. Then I want you to find them, the uniforms, that is, and ask them the same questions."

"What questions?"

"You find out from Ms. Kindernecht what she remembers about the raid and then you confirm what she said to the officers on the scene."

"Should I talk to the INS agents, too?"

Phelps thought a moment. "Only if our guys develop a case of amnesia and can't remember anything, which, when I think about it, they just might."

"That's it?" Officer Gutierrez looked disappointed.

"That is all of it. Detective work, Officer Gutierrez, is about asking questions, looking for discontinuities, and then chasing down leads." He noticed Gutierrez frowned at *discontinuities*. "It's not about patrolling and collaring bad guys in the act. How did your ride go, by the way?" Gutierrez's expression changed as quickly as the sun coming out from behind a cloud.

"Like awesome," she gushed. Phelps winced. He'd once entertained thoughts of becoming an English teacher, and "awesome" sat squarely at the top of the list of words he wanted to be declared a felony offense if uttered in public.

"Okay," he said. "If you want to ride again, you get on this program tomorrow, pronto."

"WHAT WERE YOU PLAYING at this afternoon?" Brad Stark's voice shook. His wife's interference in the interview had nearly ruined everything. "That man is a potential major donor and you sat there, were rude to him, and if that wasn't bad enough, you practically became an extortionist. What chance do you think I have now of prying a gift from him?"

"This may come as a flash, Brad, honey, but that man isn't going to give Scott Academy squat. He has not attended a reunion in fifty years. He never answers mail, returns questionnaires, or sends in news for the alumni bulletin. He has serious issues with the school. You and Darnell are so starstruck by his celebrity status, the big TV series he used to have, you aren't thinking straight."

"How do you know so much?"

"I read your files. You should, too. The man is moderately well-off, that's all. In addition, his wife has been missing, presumed dead, and the possibility exists that he's responsible. He is a 'person of interest,' as they say in the papers. But whether he is or isn't guilty, he's got more things on his mind than coughing up a gift to Scott—now or ever."

Brad collapsed on the sofa and held his head in his hands. What did she know about…anything?

"What made you ask for money for a release? You think he'd pay for a release?"

"I figure we could use the money. Face it, your tenure here is about to end. Darnell isn't happy with you, the board is asking questions, and somehow, in spite of that, you get involved with this mystery thing. It is the last, the absolute last, thing the board, Darnell, or any sensible person wants dragged up again, and there you are. Let's face it, we're on our way back to Pittsburgh. I made Daddy promise to give you your old job back."

"Daddy? Who said anything about Pittsburgh or your father? Not now. Not after what you've done. Attacking Smith was the worst thing you could have done. It only made him suspicious of me, like I might have something to do with those kids' disappearance."

"Didn't you?"

"No, of course not."

"Well, they don't know that."

"Thanks for the talk. I think it will help…well, I hope it will." Robert drove carefully, his eyes fixed on the road.

"I hope so, too, but you never know. The trouble with people my age is we are never certain about things. There are two kinds of old men, Robert, those who impart wisdom, and those who impart information. The problem is that the men in the second group don't know the difference." Robert nodded absently, and Frank realized he'd just wasted a perfectly good aphorism on his son-in-law, who seemed lost in a world of his own.

Frank stared out the window trying to picture a stream that ran through Old Oak Woods. Fifty years ago—a very long time. How much did he really remember? Robert dropped Frank off at the front of his hotel. Back in his room, he switched on the desk lamp and glanced at the array of papers strewn across every available flat surface. Somewhere among them he knew were United States Geographical Survey maps of the campus, one old one and one more recent. Maybe those would help. The face on his cell phone announced in block letters that his battery was charged and that he had missed a call or some calls. That would be Rosemary from earlier, he thought, and put the phone aside. He spread the maps across the bed and studied first one and then the other.

DEXTER LIGHT'S HANDS SHOOK. This is not the DTs, he said to himself. If I were going to have *delirium tremens* they would have kicked in yesterday. But his hands still shook. A drink would help. Two drinks, ten. Smith, the arrogant bastard, who did he think he was bossing people around like that? He didn't have to go. Smith couldn't make him and he wouldn't. That decision made, he turned his attention back to his conversation with Harlan Mosley. He removed the bottle of scotch from beneath the sink and set it on the table beside the bed. The springs squealed as he sat down heavily. He'd never noticed the sound before. Benefit of being drunk every night. He stared at the bottle as if he could levitate it if he concentrated hard enough. It sat exactly where he put it, refusing to move.

"This is the end, you know," he said to the bottle. The bottle remained silent. "The lawyer just took away the last of your excuses. She's dead and now I know all I will ever know. And I blew the best years of my life away because of that, because of her." He lowered his head and buried his face in his hands.

"WHATCHA GOT, GUTIERREZ?" Dominic Pastorella leaned over her shoulder, a little too close. By three-thirty in the afternoon, Pastorella's deodorant deserted him, and he had the symptoms of early gum disease, as well. She also knew that he came up behind her that way so he could cop a peek down her blouse.

"Step away, Detective." He seemed genuinely shocked at her reaction, but he stepped back. "This is for the lieutenant. He wants me to check out some woman named Kindernecht."

"Well, I can help you with that," he said, still keeping his distance. "She's a screwball. Calls in reports all the time. Missing this's, noisy that's, suspicious characters in her backyard or on her roof."

"Her roof?"

"Yeah, even on the roof—screwy."

"So okay, the boss wants her checked out, so that's what I'm doing."

"Hah, he's giving you the rookie runaround. Turn you loose

on a nutcase and watch you go in circles. Be a big joke back at the station. My first time up here—they had me tracking down a serial killer in the department. But spelled differently, only I'm a rookie and I don't know they mean the cereal killer—that was O'Rourke, who ate cereal for lunch. Serial—cereal, get it?"

She got it. "These reports have your name on the checkout tab, Pastorella. So what did you get out of the old lady's report?"

"Get? What's to get? I told you, she's an old bat. She just went on about some other broad she saw get in a van a couple of weeks before. She thought there was a weapon but when the uniform asked her if she saw one, she says, 'No, but they might have had one.' Might have had one—jeez. They get old and there's no telling what they'll think up."

"Thanks, I guess. No need bothering with this, then. I'll just tell the lieutenant there's nothing here."

"Wouldn't do that, Gutierrez," Pastorella said. "If the boss is playing with you, you bet he will know if you slacked off. Better work it like it meant something."

She sighed, let him take his quick peep, and gathered her folders together and rose. She'd get back to this in the morning.

THIRTY-EIGHT

FRANK SIPPED HIS COFFEE and waited until seven-thirty. Light did not appear. He assumed that meant he'd be a no-show. It didn't matter that much. He was pretty sure he knew what Light might have said. He hoped his call the night before put the fear of God into him so when he received the next summons, he wouldn't hesitate. Of course, that would depend on whether Rosemary could persuade her friend the judge to do her a favor.

He ordered breakfast and skimmed *The Baltimore Sun*. Frank had given up reading newspapers a few years back. He found himself criticizing the editorial pages and grousing at the poor writing and the shallowness of the reporting. He had a brief fling at journalism right out of college. He remembered all the blue-penciled copy his editor dropped on his desk nearly every night with a terse "Do over" scrawled across the top. Bylines were earned and only after a year at least. And then they did not accompany everything you wrote—only the good stuff. Now reporters who couldn't recognize the difference between an allegation and an accusation, between the issuance of a memo and an action taken because of it, filled the papers with their poorly constructed prose and badly researched stories. He'd grown tired of being a curmudgeon and so canceled his subscription to the *Arizona Republic*. He did enjoy reading out of town papers or, when he traveled, the locals. He didn't think they were remarkably better, but some of the writing caught his eye. He folded the paper and left it for the next occupant of his booth, paid, and walked the short distance back to his hotel.

There were several new messages on his home answering machine but none relating to any new developments. He wondered about that. He expected some sort of follow-up by now, but nothing. The optometrist had called to say his new glasses were ready, the Phoenix Symphony wanted to know if he'd consider renewing his season ticket. He'd canceled after Sandy.... The woman next door called to tell him the police had stopped by and wished to speak to him—he bet they did—and, she added, they had dragged the lake on Monday looking for something, which is what she wanted to tell him before. She wondered if it would have anything to do with his problem? A very delicate way of putting it, he thought, *his problem*. Frank hung up and stared at the phone. So now they had his gun. Well, it took them long enough to go after it. Why were they taking him seriously now? He told them where to look years ago. Now that they had it, what would they do with it? It would be too far gone to do ballistics tests on it, or would it? He needed to update his forensics if wanted to keep writing about crime. There were too many new things in police labs for him to coast along on what he knew ten years ago. As for the gun, it didn't matter to him one way or the other. They would try to connect it to Sandy, but they wouldn't.

He changed into some blue jeans, pulled on a sweater, and laced up the heavy boots he'd brought because he'd planned to take the boys for a hike. They preferred video games, so the hike never happened. As it turned out, he had a use for them after all. He made a pot of coffee and sat down to wait for Rosemary.

He didn't have long to wait. He heard the lock grind open and she stepped in carrying a small gym bag.

"Oh," she said, startled. "I thought you'd still be with Mr. Light. I was going to change while I waited for you."

"Light didn't show."

"Oh, dear, is that bad?"

"No, I don't think so. I think we can piece his story together from what we know already. We'll catch up with him later."

She stood in the middle of the room holding her bag in front of her with both hands. A cloud crossed her face. "I suppose I could use the bathroom," she said and glanced anxiously at him.

"I will go down to the lobby and wait for you," he said, a little too loudly. "Be sure to dress comfortably and bring a jacket or sweater. The weather could change." With that, he stepped into the corridor and closed the door behind him. He'd made it as far as the lobby when he realized he'd left his cell phone on the desk. He shrugged. Probably wouldn't need it, just one more thing to have to lug around. He patted his pockets to make sure he hadn't forgotten anything else and, reassured, dropped into an overstuffed chair that gave him an unobstructed view of the elevators.

Ten minutes later Rosemary stepped out of one of them. Some people, he thought, look good irrespective of how they dressed. She qualified as one of those people. She wore faded blue jeans rolled up at the cuff, a muted plaid shirt over a darker forest green shell. Her shoes were sensible and, he guessed, probably cost over one hundred dollars. She had a sweater tied around her waist and her hair tucked up in a ball cap. A platinum ponytail poked through the gap above its sizing strap.

"How do I look?" she asked, her smile tentative, as if, if he were to say not good, she'd reverse her field and try on some other outfit.

"Terrific." She smiled and gathered her purse, a rather large and bulky leather one, adjusted its strap over her shoulder, and waited. He heaved himself up from the sofa and they headed out the door.

"May I ask where we are hiking to?"

"You may," he said. "We are going to Old Oak Woods. If my memory does not fail me, we are going to find the boys, in a manner of speaking."

"Frank, do you think you know?"

"I think I might."

THIRTY-NINE

"WHAT ARE WE LOOKING FOR?" she asked. Frank led her deeper into the woods and then paused, trying to establish his bearings. Fifty years had passed since he'd walked this way. Trees had grown to maturity, died, and been replaced by new ones in that time span. It startled him to realize that some of the larger trees had been saplings the last time he passed this way. What made him think he'd ever be able to find it again?

"I've got to find it first. If I can't, then we're done here and we will have needlessly raised too many people's hopes and wasted a lot of their time." He paused a moment and looked around. He thought he could smell the new growth pushing up under the leaves that blanketed the forest floor.

"Tooth and Jesse wanted me to build them a tree house and, of course, their mother said no. So I began to tell them about how Jack and I used to come into these woods and make forts and hiding places and so on. It got me to thinking... Ah, we go this way first."

They walked a hundred yards north of their entry point to a mound of honeysuckle. He pointed at the growth.

"You see this bank of honeysuckle and forsythia? Well, Jack and I would get into the middle and trample it down to make a hiding place." He pushed through the brittle stems, treading them down with his feet. "Well, well, it looks like someone has been here before us, and recently. See, this area here is collapsed. Come on." He took her hand and led her into the center. "It's not as big as I remember, it," he said.

Rosemary high-stepped her way to a fallen tree that cut the clearing into two unequal halves.

"You're right about someone being here," she said. She leaned down and retrieved some scraps of paper.

"Probably an alumnus," he said. "The possibility that no one stumbled onto this hideaway in fifty years is pretty remote. Students, campus kids, spent hours in these woods. Someone was bound to find it."

"It looks like a photograph," she said. She picked up some more bits and laid them on the tree trunk like puzzle pieces. "An old photograph at that. Come look at this, Frank." She searched the thicket for more scraps. Frank leaned over the picture and studied it. A face emerged as she arranged and rearranged the pieces.

"Unless I am off my rocker, that is our friend and *femme fatale,* the lovely Luella Mae Parker. Now what or who do you suppose brought this picture here and shredded it?"

"I don't know, but I can guess."

"Are you going to share, or is this something you don't think fitting for a lady's ears?"

"In a minute, I promise. I need the whole of it first. Okay, now we head the other direction, downstream."

"This isn't what you wanted to show me?"

"Only part of a larger picture, in a way. I'm not sure. I could be wrong and I want to check out one other thing before I commit."

"That's the trouble with men," she said. "Always afraid of commitment." He checked to make sure she said that with a smile. She had.

"This way." They picked up the stream and followed its course. "Look for an old beech tree with an X carved into the bark. Jack and I marked the place with an X. Original, huh?" He scanned the trees on the way.

"An X carved into the bark of a tree? You're kidding. That would have been fifty years ago, Frank. The mark would be overgrown by now."

"Not on a beech. They have this smooth gray bark and the marks last as long as the tree. They look like they've been painted. No, the problem we will have is whether the tree is still standing. It might have fallen, or the school may have logged out the older hardwoods. They do that from time to time, I hear. There's a substantial profit in it and it will thin the forest, which some people think is a good thing for the ecology." They walked slowly along the stream bank looking for beech trees.

"It would help if I knew what we were looking for—besides X marks the spot."

"It'll be somewhere along this stream."

"Frank, I don't know much about geology. I took a course in college. I had to have one science, and freshman geology was a snap course. We all took it. Anyway, if I remember correctly, this is a meandering stream. It could have changed its banks and course a dozen times in the past five decades. We may be twenty yards away from where whatever we're looking for used to be."

"Yes and no," he said, his eyes still searching. "Can't see the trees for the forest. How much a stream meanders depends on the fall—the rate of descent to its mouth. This stream flows into Chinquapin Run about a mile and a half from here. The drop is nearly four feet. Doesn't sound like much, but it's enough to make this branch flow at a nice clip most of the time. The greater the fall, the straighter the course. When Jack and I were here, the stream bent to the right and then back to the left. In fifty years, I'm betting it is running straight past that point, and what we're looking for can't be, at the most, more than five or ten yards from this side of the stream."

They picked their way through the underbrush. Frank shook his head.

"You know the trouble with people," he said, squinting at a beech he knew had to be too young to carry his mark, "is that we rely too much on our memories. Scientific evidence points to the fact that of the many mental faculties God gifts us, memory is the least reliable. You have four people witness an automobile accident and you get four different stories. The longer you wait to collect the stories the greater the variation. Half the time they can't even agree on the color of the cars. I don't know why, at our age, we worry so much about losing our memory. It was never that good in the first place. Old people should rejoice in their memory loss. If you have to lose something, why not dump the least reliable?"

"Thus spake the voice of the 'experienced' minority. Say, do you think there might be a benefit in it for us?" she asked.

"A benefit? How so?"

"Well, our gray cells are being logged out, so to speak. Maybe there's a neurological benefit for our brains like logging out creates an ecological one for the forest."

Frank laughed. "It's a happy thought, but I feel like I've been clear-cut. Nothing left but stumps." He caught sight of the small rise.

"There," he said, "you see that low ridge running parallel to the stream? That's the old bank. When I last saw it, it was almost eight feet high, but the stream has straightened out its course and natural erosion over the years has smoothed it out. In another twenty years, you won't be able to see it at all."

Then he saw the tree. In the forest with its high canopy, the beech had grown straight up, reaching for its share of the sun. Its trunk bore the evidence of hundreds of boys with pocketknives—an allowable possession in years past, contraband nowadays. Initials and semi-obscene phrases covered the surface six feet up the trunk—and in the center, Frank's X. He looked around and his mind drifted backward fifty years. It was cool in the forest's shade, but Frank sweated. He walked to the old bank, stepped over the ridge, and stared at the depression.

"This is the place," he said.

FORTY

ROSEMARY CLEARED PAPERS away from one edge and flopped down on the bed. "I need to get to the gym more often," she said. "That walk couldn't have been more than four miles and I'm whipped."

They'd returned to the hotel in relative silence. Frank knew she wanted to hear it all, but he wanted time to think it through. He could be wrong. How good was his "logged out" memory and what were the possibilities that all of his and Jack's work had survived a quarter of a century? The clearing in the honeysuckle thicket didn't prove anything. It could have been discovered and rediscovered numerous times over the years and easily repaired.

"Are you up for lunch?" he asked.

"Not looking like this," she said.

"You look fine."

"I am sweaty, tousled, and in my grubby clothes. I need a shower, a session with my makeup, and at least a half hour to get myself moderately presentable. And don't tell me I look fine. Men say that all the time. Here's a flash—women don't care whether we look fine to them or not, it's everybody else we're concerned about."

"I hear you. Tell you what. Since there's no room service, I'll just wash up, take my cell phone to the lobby, and make some calls. You can meet me there when you are sufficiently repaired to face the world. Then we'll have lunch."

She sat up and pulled off her cap, spilling her wonderful platinum hair around her shoulders. She shook it out and began unbuttoning her blouse. He grabbed the phone, checked his pockets, and left without washing up. In his rush, he missed her grin.

HE WAS STARING AT THE PHONE when she emerged from the elevator. He didn't notice her and looked up only when she stood in front of him.

"Frank? Hello, anybody home?"

She came into focus. He exhaled, but his eyes were still fixed somewhere in space. "Right, are you ready?" he said, voice flat. She pirouetted in front of him.

"Ready as I'll ever be. How about you? Did you manage to find a washbasin?"

He raised his arm, wagging his wrist toward the restrooms. "Yeah. If it's all right with you, I'd like to skip the idea of driving somewhere. Is it okay to go next door to eat? I have some things to do this afternoon…I need some time…."

"Frank, are you all right?"

"Am I? No. I don't know. I'll tell you at lunch."

There were only a half dozen customers in the restaurant. He glanced at his watch and discovered it was after two. They ordered and sipped their drinks.

"What's up, doc?" she asked. She leaned forward, smiling, trying to see behind his eyes.

He looked up. His hands were palms down on the table's surface, and his thumbs moved back and forth, making squeaking sounds. "I have to go home," he said. "Right away, tomorrow, as soon as I can get packed. I need to talk to my daughter…she may want to go with me."

"What's up?" she asked again, this time seriously.

"They found Sandy's body. Four years and they finally found it out in the desert. I have to go home."

"Found? Frank, who found your wife's body? The police?"

He nodded and brought his thumbs under control.

Their lunch came and they ate in silence. That is, she ate. Frank picked.

"This changes everything," he said. "I'll have to call the airlines, change my ticket again…check out of here, leave…this… you…."

"Of course you do. Can I help? I have a travel agent I can call. She can at least take that job off your to-do list."

"Yes, thank you, if that's not too much trouble. I need to call Barbara." But he didn't move to make the call. "The truth is, I'm afraid to call her. I don't know what the cops are going to do to me when I get there."

"Well, there's no sense worrying about that now," she said. "Give me your phone and I'll call the agent. I'll tell her to book reservations in both your names. If you need to cancel one you can." She phoned the agent. "When did you want to fly out?"

He thought a minute. "Late tomorrow afternoon would be best. That way, I'll have a little time in the evening to get myself organized before the cops descend on me, I hope. And it will give us a little time to clear up this missing boy business." She raised her eyebrows at that, murmured into the phone, then snapped it shut.

"You still want to? I mean, do you think we can?" she asked. "It's really important you don't leave with this thing still hanging. We owe it to those families. We opened up that box of horrors again. We can't just drop it. They need closure. Everyone does. But under the circumstances—"

"I think we can do it, Rosemary. But I'll need a favor from your friend the judge."

"I don't know about that, Frank. He'll certainly try to do something, but the last time, the police wouldn't give him the time of day."

"I don't care about the police. I want him to write some official-looking order requiring certain people to meet me at the school's main gate tomorrow morning at eight o'clock."

"Can he do that? I mean, order people to do that?"

"I don't think so, but they may not know that and even if they do, their curiosity will bring them out. At least one of them will be there."

"Who?"

"The guilty one."

"Are you going to tell me who that is?"

"Yes, in a minute."

"Why not just call them yourself?"

"I have no clout in these parts. I'm just an old man—"

"Experienced."

"Not this time—old. An old man with an idea. And I need them all there. I am not Hercule Poirot and do not have Inspector Japp to insist they attend."

"Or Nero Wolf...no Archie Godwin to round up the cast of suspects."

He smiled. "No, or Nero Wolf, either. You're my Archie. That's why I need your judge. He will sound sufficiently authoritarian to get them there. He should use language like *official reopening of the investigation* or *important new evidence,* things like that. It will get them. Oh, and you should invite your friend the ex-cop, the one working the cold case who gave us all the documents. He deserves to hear this. One more thing, I need couriers, messengers to deliver the judge's orders to them all ASAP."

"I'll call in some favors from George's old buddies. They have the muscle to pull this off. Okay, we need a fake court order and a messenger service to deliver them today. Consider it done. Now, are you going to tell me what happened, or do I have to wait until tomorrow, too?"

"I don't know."

"Why?"

"I don't want to see you cry."

"Try me."

He told her the story. She did cry—a lot.

FORTY-ONE

PHELPS LET LEDEZMA AND Pastorella stand while he shuffled papers into a pile and swept a handful of paperclips into the middle drawer of his desk. He didn't have anything against the sergeant or his partner, but he didn't like time wasters either and Ledezma, at least, had wasted time and resources. He looked up. Ledezma was inspecting the putter on the desk.

"It's a Ping," Phelps said. "It needs to be cleaned and re-gripped. Dave Fowler gave it to me." Ledezma took his eyes from the putter and looked at him. He seemed uncomfortable. He knew where the putter came from. Good, Phelps wanted Ledezma to be second-guessing. It was time to finish this business once and for all. He waved Officer Gutierrez in and motioned for her to sit. Ledezma looked at the rookie and started to say something.

"Sit," Phelps said and gestured toward two gray steel chairs. "Since Officer Gutierrez is our intern, I want her to hear this. She can learn something before she gets shipped off to traffic. Bring me up-to-date on the Smith case."

Ledezma cleared his throat. Pastorella looked nervous and dug a notebook out of his jacket pocket. Phelps couldn't be sure if he would be reading from it or writing in it. Pastorella never struck him as the sharpest tool in the shed.

"We are getting closer," Ledezma began. Pastorella nodded. "The body they found in the desert is the wife. We have a pretty good circumstantial case on him and once we confront him with it, he'll crack."

"You had a crew of divers in a lake behind his house on Monday. What for?"

"Right, we found his gun."

"His gun. That all?"

"Yes, but it's the right caliber for the wound in the body's skull."

"The dive team leader says you kept them in the water three hours after they found the gun. What was that all about?"

"I thought we'd find her jewelry."

"Her jewelry? Why did you think you'd find her jewelry in the lake?"

"Well, it wasn't on her at the crime scene. That means he must have taken it—"

"And then threw it in the lake?"

"Yes, sir."

"You buying this, Pastorella?"

"Well, it does tie together."

"Who did you talk to this week?"

"Insurance salesman, the guy who sold Smith the million dollars on his wife, double indemnity, no less."

"What'd he say?"

"Um…not much. He tried to tell me that buying the insurance was her idea or something. But that don't seem too likely, under the circumstances."

"Why?"

"Well, he clipped her and he gets the money. What's in it for her? He's lying."

Phelps leaned back in his chair and folded his hands on his stomach. "Tell you what, why don't you lay out your case for me exactly as you see it. The body, the gun, the jewelry—all of it."

Ledezma perked up and pulled out his notebook. "Okay," he said, "I figure it this way—Smith decides to kill his wife. They're fighting, another woman, something. The woman next door is my guess—hot-looking fifty-something. He's a smart-ass mystery story writer who thinks he's the guy to commit the perfect murder, only he isn't." Ledezma looked around and got an encouraging nod and a weak smile from Pastorella.

"So he says, 'Let's go out to the desert and take a walk,' or something. They get out there and he says, 'Take off your jewelry.' Then he pulls the gun. She drops on her knees and begs him, something like that. He steps up behind her. She starts to pray. The ME says she had her head down like she was praying. And he pops her."

"Why does he take the jewelry?"

"Don't know. Maybe to give to his kids, maybe for the bimbo he's got on the side, maybe to make it look like a robbery."

"Why'd he toss it in the lake, assuming he did? You never found any jewelry, did you?"

"No. See, they'd be pretty small and in all that mud, they'd be hard to find. I'm thinking when he feels us closing in, before we got the warrant to search his house, he got spooked and threw the gun and the jewels in the lake. Up to then he could sit on them. Or he could have ditched them somewhere else."

"Or given it to the girlfriend," Pastorella chimed in. "Assuming there is a girlfriend. Did either of you check that angle out?"

The two detectives exchanged glances. Ledezma shrugged.

"One more question for you two," Phelps said. He sat up in his chair and took them both in with eyes that had gone from friendly sky blue to steely gray. "Did either of you check any incident reports for the area for that day or anytime within, say, three months, just in case?"

"I did," Pastorella said, and opened his book.

"Did you read one called in by a Ms. Kindernecht?"

"The screwy broad? Yeah, I glanced at them. She's a nut. Elevator doesn't go all the way to the top floor. She calls stuff in all the time. She sees suspicious people in the neighborhood, her cat's missing, the neighbors are making too much noise, can we reroute the planes from Luke Air Force Base. The woman's a pain in the butt."

"But you did read them?"

"Well, yeah."

"Anything?"

"In her calls? You're kidding, right?"

Phelps considered what he should say next. These were good police officers. Ledezma had a future. Pastorella, maybe, maybe not. Sometimes a man gets an idea and won't let it go. When that happens, when the need to be right overshadows the need to be careful, bad guys walk, innocent guys get hassled or maybe even do time. Ledezma had been on the writer's case from the get-go and had missed things.

Phelps wished he could smoke his cigar. These sessions always went better for him in the old days when they could smoke in the office. Now, if he wanted to smoke he had to go downstairs and out the back door and stand by the Dumpster. He sighed.

"Okay, this is the way I see it. Ledezma, you got a bug up yours about this guy. You want him way too bad. And because of that you aren't paying attention and are going to blow this one." Ledezma squirmed in his chair.

"You two need to learn to play *what if.* When a case goes this cold, a *what if* can break it open."

"A what if?" Pastorella asked.

"Yeah. Look, you say to yourself, what if there isn't a girl-friend, what if the insurance man is telling the truth, what if the screwy woman said something important, what if Smith is not the guy. What then?"

"But he is the guy," Ledezma almost shouted.

"You say so, but what does the evidence tell you?"

"Lieutenant, I know it's circumstantial, but it's there."

"That's the point, Manny. It's not there, never was. You wanted it to be there, so you only pushed in one direction."

Ledezma's face reddened. He started to say something. Something Phelps feared might have career-altering consequences. He lifted his hand off the table, palm out.

"Listen to me. What did the ME say? In his final report he says, after the details about the condition of the body, et cetera, he says, 'The victim was probably shot while kneeling. She most likely was holding her hands together, one over the other because her left ring finger had been cut off. This would indicate a brutal assault on her before the fatal shot was fired.

Her head was bent forward, probably in response to the pain in her hand.'" Phelps looked up. Ledezma sat absolutely still. He opened his mouth to say something and then stopped.

"'Parts of her clothing,'" Phelps read, "'what appear to be shorts or capri pants, while showing the effects of being in the open and subject to insects and rodents, appear to have been removed and then placed with her body before the canvas was put over her. This would indicate a possible sexual assault, as well.' And then he says, 'The body is too badly decomposed to extract DNA with any certitude, but we do have possible residue on the clothes which we will test and put into the computer.' You with me so far?"

Ledezma's face had faded from red to gray. Pastorella looked confused and a little worried. He kept shifting his attention from Phelps to Ledezma.

"Now here's the next piece. You never went back to the ME for the final?" Ledezma shook his head. "Okay. 'The body had been covered with a scrap of canvas measuring five-and-a-half feet by six. It had a trim piece of vinyl on one edge, indicating it was once part of an awning or perhaps a covering for a table.' That ringing any bells, Pastorella?"

Pastorella frowned and chewed on the end of his pencil.

"An awning? Anything? No? Well, we move on. The ME adds as his final note, 'In conclusion, it is my professional opinion the woman, Saundra Smith, was murdered after she was beaten, raped, and robbed. Her finger was removed by a very sharp knife probably because she could not get her wedding band off quickly enough for her attackers. She was pushed to her knees and shot on the spot. A second search of the scene produced the bullet buried in two feet of dirt on the trajectory such an analysis suggests. The finger has not been found. The assumption must be made that some animal found it and took it away.'

"Now, let us go through the incident reports for Mrs. Smith's neighborhood. This would be your area, Pastorella. Do you remember anything coming down about that time?" The two men looked blank.

"Two months after she disappeared, our people and the INS raided a house on a street ten blocks from where she lived. They removed forty-five illegal immigrants that day. Another half dozen beat it over the fence and got away. You with me?" They looked at each other and back at him.

"Let me give you a quote from our Ms. Kindernecht. 'I told your men before there was something funny about that house. I told them about the nice woman they ran after and took away in the van.'

"Now we go back to the day Smith's wife disappeared. Incident report for that day, one of a couple of dozen. Easy to overlook, especially if it's from Ms. Kindernecht. 'Three men came out of the house and stopped a nice looking lady, I think I've seen her before, and then they put her in a van and drove away.' The receiving officer asked, 'Did they force her in any way?' She replies, 'No, but they might have had a knife or a gun, mightn't they?' Officer: 'Can you describe the van?' Ms. Kindernecht: 'It was brown and had a picture of...' Are you ready for this? '...an awning on it.'" The two officers sat on the edge of their chairs. Phelps couldn't even detect breathing.

"Here's the way it went down, boys. She goes for a walk, like the husband says. She's on the street where the illegal immigrant smugglers, the *coyotes,* have set up their drop house. She sees something. Maybe a shade goes up by accident—whappa, bap, bap—something, she turns at the sound and she's eyeballing a gang of illegals standing around in the living room. She stands there gawking, and while she's wondering what to do, three *coyotes* slip out the door, put a gun or a knife in her back, and drive her away. Maybe they're headed to Nogales anyway. They drive into the desert, God only knows what they did to her out there, and then they shot her. They cover her up with a scrap of awning from the van and leave her. There's a report from Mesa about a stolen van, by the way. It turned up in Bisbee later."

The three men sat in silence. Ledezma and Pastorella studied the shine on their shoes as if they might be inspected by the

President of the United States and their entire future depended on him approving it. Gutierrez sat with her mouth open.

"Now what?" Ledezma said.

"Now, Manny, you go apologize to Frank Smith. Pastorella, you, too."

Ledezma looked at Phelps. "Does this go in my—"

"Jacket? Not this time, Manny. We all get one of these sometime in our career. We just know that we know. And then it turns out we're wrong. Been there myself. And I need all the men I can get. But you find Smith and you make nice, or I could change my mind."

FORTY-TWO

THE JUDGE'S OFFICIAL-LOOKING order had the desired effect. At eight o'clock the next morning, eleven people gathered at the school's main gate. Felix Darnell looked irritated and kept brushing his thinning hair out of his eyes. Too early to mousse, Frank thought. Dexter Light seemed a little the worse for wear, but Frank couldn't decide if that was the result of a night of booze or several days without it. Stark had brought his wife with him, or perhaps it was the other way around. Elizabeth Roulx looked sleepy but interested. Mrs. Sands looked around anxiously. Her ex-husband had refused to come with her. Rosemary's friend, the ex-policeman, and two active duty cops rounded out the group.

"This way, please," he said and led them into the woods. They moved easily along a bridle path until they came to the stream. He then sent them on through the underbrush. Judith Stark, for reasons that made sense only to her, had worn high heels and had a hard time of it. Finally she removed her shoes, sacrificing a pair of new pantyhose in the process. They stepped carefully through generations of leaves and branches. Since the order to appear at a time and place said nothing about where they would have to go, only Frank and Rosemary were appropriately shod. Darnell looked at his Gucci loafers, now scratched and muddy, and cursed under his breath. The cops seemed perfectly content with the circumstances. They were accustomed to shoe disasters. The trees were in early bud. The maples had leafed out but the birches and oaks seemed to lag behind as if they wanted to see if the maples were going to make it first. Here and there, Frank saw a wild azalea with pale pink blossoms and unkempt forsythia making bright yellow splashes against the green and purples of the brush and trees.

When they reached the beech tree, Frank stopped them. He formed them in a circle and carefully studied each of their faces.

"One of you," he said quietly, "could tell this story far better than I. Before I start, I would like to give that person the opportunity." He waited. No one stirred.

"Very well. Over there—" he pointed to the X in the tree "—is where my brother, Jack, and I marked this spot. If you look over there—" he pointed to a slight V-shaped notch in the embankment "—this is where my brother, Jack, and I once dug a cave. It wasn't much of a cave, but we were proud of it. We had bought army surplus entrenching tools and needed a project. After the war—that would be the Second World War for those of you too young to remember. After that war, surplus military supplies were everywhere. Jack and I bought those entrenching tools and a parachute at Sunny's Surplus in Pikesville, I think. We spent a great deal of time in the woods back then, Jack and I. I guess there isn't a square foot of this and all the woods and fields around here we didn't explore at one time or another. It was a wonderful time. A great time to be young...." He paused and cleared his throat. He could do this. He felt Rosemary's hand squeeze his arm.

"The strange thing is, in the five decades since I last walked these woods, everything has changed. It took me nearly an hour to get my bearings. I had to find a small copse Jack and I created before I could make my way here—I should say, *our* way here. Mrs. Mitchell and I came this way yesterday. Well, at any rate, the stream bank along here rose to something like eight feet then. It doesn't look like it now, but fifty years ago it did. We dug our cave straight into the bank, there.

"It turned out to be a fine place to hide. We brought cigar boxes with the things we didn't want our parents to know we had, and hid them in the cave. I don't know for sure, but I think the roof would have been at least three feet thick then. The soil here is dense but sandy. Pre-sandstone, I would call it. Boys do stupid things and we were no exception. We climbed in and out of the cave for months. The idea that to do so might be dangerous never occurred to us. We'd made a number of forts and hideouts in the woods. Some of them were discovered by other kids years later. The hollow in the honeysuckle north of here, for example, has been used by a lot of people over the years. Even recently, if I'm not mistaken, but Mr. Light would know more about that than I."

Light shifted his feet, looked startled, and then directed his gaze back up the streambed in the direction of the copse. He nodded.

"Now, here's the situation as I see it. Those of you who lived it may jump in at any time and correct me if you wish. I am, of necessity, only speculating what happened. But, then, I write stories. Those of us who write fiction succeed or fail in our ability to visualize things that are plausible, and make them seem real to our readers. We get pretty good at it and sometimes surprise ourselves by how real we can be.

"Take today's story, for example. It actually begins sooner than we've been led to believe. At one-thirty, or thereabout, on that Saturday afternoon, five boys entered the woods somewhere around here."

"Four boys, and it was nearer to two," Stark interrupted. The ex-cop nodded.

"No, that's the first error. Nobody checked the time because it didn't seem important then. Mrs. Parker said two, definitely, and so two it was, even though Sam Littlefield, who'd timed his run in and out of the city for years, said one-thirty. Who's going to take the word of an African-American bus driver over a faculty member? It was one-thirty, wasn't it, Mr. Light?" Everyone swiveled around to look at Dexter.

Dexter Light looked to his right and left and nodded. "Yes," he said.

"You went along with Mrs. Parker's version because the two of you thought you could cover your affair. If the disappearance occurred at two, you were covered and so was Mrs. Parker, who

could not have been with you in the woods. So one-thirty it was.
That means you, Stark, have to account for your behavior at the
time, as well. You were with the other four, and that makes five
boys."

"I had DISH, I wasn't here."

"Mr. Light had DISH, too, but he was here and so were you.
DISH began at two, not one-thirty. You had plenty of time to be
in the woods and still make it back to the study hall."

"I don't see where this is going," Felix Darnell grumbled. "I'm
at the point of asking these good gentlemen—" he gestured to
the policemen "—to put an end to this."

"Patience, Dr. Darnell. You will be pleased when we are done
here, but you will have to wait a little longer. Surely the school
can only benefit by bringing this tragedy to a close." The two
officers did not move.

"I take it, then, you dragged us out here to tell us what happened to those boys?"

"That is correct," Frank said.

Mrs. Sands uttered a barely audible "Oh, my God."

Elizabeth Roulx slipped her camera from its case and began
to take pictures.

"Mr. Stark, do you have anything to add so far? You were a
witness," Frank said.

"Don't say anything," Judith Stark hissed. "He doesn't know
shit."

All eyes swung around to stare at her. She stood next to her
husband, her long dress mud spattered at the hem and her shoes
in her hand.

If Darnell's eyebrows rose any higher they would have slid
down the back of his neck. "I'm not sure I appreciate…" he
began, but his voice trailed off.

"Screw you, you old letch. You didn't seem to mind how I
talked at the Christmas party." Her gaze swept the group and
she added, "The man's an octopus."

Darnell's face turned a garish shade of red and he started to
sputter a response. Then he noticed Elizabeth Roulx's camera

pointed his way, reversed his field, and managed a sickly smile for her benefit.

"Mr. Stark, before your wife decided to entertain us, I asked you a question. You were a witness. Anything to add?"

Stark squeezed his wife's elbow just as she started to say something.

"Shut up, Judith," he said through his teeth. Frank waited for more. Stark said nothing. He turned back to Light.

"Okay, five boys enter the woods. Did you know they were here, Mr. Light?"

"I heard their voices. I wondered…"

"Wondered what?"

"If they'd seen me with Mrs. Parker."

"We did," Stark muttered.

"She left and I decided to follow the boys and find out what they knew. I couldn't have them talking to their parents or Daigle."

"Who's Daigle?" Darnell wanted to know.

"One of your predecessors," Rosemary answered.

The retired cop stared at Light. "So you did what to them?"

"Nothing. I followed their voices and then I didn't hear them anymore. I lost them. I searched and then left for DISH."

Frank waited. "Mr. Stark, anything?"

Silence.

"It's been a funny week," Frank said. "I came here for closure on a part of my life that ended badly. My brother, Jack, killed himself because some of my classmates thought it would be amusing to embarrass him by reporting he was gay. They didn't know it would end in his suicide. It turned my father into a bitter old man and broke my mother's heart. But they couldn't have known it would end that way. It was just an impulsive and stupid thing to do. Boys, I have come to realize this week, are given to doing stupid things. One of my grandchildren, for example, nearly knocked his brother out with a lacrosse ball. He just took it into his head to fling it. He never considered what might happen if he actually hit him.

"Then I heard on the news that two boys nearly died when some scaffolding they were playing on collapsed. The construction site had been sealed off, but they found a way in and the chance to climb irresistible. They clambered up on scaffolding that was in the process of being dismantled. They didn't know that, and certainly could not ask. When part of it collapsed, they didn't have a chance. Then yesterday, a family smashed into a bridge abutment because some idiot threw a stone onto the highway and hit their windshield. A stone thrown at thirty miles an hour hits a windshield moving at sixty miles an hour. They didn't have a chance, either. I don't suppose we will ever know who threw the stone.

"That brings us to this place. Jack and I dug a cave right over there. We never considered what might happen to us if it were to fall in. More importantly, we never considered what might happen if it fell in on someone else. When we grew older and were not interested in playing fort, we should have collapsed it. But when I left, the last thing on my mind was Old Oak Woods.

"So twenty-five years later, Ned Sparks finds our cave and takes his friends to see it. They all crawl in and talk. What did you talk about, Stark?"

Stark did not answer. He stood barely breathing—as still and as pale as one of the white birch trees at his back.

"I don't suppose it's all that important. Now here's the part I'm not sure about. Stark had to leave. He had DISH. Light is moving this way, but he has DISH, too. Within minutes, they must head up the hill to school. If we knew what happened in that brief moment, we could put an end to this twenty-five-year-old mystery. Stark? Light?"

Light shifted his feet. "I told you what happened. I walked this way from that copse you talked about. But I lost the voices. I searched back that way and then hurried up the hill. That's it, I swear."

"I'm inclined to believe you," Frank said, "because of what I said before about kids doing impulsive and stupid things. When Jack and I dug the cave, its ceiling would have been nearly three feet thick, but every now and then a chunk of dirt would fall in, and you could tell it would eventually collapse. It's not something we thought about then. Only now I see its importance. I guess I have to take some responsibility for what happened next. When you and your friends crawled in, how thick do you think the ceiling was, Stark?"

He shook his head and his face began to change from birch white to beech gray.

"Well, I would guess it was probably no more than a foot at the dome, maybe less." Frank paused and let the picture of a rough cave form in the minds of his listeners. Rosemary, who'd heard it before, felt a tear slide down her cheek. She dabbed at it with a tissue.

"Stark, I think you crawled out. You said something like, 'I've got DISH, I gotta go.' And you start to walk away. Then you think, 'I'll scare the bejesus out of them,' and you climb up the bank and stand over them on the surface. 'I'll jump up and down and knock some sand down on them. Then they'll come flying out like bees from a hive.' It was a stupid, impulsive act. Not intended to hurt anyone. But what happened, Mr. Stark?"

Stark's eyes raced around the circle of people looking for help. Mrs. Sands moaned, "Oh, my God, Bobby…"

Judith Stark folded and sat heavily on the ground. "I told you not to come. Now it's ruined."

"It was an accident," Stark whispered. "I only jumped once. One time, I swear, and the whole roof fell in. It made a sound like, wuff, and then, nothing. I stood there and I knew there wasn't anything anybody could do. They would be dead before I could get help."

Mrs. Sands began to sob.

Elizabeth Roulx spoke for the first time. "So you walked away and left four families in perpetual mourning. Never said a word.… How could you?"

"I was just a kid, I didn't know. I was scared, I didn't know…

and then, later…I guessed it was too late….” Stark dropped to the ground next to his wife and sobbed.

Frank turned to the two police officers. “You can dig here,” he said and pointed to the ground at his feet.

EPILOGUE

THEY WATCHED THE LAST of the cars drive away, and finally the two of them were alone. The woods grew quiet. Only the splashing of the stream in the background and a pair of blue jays yammering in the distance broke the silence.

"So what happens now, Frank?"

"Happens? Well, I leave this evening for Phoenix."

"Is your daughter going with you?"

"No, she said she couldn't on short notice, although her husband said he could watch the kids, but…she's still not sure about me…the police and all that."

She waited.

"Would you…?"

She turned and searched his face. "Would I what?"

"Well, since I lost my traveling companion…"

"Are you suggesting—?"

"There are almost no bugs in the Valley of the Sun."

"Just scorpions, snakes, and rabbits eating your lantana."

"That's pretty much it."

"And coyotes."

"Yes, and coyotes."

She waited.

"Come with me, Rosemary. I can't promise you anything. I may be in jail five minutes after we get there and need a bail bond—"

"I'm a very rich woman, Frank. I can raise the bail."

ROSEMARY HAD TO HURRY to keep up with Frank, but she nearly ran him over as they cleared the security area and entered the main lobby of Sky Harbor's terminal four. He stood frozen in place, his gaze directed across the seats set aside for people waiting to greet arrivals.

"Why are we stopping?" she asked, then followed his gaze toward two men who slouched uncomfortably against the wall.

"Wait here." He walked toward the men. She followed anyway. "Sergeant Ledezma, what a surprise, and you, too, Pastorella. Is this a social call or are you here on official business?"

Rosemary's heart went to her throat. This is it, she thought. The one she thought must be Ledezma looked at the floor and then at Frank.

"Mr. Smith, we came to offer an apology."

"A what?" Frank's expression shifted from anxious to unbelieving.

"Ah, you probably know we found your wife's body—"

"Yes, I got your call. A little late, I'm afraid. I came back as quickly as I could."

"Yeah, we, that is to say…since Pastorella here called about that, we've been looking at the evidence at the scene, where they found her…remains, and other things we uncovered just recently indicate your wife was probably killed by *coyotes*. We think she must have witnessed something and they couldn't let her live. Sorry. We don't have anybody in custody, but we do have some DNA samples and a possible match. I'm sorry."

"How did she die?"

Ledezma shook his head. "She never knew what hit her."

He's lying, Rosemary thought. He's lying because he's feeling stupid about all the time he wasted harassing Frank and not looking for real killers. And he's lying because she must have died a terrible death and they don't want him to know, because he's had enough.

"You can tell me the details later. You're done with me, right?"

"Yes, sir. This envelope sort of spells it out, there's the death certificate…and all. We've notified the insurance company and told them to release the benefits." The three men stood staring at each other. Finally, Ledezma shrugged his shoulders.

"So, we're okay? Sorry."

She stepped away from Frank as the two policemen walked away. What kind of night would she have now? He would need her eventually, but maybe not right away. She'd wait as long as it took.

You were right, kiddo. Congratulations.

"I won't need you anymore," she said, this time very softly, and knew she was done with her voices forever. He turned to her and she took his hand.

"Let's go," he said. "I want to show you the desert."

* * * * *

REQUEST YOUR FREE BOOKS!

2 FREE NOVELS
PLUS 2 FREE GIFTS!

MYSTERY **W⊕RLDWIDE LIBRARY**®
™
Your Partner in Crime

YES! Please send me 2 FREE novels from the Worldwide Library® series and my 2 FREE gifts (gifts are worth about $10). After receiving them, if I don't wish to receive any more books, I can return the shipping statement marked "cancel." If I don't cancel, I will receive 4 brand-new novels every month and be billed just $5.24 per book in the U.S. or $6.24 per book in Canada. That's a saving of at least 34% off the cover price. It's quite a bargain! Shipping and handling is just 50¢ per book in the U.S. and 75¢ per book in Canada.* I understand that accepting the 2 free books and gifts places me under no obligation to buy anything. I can always return a shipment and cancel at any time. Even if I never buy another book, the two free books and gifts are mine to keep forever.

414/424 WDN FEJ3

Name	(PLEASE PRINT)	
Address		Apt. #
City	State/Prov.	Zip/Postal Code

Signature (if under 18, a parent or guardian must sign)

Mail to the **Reader Service:**
IN U.S.A.: P.O. Box 1867, Buffalo, NY 14240-1867
IN CANADA: P.O. Box 609, Fort Erie, Ontario L2A 5X3

Not valid for current subscribers to the Worldwide Library series.

Want to try two free books from another line?
Call 1-800-873-8635 or visit www.ReaderService.com.

* Terms and prices subject to change without notice. Prices do not include applicable taxes. Sales tax applicable in N.Y. Canadian residents will be charged applicable taxes. Offer not valid in Quebec. This offer is limited to one order per household. All orders subject to credit approval. Credit or debit balances in a customer's account(s) may be offset by any other outstanding balance owed by or to the customer. Please allow 4 to 6 weeks for delivery. Offer available while quantities last.

Your Privacy—The Reader Service is committed to protecting your privacy. Our Privacy Policy is available online at www.ReaderService.com or upon request from the Reader Service.

We make a portion of our mailing list available to reputable third parties that offer products we believe may interest you. If you prefer that we not exchange your name with third parties, or if you wish to clarify or modify your communication preferences, please visit us at www.ReaderService.com/consumerschoice or write to us at Reader Service Preference Service, P.O. Box 9062, Buffalo, NY 14269. Include your complete name and address.

WWLI1B